BEWITCHED BY YOU

KENDRA MASE

Bewitched
— BY —
YOU

BEWITCHED BY YOU

Copyright © 2022 by Kendra Mase

All rights reserved.

Editing by Jovana Shirley, Unforeseen Editing, www.unforeseenediting.com and My Brother's Editor, mybrotherseditor.co

Cover Design by Sam Palencia, Ink & Laurel, www.inkandlaurel.com

In accordance with the U.S. Copyright Act of 1976, no part of this book may be reproduced in any form or by electronic or mechanical means, including information storage and retrieval systems, without written permission from the author, except for the use of brief quotations in a book review.

ISBN 978-1-7373179-8-2 (ebook) | ISBN 978-1-7373179-9-9 (paperback)

This is a work of fiction. Names, characters, places, and incidents are either the products of the author's imagination or are used fictitiously, and any resemblance to actual persons, living or dead, business establishments, events, or locales is entirely coincidental.

*For those hoping for their better **next**.*

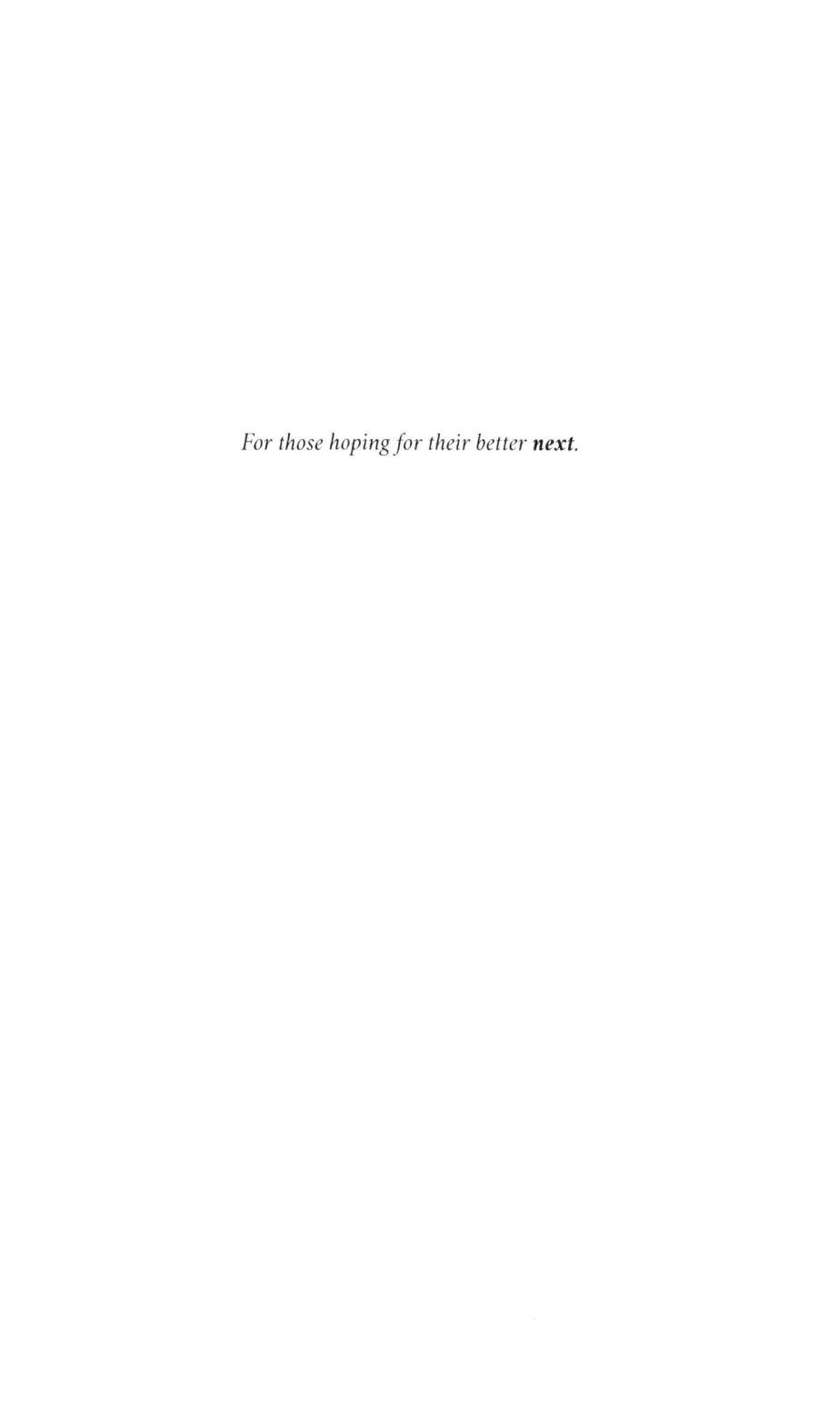

1

I'd truly thought if there ever came a time where I'd be forced to sit outside the Barnett University dean's office, it would be for something more interesting. Found drunk and spread eagle in front of the chairman's house came to mind. So did accidentally setting something aflame or even something as stupid as toilet-papering one of the last remaining fraternities on University Row.

I kneaded the sharp, pointed end of my crystal hanging in the center of my chest. Even if I didn't want the graciously gifted talisman of deceit from one of my coven members—who, once again, was trying to intrude on my life—I needed to suck up as many good vibes as I could. I hadn't planned on being here, sitting outside the dean's office like some overachiever or delinquent, but it wasn't as if I hadn't volunteered myself. The student life events coordinator transferred me here. This was my final step to see my closely organized plans come to life.

Though I already knew what they were going to tell me. It wasn't as if they were going to say yes to an on-campus Samhain celebration on the full moon. Something that only happened every twenty years.

Absolutely not! I could basically hear one of the old administration lady's voices ringing in my ears. *We define ourselves with puritan pride, achievement, and greatness being within every student's grasp. What kind of liberal arts campus do you think we are?*

The type that let in witches to begin with. That kind.

The heel of my black boot clicked as I bounced my knee up and down to the tick of the old wooden grandfather clock sitting across the room, proudly displayed in contrast to the slick marble floor.

They were absolutely going to say no.

Then where would I be?

Figuring out your life—that's what, a little, dark fury in my head whispered haughtily. Perhaps it was a goddess herself. If so, I could only imagine her wise advice also included laughing at me. I was so full of fodder for her amusement from the fact that I was being badgered by not only my coven, but now also the registrar. They sent me more than a few reminders to pick a major. Instead, I spent my time debating which name for the possible party I was throwing sounded less cringeworthy.

Fall Fest? Or Halloween Extravaganza Spectacular?

My life had reached its peak, as low as it was, and now was promptly going down the drain.

I gripped my pendant harder before glancing back up at the clock a second time.

I got here way too early.

So had the guy next to me by the looks of it. Long lashes shadowed his light eyes, which were zoning out at the wall opposite us. Blinking, his gaze flickered, catching my glance. "Hi."

"Hi," I responded slowly.

"I'm Ryan, by the way." He gave an easy smile. Perfectly straight white teeth flashed.

I tipped my chin back in acknowledgment, but nothing else. I knew who he was. I didn't try to commit his name to memory, but it was hard not to know the star football player on BU's consistently losing team when everyone acted like he was America's golden child.

It was also hard to forget the guy who made fun of you at first-year orientation. He'd had a lot more strawberry-blond-colored hair at the time. I remembered how it dipped over his ears and struck an even darker shade when coated in sweat after whatever practice he had been at prior. Yet he still had the audacity to call me the weird one who looked like I was coming to steal their souls.

The riffs got a few laughs from his friends while I stood off to the side, trying to hide the way my lip curled back in repulsion. I had yet to find my friend from then on, Vadika, until later in the evening. Looping her arm around mine in the middle of the menial social gathering over plastic cups of lemonade and soda, she'd proclaimed easily that I would be her best friend—with the condition that she was allowed to squat in my dorm room when she didn't want to commute home to and from campus on the weekends, though it never happened often.

It was a codependent sort of relationship, but we survived the past few years together. Vadika made me do things on campus that weren't just essays and counting down the minutes until my weekly coven meeting in town ever since she had made it her mission to have the full college experience. I … well, she assured me I did something besides bring interesting conversation and being able to tow her back to my dorm bathroom after trying purple jungle juice at a party down the row, where people—like the jock next to me—were a constant sight.

Only now, compared to usual, the renowned Ryan Gardner was much more put together. His hair fell over the crown of his head in a cropped swoop, and his jawline was shaved, squared off, and defined from the young first-year who had situated me as the butt of a joke. I wondered what he thought of me now.

In the past three years, my hair had been chopped, styled, and dyed. My wardrobe, thanks to Vadika, turned from the clearance rack specials my dad often tried to help me pick out to a much more bohemian fusion of clothes.

"Less scary, more dark feminine divinity," Vadika had described it, often with a flourish.

"What kind of rock is that?"

I turned back to face Ryan. His eyes trailed between my face and where I clutched at the carved pendant.

I twisted it for a better view, poised between fingertips. "It's labradorite."

"Oh." Ryan nodded, as if he were stupid not to have realized and knew exactly what it was for instead of, more likely, that he couldn't care less. "Cool."

I gave him a single nod. *Very.*

"Does it mean anything?"

Is he for real right now?

"It's supposed to be good for luck," I carefully explained. It was also supposed to guide people in the right direction in life when stuck between a rock and a hard place. Another jab from the crystal gift giver, Celeste. "Sort of."

"Like a lucky charm?" he asked.

I lifted my gaze to stare at him. "No."

"Huh. Do you have anything that could fix this?" Ryan gestured down toward his leg.

On another one of Vadika's university experience excursions to one of the first football games of the year, I had seen what caused the injury to happen firsthand. Still, I expected the damage to be worse. Ryan was carted off the field after everyone in the stands sucked in a sharp breath at the hit. A pained expression marred the black swipes of paint over each of his cheeks. Still, he had given a thumbs-up to the crowd before disappearing into the locker rooms.

A heavy brace now circled his knee. Crutches leaned against the uncomfortable woven chair beside him.

His shoulders drooped.

Before I could say anything, the door creaked open behind us both.

"Luella Pierce?"

Immediately, I stood, turning on the edge of the short heel of my boot. "That's me."

"Come into my office." The dean waved me inside. He shut the door almost completely behind me, leaving a small gap between the frame and handle.

Glancing back as I found the chair across from the dean's desk, I could still see the side of Ryan Gardner's leg stretched out.

"Make yourself comfortable. Can I get you some water or anything?"

I needed to focus. I'd never met the dean before. I was sure I must've seen him somewhere on campus; still, when I had been sent to the big, old building, I'd expected someone older. I'd thought I would be pleading my case to someone who was more set in his ways than this one, clad in a loose polo that matched his dark, slicked-back hair. The pleated pants also looked like something forced on him by his wife, according to the freshly shined gold ring on his fourth finger.

A fresh wave of confidence grew. Maybe this whole thing wouldn't turn out so bad. He might be new to Barnett. He might want to shake things up here and make his mark—at least slightly.

"I'm good, thanks," I answered his question, continuing to look around the office.

The cohesiveness was hard to ignore from the spirited green-and-white cooler of mini water bottles for the taking to the wall of Barnett sports memorabilia. To top it off, I saw the bachelor's degree that looked very similar to the one I would hopefully receive next year.

"You went to Barnett?"

"I did." The dean flashed his overly white teeth. He joked, "I consider myself one of the most involved alums. So, what is it that I can do for you?"

I cleared my throat, feeling as if something were lodged in the center of it.

Maybe this would be more difficult than I thought now. I tried to cover the sound as I lifted my binder from my tote bag, setting it on the edge of the large mahogany desk. Opening it up, I twisted it around to display its contents. "Well, I started a project of sorts for campus. I brought it to the student life department specifically, but since I'm not a club, they directed me here."

The dean slowly looked over the plans I'd spent hours on, flipping back and forth between three-hole-punched pages of photographs and lists. A cost spreadsheet was included. The entire event in and of itself—once he got over the type of event I was promoting exactly—turned out to be very reasonable after I'd gotten a bit creative and enlisted the help of my coven on whether or not they'd volunteer.

"A fall festival?" the dean clarified, saying each word slowly, as if he were the person trying to explain the idea to me. He continued to look over the next section of details and cocked his head to the side, one page after another.

Before he could say anything else unintentionally degrading, I spoke up. "Not exactly a festival. I've been thinking of it as more of a gathering surrounding the holiday. It would be more put together than the parties that happen on campus."

His dark eyes flickered up from a page held between his thumb and pointer.

"Safer as well," I added. Why did I sound so meek?

"Of course. You do know that Barnett has a September pep rally and homecoming day, correct? It coincides with fall and the first weekend in October."

I blinked. Fall started this Tuesday, but either way, I knew what he was getting at. That was correct. I, however, *still* wasn't talking about fall or the equinox sneaking up on us. I was talking about Samhain.

Then again, I was also not talking about Samhain.

To talk about the pagan holiday, no one could pronounce their first time properly, would be to open Pandora's box in an otherwise neo-Christian campus setting. I was not going to get into that today. Ever, if I had it my way.

"Right," I said. "But like I said, this would be different. The celebration I'm proposing wouldn't surround sports, for one. Less burgers and hot dogs and more … festive. Everyone could participate. Also, it would be more meaningful. You know, with Halloween and everything." Was my voice coming out higher than normal now? My gods, I was pretty sure it was, even if the meekness was dissipating.

Again, I cleared my throat.

The dean grimaced at the guttural noise.

"It could also be open to whoever wanted to come both on campus or in town if we put up some flyers to fully include our Barnett community," I went on.

"We also have our tradition of trick-or-treating for the staff and town kids, you know, of course."

"Of course." I blinked. "Again, this wouldn't be like trick-or-treating."

The dean turned his gaze down to my spreadsheet. "Hmm."

Hmm?

"This would be Samhain," I finally came out with, knowing I was fighting a losing conversation. The word struck a tone. On the tip of my tongue, it stirred magic that even the dean seemed to feel, strong and effervescent in the air. "Halloween is the witch new year, you know, of course," I said, using his words.

"I'm somewhat aware." He looked me up and down in a sweeping motion, as if suddenly wondering where my pointy hat was.

"Thinning of the veil and all that," I explained as if this were common knowledge. "Samhain is a time for new beginnings—letting go of that which does not serve us and starting new. It would be educational as well as fun to this autumnal party. It would be outdoors in the evening to celebrate. There's also a full moon this year, which doesn't happen often. If we manage to turn out the lamps near the quad, it would be great to see the stars, which I know some students from the bigger cities don't often get to see."

"This looks very ... well researched," the dean attempted. He shrugged, closing the cover of my white plastic binder in his hands. Instead of handing it back over to me, however, he pulled it farther away, as if he meant to keep it. "We will, of course, have to put this up for a vote to the student council."

A vote. *A vote!*

I was somehow moving forward with this even if I thought the dean of campus life could snap his fingers and be done with it. All I needed was to get a silly vote done by the student ...

"Student what?"

"The student council," the dean repeated, as if it made whatever he was talking about clearer.

The only thing that it did was cause my stomach to drop.

The student council. I pressed my lips together as I thought of the few people I remembered putting posters up last spring for a coveted spot on the single, slightly governmental organization on campus.

"The student body president and the rest of the student government will decide if this is a sort of event that people will be interested in as well as the ramifications to the school to promote with funding. There is, as you know from your extensive planning, only so much to go around."

"Don't you make that decision?" I asked.

"We encourage our students to take an active role in their university experience, Luella."

I blinked. *Right.* That is, if it wasn't me right here and now, it seemed. I forced myself to smile, sparing no tooth so I wouldn't glare.

"I will keep this." He lifted my slim binder an inch off the desk before letting it slap back down. "And I'll pass it on. You should hear of the decision by the end of the next week if all goes well."

"And if I don't?"

"Then, I applaud your excitement and ambition so early in the school year. But I will have to say, if the event you planned ends there, perhaps it would be a good thing."

"Excuse me?"

"I noticed that you've yet to fully commit to a major as of last spring," the dean commented casually. "Nearly all of our fourth-year students usually have one sorted by now, so they can commit to their chosen study and graduate on time."

"I have a major," I said, though my voice shook. What was happening to me? What was happening here? I had come in to talk about a celebration more exciting than the stamp club's annual exhibition, not myself. Now, I had a stutter as prominent as Pinocchio's nose, branding me a liar.

"A few started, it looks like," the dean agreed. "I'm interested, to say the least. English, biology, marketing, art history, anthropology, French—and not to mention, your longest interim, working in our graphic design department. Which one are you going to end on? Any thoughts?"

I paused, unsure of how to answer. "I'm still going through the pros and cons."

He closed his eyes that looked much less concerned than he'd proclaimed. "A wise choice. I suggest you take the time to think strongly."

"Thank you for that ... advice."

"Thank you for your time. Have a good rest of your week."

Blinking, I glanced toward the clock, still ticking by, not ten minutes from the last time I'd looked out in the hall. "Okay. Thanks."

The dean stood up, gesturing with one hand back to the door where he'd welcomed me. He was the picture of oddly handsome academia that belonged more in the Hamptons than small-town Barnett.

Still, it made no sense.

Was I just mind-fucked by the dean of campus life?

Either way, I was directed out in the hall. The prized football player stared between the two of us from where he slouched in his chair. Eyebrows raised, he pursed his lips, as if unsure of what had just happened between the dean and me.

That made two of us.

I'd thought that my entire project would be up to the actual people who ran the school, not the people who sat next to me in art, economics, and biology with obnoxious enamel forest-green pins on their backpacks to show their BU pride. People like my roommate. My awful, loud—more often than not—rude, *made her side of our tiny double look like something out of a first-year university advertisement* roommate.

The dean spoke up past me as I tried to understand how such a status quo world of pretty girls and boys running the world past high school was still in fashion. "Mr. Gardner, come into my office and get situated if you'd like. We are still waiting on one other person to join us."

Wide shoulders shifted as Ryan blinked from his seat, his gaze for some reason still eyeing me. Ryan scooted himself up from a nearly horizontal position. He reached for his crutches and easily slipped them under his arms. "All right."

As we passed, he flashed me an attempt at a comforting smile before he disappeared into the office. The door shut fully this time, unlike for my meeting, and the sound of the old brass tumblers clicking into place was enough to startle me. I swung my backpack over my shoulders and headed straight out the door and into the east campus.

Hopping down the steps, I started to walk around the curved sidewalks. Trees loomed over me, casting a shadow on my steps.

The foliage, of all things, was one of the reasons I'd chosen to go to school at Barnett. The pictures alone sold me. I liked the trees. The river nearby was usually gray, but some days, the water carried itself majestically. Blue and clear enough to dip your feet in, if you were picnicking at the right spot. The nature curved around you, looping over your shoulders like a cool, comforting blanket.

Now, I couldn't pull myself far enough out of my mind to even think of how the leaves rustled in the wind, picking up.

What in the name of all the gods had just happened?

I had taken one step inside the office, and suddenly, I'd turned into mush. I turned into that shy and abrasive little girl I'd left behind in Columbus, unable to say what I thought and stand up for myself. I should've demanded and fought for my right to be a part of the campus, just like anyone else.

Stars, the dean had barely glanced at me or my plans before swiping them away. Dismissed. Done. To him, I was no one but another random student who was too indecisive to pick a stupid major to be defined as for the rest of her life.

I took a few deep breaths. Nothing eased the tight strain between my eyebrows. I'd had one chance that felt right, and now, it was gone. Even if the student council, or whatever they called it, was going to give me the time of day, I knew I wasn't going to get much further than that, especially not if the person I had to see at least once a day had any say.

Natalie, my housing lottery-won roommate, practically reveled in the fact that people looked at me like a weirdo or just ignored me altogether. Her reminders of that, however, didn't bother me. Not much anyway.

My backpack was yanked back away from my shoulder, nearly taking me with it.

I caught myself, my feet luckily finding themselves back underneath me before my perpetrator went down with me.

"So? I've been looking for you ever since your meeting started. I didn't want to call you and interrupt." Vadika chuckled as she leaned around my shoulder to get a better view of my face.

A swath of dark hair swung free of her loose bun as she spun around in front of me. At some point from the offices, I'd managed to wander across campus. Around the corner, and I'd be in front of the science building, where my friend spent most of her time, and thus, so did I, especially when finals came around.

While Vadika had on her protective goggles and shot pipettes across the room until one a.m., I slipped on my wire-framed glasses and worked on my laptop, eventually able to ignore her tiny whispers to herself as she counted microorganisms in a petri dish.

"Tell me, how did it go? What did they say?" she asked.

I readjusted my bag's strap digging into my shoulder. Slowly, we continued to walk forward, Vadika directing me back toward the center of campus, where I knew she met up with her commuter group once a week. It was a mandatory club to make sure they were all adequately participating in Barnett culture even though they didn't live there full time.

Vadika complained about it, but she always went back for the free, fresh donuts they laid out like a strange commuter's anonymous meeting.

"He said maybe."

"Maybe?" My sweet friend acted as if he were the crazy one.

Now, I wasn't so sure.

Was the idea crazy? Sure, I'd basically blurted out that I wanted to have a live ritual going on campus for a pagan holiday, but what more was there besides honoring the full moon and having a small bonfire? There was a nature walk and food and dancing and pumpkins and shit.

I was basically serving up an all-inclusive trip to Starbucks … just more outside.

I lifted a shoulder. "He has to run all nonacademic events by the student council. They meet at the end of the week."

Just another hoop to jump through. Only this time, I was sure that I'd trip halfway and come crashing down on my face.

"The council? Or is it still the student association, meant to be whispered in reverent, hushed tones?"

"Does it matter?"

Vadika didn't have anything to say to that, lifting a hand to push back a strand of hair behind her ear, lined with gold piercings. "Isn't *she* on the committee?"

I could've almost smiled at how she referenced Natalie. Vadika always tried to give people the benefit of the doubt, but after the last time Natalie had tried to get me kicked out of my room last month for the few unlit candles I had sitting out on my desk, Vadika's mind had been made up.

"She is."

Pretty sure she was anyway. It fit.

"Well, damn."

My internal monologue exactly.

"It's way too late to get on that girl's good side, huh?" Vadika mumbled.

Way too late. I was screwed. No matter which way I put this to make this entire scenario seem a little better, unless Natalie suddenly had a personality change and the world had a minor apocalypse, there was no way Natalie was going to vote for me. The rest of the committee, however, I couldn't be one-hundred-percent positive. They were likely easily swayed.

It wasn't as if the student council was bad. It was simply that the only things that ever got passed through Barnett's committee were those created by the committee. The bland, boring traditional college event–creating committee.

This place was basically a democratic dictatorship.

I groaned.

"It's not the end of the world."

"Just the end of my plan," I sighed.

Vadika bit her lip.

"Don't."

"You know you only started this to get back at Celeste," Vadika said anyway.

"That's not true." It was only partly true.

Everyone seemed to know it before I did.

I'd finally gotten back to Barnett a week before the start of classes after spending too much time with my father and grandmother, who spouted the Old Testament at me along with warnings to my father that I was becoming a Satan worshipper. Coming back to Barnett and my coven felt like coming home. I was at ease.

Then, Celeste, one of the few women in my tiny yet fantastic coven, had had to ruin it all. I hadn't realized that I was trading one crotchety old woman for a middle-aged one who suddenly decided she wanted to have more input on my life and made everyone else agree with her. Or more specifically, the fact that I needed to start making decisions, like my major and doing more "young people things." Basically, live more.

As if I wasn't already.

Why wasn't I going out with Vadika more? Where was my boyfriend, girlfriend, or nonbinary partner? They didn't care which. What did I plan to do when I graduated next year? Did I know that I couldn't hang out with them in our high priestess, Gertrude's, garden and inside her lilac-and-green Victorian home alongside the river forever?

My friends were turning into cranky aunts.

Anyway, I'd told them that I already had enough on my plate.

"Like what?" they had asked.

Well, the Samhain celebration that Vadika had—but also hadn't—suggested I plan on campus. The celebration that I then had to plan quickly and efficiently, as if they hadn't seen through my terribly delivered lie to begin with.

Gertie had to cover up her laughter when I admitted the truth to her.

For now, however, everyone got off my back. I had until the holiday to make it all happen. Just like magic, I'd prove myself to Celeste, even though I insisted I truly didn't care what she thought of me in comparison to her fifteen-year-old daughter, who was, according to her, destined to take over the coven one day.

I huffed. "She just gets on my nerves."

"I know."

"I wanted to prove her wrong."

"I know."

"I know you know, and I appreciate you." I stared up at Vadika with soft, large eyes as we stood outside the Student Union Building—a.k.a. SUB. Inside, in one of the slightly mildew-smelling conference rooms, was a bunch of other commuter students less acclimated to Barnett than Vadika. There were also the gooey and delicious snacks the club adviser brought every other week.

"I can't steal you any more donuts."

"Like they would notice."

She smiled, shaking her head. "I'm stopping in for all of five minutes, and then my parents are coming right after to pick me up for the weekend. Wish me luck at another joyous family wedding."

"Don't get hitched without me."

The last time she had gone to a wedding with her family, she'd sent messages—which I still saved—about her aunts sticking her in a closet with a much younger boy, who they believed she'd have such beautiful little babies with.

I'd nearly died with laughter at Vadika begging me to call the National Guard to come and save her.

"I'll take pictures of my many potential suitors."

"That will help me make it through the weekend, thank you."

"Don't look so sad," Vadika complained. "I can't stand it. You're going to make me sneak you inside again. No one believes you're a very distant cousin visiting campus."

I shook my head. "I'm okay. I'm just going to drop some stuff off in my room and take a walk."

"Say hi to the sunset for me."

"Say hello to your future husband for me."

She groaned, throwing her head back as she headed inside.

2

As one of the smaller residence halls on campus, most people never realized the old tree-covered building was there. Or they thought it was another set of tiny offices where they stuck the adjunct professors. After being placed there against my will when the housing came around at the end of my second year, I had gone searching for the space and easily fell in love.

Old windowpanes were chipped with layers of history and paint. Creaky radiators always made the room a little too warm or too cold, and yet it felt right. It felt perhaps the most *Barnett* than any of the other updated buildings. I could imagine other students sitting right where I was. I could feel the marks they had made where they lived and worked, both physically and in the stale air that hung in the stairwell.

Or I did love it when I had a roommate who didn't terrorize every moment of my waking time inside of it.

Natalie didn't win the housing lottery this past year either, and she was much less enticed by the hall's unique charms.

If I hadn't already known that, it wouldn't have been difficult to figure out. She tore in and out of the room on a daily basis like the space was poisonous as well as an eyesore. Today, however, she scrubbed her desk, and the world's tiniest hand vacuum had been left in the middle of the ugly pink-and-green rug, which reminded me of watermelon.

An armful at a time, she threw out vanilla-bean protein bar wrappers and old coffee cups that had been littering her side of the room into the community hall trash.

Not saying a single word, I headed directly toward my side of the small cube. I'd coveted the idea of having a single all to myself, but I just couldn't consider the extra few hundred dollars that came with the privilege.

Now, I regretted such a frugal decision.

Previously, my roommates had lived their lives, and I'd lived mine. When it came to my living space, it wasn't ever a happy home at Barnett, but at the very least, it was a peaceful coexistence for the academic year. Natalie, on the other hand…

"My boyfriend is coming for the weekend," Natalie announced.

I kicked off my shoes that pinched my toes. I was ready to do the same with my jeans and switch into my sweatpants as I figured out what I was going to do for the rest of the night. I still wanted to take a walk, my entire body tense and tired, before I headed to the library to get some work done.

"Okay?" I stretched out the word, waiting for more.

"He'll be here soon. So, no offense …" She paused, as if weighing the phrase. "I would rather you made yourself disappear."

Pausing as I leaned down over my drawers, I turned back to stare at her. "Excuse me?"

My roommate continued to fluff her flat down pillows before walking over to the one thing I had brought in the room that she didn't seem to have a problem with, turning on the small essential oil diffuser. "Don't you have anywhere better to be tonight? It's Friday. You have friends, right? That Indian one you bring around here? Plus, I don't think you'll want to stay here with us all night after we get back."

She had to be kidding.

Natalie raised her eyebrows. "If you get what I mean."

Oh, I understood all too well Natalie's not-so-subtle meaning.

"Could you make sure that your weird stuff is … I don't know … put away? That way, my boyfriend and I don't have to look at whatever sort of print that is. Not to mention your collection there." She waved toward my desk, covered in notebooks, tea, and crystals. They were many of the same ones that had been "unintentionally" knocked off the windowsill the last time they were charging.

I turned my attention then to my poster, knowing exactly which one she was talking about. She could be rude about my lifestyle, but her taste in art was just willfully distasteful. "It's Gustav Klimt. Art nouveau?"

"I don't care if it's the *Mona Lisa*," she said. "It's art that I'm not a fan of. I don't want to see some chick swooning while I'm already squeezed in my obnoxious twin bed with *my* boyfriend. I get to see him once every month or so. So, get what you need to get and leave, please."

"Why, yes, Natalie, I will just completely uproot myself from my room for the whole weekend because you decided to invite someone over without asking me if I had anywhere to stay." I crossed my arms as I glared at the wall, displeasure clearly coating my tone.

I certainly didn't want to stay here and risk hearing whatever it was Natalie did at night with her boyfriend. Usually, when this sort of thing happened, I would crash with Vadika at her parents' house, which wasn't the worst thing in the world. They fed me and treated us like friends having a sleepover–only that wouldn't be the case this weekend.

"Perfect." Natalie smirked in a way that was not at all sincere as she grabbed her bag off the hook of her bed before heading to the door. "Be sure that you have everything you need and are out by the time I get back from the sorority dinner please. He's meeting me there."

I stared at her as she left, leaving me there in the center of our room.

She had to be kidding. However, in this strange logic of Natalie, I knew she wasn't. I didn't want to give in. I wanted to take a stand. I was still unsure just how far Natalie would take spending the night with her boyfriend across from me.

Groaning, I slipped a more comfortable pair of boots on and knotted the laces. Grabbing my backpack, I shoved in a fresh set of clothes and my laptop. Maybe I could still ask Vadika if I could stay at her parents' place even if they weren't going to be there. They had at least three cats that could probably use the company.

By the time I made it back outside, I took a turn onto the dirt path that ran along the outskirts of campus. I noted Natalie not far away, laughing with another one of her friends, wearing an oversize football jersey that dipped over her shoulder.

Her laughter faltered as she noticed me. She raised her eyebrows, as if I was about to dare come near her in public.

I rolled my eyes and kept walking.

First-year residence halls were always loud, music and voices sneaking through the cracks of the windows. Academic buildings were turned dark, except for a few rooms still lit up from students likely making a home for themselves for the evening before everything was automatically locked up. I passed all of it as I headed farther up the hill Barnett sat on.

The space was also popular with people who needed to escape and smoke in the afternoon after classes. I mostly used it for the former.

The inlet on the hill was right on the edge of the cemetery behind campus. The grass was slightly too high, and it tickled and scratched my skin, but the view was worth it. Looking out over Barnett the campus glowed. Quaint houses were nestled in patches of thick trees. The wide, ever-flowing river glistened as the sun began to go down in a flurry of oranges and pinks, seeming so far away.

Lifting my phone up to my ear, I propped it, holding it between my ear and shoulder, as I swung my backpack to the ground. I riffled through the pockets, making sure I had everything one more time before I had to live out of my backpack for the weekend.

The buzzing droned on for lack of service until my call connected.

"Hey, Lu. What's up?" Vadika asked. I could hear the smile in her voice. "Did you tell the sun hello for me yet? Or is it goodbye at this time of day?"

I smiled. Neither really, but this was good. I wanted to catch her while she was still in a good mood.

"I need a favor."

Vadika chuckled. "O-kay."

"Do you think your parents would mind if I headed over to your place for the weekend? I'll take care of the cats and everything."

"What happened?"

"My archnemesis kicked me out of the room because of her boyfriend." I rolled my eyes as I leaned against one of the slopes of grass.

"Lu, I'm sorry. We all just left. My parents came to pick me up a little while ago," Vadika apologized with a sigh. "I wish I had known."

"Oh. To be honest, I'd sort of figured." Blinking, I kept staring out at the sun, though the air still felt cool and not so comforting any longer. "It's fine."

"Are you sure? I could ask to see if we could call a neighbor to get you a key."

"It's no big deal, Vad," I assured her. "I'll be good. Just another night in the library before I sleep on the common room couch."

"Gross. I'm sorry."

"Don't be. Forget I asked," I said. "Have fun at the wedding and make some young groomsman's night."

She snorted. "Don't joke. Good luck."

"You too."

I waited until the sun was almost the entire way down and watched as the lamps on campus began to turn on one at a time, lighting the way. It needed to be now, or I wasn't sure that I would ever get up, so I stood, looping my backpack around my shoulders. Still, I took the longer way, heading through the cemetery to get on the main path.

It seemed that out of all the campuses I'd visited before I settled on Barnett, most of them had a cemetery on or very near campus in an oddly foreboding fashion. Gravestones were faded or toppled over, some dating back centuries, as I wandered through the rows.

Today had been a rough day, and it wasn't even over yet. I still had work to do on my computer and a couch to proclaim as mine for at least five hours, so no drunk partygoers would sit on top of me in the middle of the night.

What a joy.

I kicked at a loose patch of grass before pausing altogether, halting my motivation to go another step. What was I doing here? In the cemetery or on campus? I was basically a loser witch whose best friends were middle-aged women. I didn't even have a major or clear understanding of what the hell I was going to do next year when I could no longer write that I was a student under *Occupation* on legal forms.

Just your average witch certainly wouldn't be applicable. Nor as well respected if I ran away.

But what else was for me here, except for the people I'd grown fond of and the work I did with Gertie in her garden? I had basically been made to be a retired old lady who secretly sold spells on the side.

Maybe my coven had a point—even if I would never say such a thing aloud.

I groaned audibly.

I needed to stop going in this loop. So what if I was happy with the simple things I found for myself? Happy enough anyway.

Right here, right now.

I didn't want anything to change. So, what if I stayed in this town forever? I could help Gertie at the house where she'd no doubt adopt another stray cat. I'd swing on her sun porch until I got old and withered and pestered other young ladies interested in witchcraft that they should have more lovers and take more chances and live more life …

I shut my eyes, walking the path before I opened them again. At that moment, however, before I could help it, a small shriek escaped my mouth, quickly recaptured as my hands covered my mouth and I stared down at a body that lay between headstones.

3

"What are you doing?" I screeched. Pulling my hand away from my mouth, dark-red lipstick stained on my palm.

A tall and bulky body indented the grass. He laid between two headstones in the middle of the walkway. Crutches and an overfilled backpack had been flung to the side. "Midterms, am I right?"

I stared down at the prone form, blinking up toward the ever-darkening sky. He had to be kidding.

"It's September."

The very much alive body shrugged. The same guy who had stared at my necklace outside the dean's office.

Ryan Gardner. Of course it was Ryan Gardner.

He turned his light-blue gaze back up to the wispy clouds in the sky with a light huff. "I'm debating the meaning of life. You're welcome to join me."

I raised an eyebrow, settling my hands on my hips as I stared down at him. "I never took you as emo."

Again, Ryan shrugged. When he scooched over, the movement caused his hair to plaster against one side of his head. He patted the ground next to him.

"Yeah, no thanks." I looked back around for anyone who must've trudged up here with him. Unfortunately, there was only him and me. "I'll leave you to it. Thanks for freaking me out. I have to go in case this existential crisis in the cemetery turns into something I can be blamed for."

"I thought it was a graveyard."

"You have to have a church for it to be a yard." I couldn't help but correct him.

"Huh." He nodded thoughtfully. "Never knew. Learn something new every day."

Right. Well ...

"Good luck with whatever is going on here. I have a few things to deal with of my own. Only in my case, I'm going to do so in a not-fucked-up place—in the library."

The to-do list I was avoiding went on and on, especially now that the one thing I had kept at the top of my list the past few weeks was likely to disappear any moment now.

"See ya around."

Taking a step away, I paused. Should I really leave him there? "Are you sure you're okay?"

"Just contemplating life."

"All right then. See ya around, maybe." Or likely not.

He lifted a limp hand, letting it fall back down against the cool earth.

Turning away, I made my way back down the rocky slope of the cemetery, glancing back twice to see Barnett's running-back golden boy still lying there. It was a feat Ryan had managed to get up here without collapsing. At least, not collapsing before he clearly wanted to, between headstones like a very alive zombie.

For some reason, I always believed I was the only one who came up there to think. There was something a bit metaphorical about the dead and the living conversing to figure out what the heck to do with the time they had so much and so little of, all at the same time.

A little morbid too.

As if to remind myself of the wonders of life, I stopped into the SUB. I got a look of concern over the amount of sour gummy worms I purchased and stuck the package into my backpack. Twisting it over my shoulder, I zipped the front pocket back up before making my way by the few others who were staying on campus for dinner. They lounged at tables, sipping on soda and laughing with one another. Some of them were already dressed for their night out to wherever the secret parties were this week. Though, in the end, they weren't all that secret when half the campus was called by some unforeseen force down to the Row or crammed into the few university apartments nearby.

I never knew how anyone ever managed to get those with their own kitchens and living spaces. Then again, I wasn't sure I would know who to live with to fill the apartment anyway. My own little dorm on the edge of campus was perfect.

I reminded myself of all the reasons why, trying to gain a little positivity after my walk and watching the sunset to clear the day away.

By the time I made it to the library, the sun was completely down. Crossing my arms over one another to keep the cold from setting in, I pushed the front door open, where the library hours were posted from seven in the morning to midnight.

I waved a hand toward the student librarian who was finishing up checking in books. They didn't wave back. I headed back farther toward the offices. There were only a few still lit with desk lamps.

The glass door made a whoosh sound when it parted open.

"I'm surprised they finally got around to fixing the hinges," I commented, remembering the screeching scream of a sound that the sliding door used to emit.

Immediately, the woman looked up from her desk. She

paused her tapping of sky-blue fingernails as she grinned. "What a surprise! I didn't expect to see you here tonight, Lu. It's Friday. Shouldn't you be out, living up the greatest years of your life or something?"

She winked from below her tight black curls to assert the sarcasm in her tone. Faith was the one who got my sense of humor during coven meetings. At the very least, she pretended to. A little flighty, Faith was also always kind enough to anyone so long as they didn't cross her. Then, all bets were off.

"Vadika is out of town with her family," I replied in explanation.

"Aw, that's too bad."

I shrugged. "What are you doing here so late?"

Her eyes widened with enthusiasm. "Reorganizing."

"Reorganizing?" I looked around her chaotic mess of an office.

"Not in here, silly. Or at least, not completely. I left for a few weeks during the summer, and now, my entire cataloging system on the Norse mythology is in shambles," Faith complained—or tried to. Her voice still sounded a little too delighted at the mishap. "At this rate, I'll never get to the French Revolution. I was hoping to have that reshelved by the Samhain. I was also thinking about starting another book club here. Good idea? Bad idea?"

I shrugged. "Decent idea."

"This year, I figured it could be themed. You'd come, wouldn't you?"

Pressing my lips together, I watched Faith pace back and forth with energy. "Of course."

"Fabulous." Her hazel eyes glittered.

I resettled myself against the wall as I watched her work until she finally paused, leaning back against the edge of her desk.

"Don't let me keep you if you have stuff to do," said Faith, peeking up from where she double-checked the slip of paper inside the next book and made a note. "I plan on heading out in a bit, so I'm not going to ask you to help me. Not yet, that is. Unless you need something?"

"Nope," I said. "Just sort of …"

"Procrastinating?" Seeing that she had gotten that mostly right, she nodded. "Go. I'll see you tomorrow, right? And on Tuesday, if you haven't already marked it down, make sure to come early! I think that Celeste is going to teach us how to make her apple pie before our Mabon ritual."

Celeste made her famous apple pie each fall. It was always crisp, yet gooey and perfectly spiced. We'd been on her about teaching the recipe for ages, even if we were going to have to make do in Gertie's slightly cramped kitchen.

"Sounds good. Have a nice night, Faith."

"Happy studying."

I gave a final wave, which Faith gleefully returned, and I moved around the circular library space until I made it to the stairs. Spaces were grouped by volume. Each floor from the basement archives upward got quieter as you climbed.

I turned left to the second floor. It wasn't that I was a habitual creature, but after the past few years, I had found exactly where the perfect spot was in the library.

On the second floor, there were no distractions, no matter the scenario. I could get work done, lounge, and hide away from the rest of the people who were also likely cramming for an exam, all at the same time.

The spot where I rarely ever had to interact with anyone was in the back corner by the large, curved window. An oversize table was set there unceremoniously but created plenty of room to stretch out.

Only tonight, someone was sitting in it.

My footfalls nearly froze before I noticed exactly who was sitting in the seat beside the one I usually filled. I walked around the other side of the table with purpose until I looked the table stealer in the face.

"What are you doing here?" I couldn't help the words that came out harsher than intended.

No matter their venom, my words didn't seem to faze him in the slightest. As I held a pencil in hand, his one foot was casually propped up in the chair beside him, enhancing the entire devil-may-care facade he was putting on.

"Fancy seeing you here."

"I told you I was going to be here," I grumbled, looking around the space.

There were plenty of other tables available, and yet Ryan Gardner had to sit here?

And for a moment there, I'd truly been curious if the self-absorbed jock who had made fun of me three years ago had somehow matured. Obviously not.

"Yet I still got here first. What a wonderful world we live in," sang Ryan.

That was true. I looked back toward his leg and crutches. How had he gotten here before me?

"You're welcome to sit down," Ryan went on, gesturing to the other side of the wide, solid wood table.

Of course I was welcome to sit down. This was *my* table. Except for unknowing first-years, no one messed with the status quo of where people sat in the cafeteria or library. Not when you saw and knew that someone else had deemed it their spot.

"Is this what is happening here? You aren't going to let up today until I sit with you?"

"Only mean girls don't share the table, Luella," he said with the cock of his head. "And I'm neither of those things."

I begged to differ.

He wasn't going to be causing another ruined part of my day, however. I rounded the other side of the table, closest to the window looking out onto the covered campus. In a single movement, I flopped down into the cushioned seat and let my heavy bag drop to the floor.

"Since you now see this area is taken, you can go," I said kindly. "Thanks for saving it for me."

It would've worked out all too well if that had persuaded Ryan at all. Clearly, the Barnett wonder boy was used to getting his way.

Ryan didn't move. If anything, he looked more delighted about how this was all turning out for him.

Sighing, I slowly pulled out my laptop and notebook, setting myself up how I always did. I was not moving, whether he thought that was the case or not. My screen flickered to life, and my hands paused over my keyboard. When I looked over the edge of my laptop, he was still there, looking back and forth between his battered-looking copy of *Pride and Prejudice* and me.

My willpower to ignore him was slipping.

"Fine. What's your deal? Is this some sort of bet you are doing with someone? A game? Or ..." I waited for him to fill in the blank, each word setting me more on edge.

Today really wasn't the day.

"It's not a bet. At first, I planned on just lying around in the cemetery for a while until one of my friends came to find me," Ryan said casually.

"So, the whole *pretending you're dead* thing happens often?"

He shrugged. "I wouldn't say I lie around in cemeteries *often*—cemetery, right?"

I nodded warily.

"But it does put things into perspective. It's quiet too. My head gets all loud and starts to race around in there sometimes, and the quiet is nice." He tapped the side of his head, as if a carnival ride were still going on in there. "You aren't the first person I scared, I will admit. Once last year, during finals, I needed a break and went up there to lie down between Lillian Hardtman and the good ol' Barnett brothers when it started to snow. A first-year stumbled across me and screamed. He was louder than you."

"I didn't scream."

He lifted his fingers. "A little bit. Anyway, I'm pretty positive he thought I was a dead body. Public safety had to come up, and we were much less amused."

"You seriously were just going to lie there for hours until a friend came and found you there and dragged you back to campus?"

"A friend did find me." He grinned at me.

We were not friends.

"What a riveting story. How does this play into why you are bothering me?"

"Oh, right. Well, I was up there, trying to figure out some things. Then, it dawned on me—the answer to at least one of my problems," he exclaimed.

"And that was?"

"You, of course."

Me?

I raised my eyebrows as my notebook slipped out of my hand against my keyboard. Ryan's pencil trembled before it rolled to the side.

He continued to smile up at me, as if the small earthquake wasn't any indication of how I was feeling right now. "You see, I heard from somewhere that you have basically taken the entire catalog of classes at Barnett."

Well, that wasn't true. At least, not completely, though I did have the habit of overloading on class credits whenever I changed my major.

"Did you now?"

He nodded, assured. "So, I figured, who better to help me out?"

"Excuse me?" I was obviously not following.

He wanted me to help him?

His smile began to falter, as did his clasped hands. Letting them go, he took a deep breath. "Look—"

"No, I mean, you look," I cut him off.

All I wanted to do was sit here for a few hours. I would get work done or maybe watch a movie on my laptop. Then, I would at least be somewhat prepared to sleep in my own confused misery tonight on a gross common room couch without Vadika.

No one was forcing me to go out to dinner or out to any parties or school events. It was just me. Tonight was mine. I hated to admit it, but I was oddly lost when it came to fun without her well-meaning involvement in my life.

"I didn't have a good day, and I really don't need anything else going on right now. I know you probably think that I should be falling over myself to help you with whatever little problem you have, but, well …" I looked down at myself in my jogger-style sweatpants as if that said enough.

With another deep breath, Ryan nodded. "I get it. Sorry. I didn't realize. Seems like a shit day all the way around."

"Is that so?"

"My coach met me in the dean's office. You know, where I saw you earlier."

I remembered. Reaching up, I touched the crystal pendant I was wearing still. I hadn't taken it off when I went back to my dorm. A little hope still stuck there—that whatever power Celeste had tried to infuse would kick in eventually.

Ryan took a deep breath before he continued, "My coach and the dean, who'd been my recruiter when I first came to Barnett, said they wanted to break the news about my leg to me together. According to the doctors and everything, there is a lot of damage to my knee. That means a lot of physical therapy before I could ever even consider getting back on the field this season. I let them know that I wouldn't be going back to playing at all. For the team or any other team."

"What do you mean?"

He sighed, shutting his eyes for a second. When he opened

them again, he scuffed his foot against the blue carpet. The other one was still propped on the chair.

I couldn't help myself as I glanced down at his braced knee. "It's that bad?"

"It wasn't the first time it happened," Ryan explained. "Either way, I was told I got lucky this time. The ACL tear was minor … ish. Course, now, well, that's it for football."

He attempted a small laugh. The short sound came out soft and a little uneasy.

"So, there is no way for you to go back to playing?" I asked calmly, peeking back up to the disappointment clearly written across his face.

"There is. But, y'know, there's that whole idea of wanting to walk for the rest of my life. I decided more or less to go with that option."

"Makes sense."

"Now, as you might imagine, they want me to get back to paying closer attention to my classes. It wasn't that big of a deal when I was playing. There were practices. Games. A lot of other things were going on every day to contend with, and I got a little leeway. That meant my grades weren't the greatest last semester … or the one before. I've been trying to squeeze in my general classes. I still have a few to get through."

I sighed. "So, in comes me?"

"In comes you." He bit his bottom lip. "I could really use the help."

"Did you even know my name before today?"

"Of course I did, Luella Pierce," he said, as if I were the one back to making jokes now.

But I wasn't.

The fact that he had answered surprised me. I honestly hadn't known if he would know my name or who I was at all. It was a small campus, sure. It was hard not to know the people you constantly walked by on it, and yet I honestly assumed when he saw me, he still just thought back to the day he had made fun of my clothes three years ago.

Satan's mistress, coming to steal their souls.

If only that were the truth. Then, I wouldn't be stressing out over whatever it was I needed to figure out to do next. In all facets.

"What's your major?" I asked casually.

His eyes widened with delight. He was getting somewhere with me, unfortunately. But I still hadn't made up my mind. He just looked so pitiful. Reaching down, he started to pull more folders out of his bag. A mishmash of papers floated out of the edges.

"I'm in elementary ed," he answered proudly. "But what I really need some help with is biology. I'm behind on a science credit. But I also have an English paper due soon—on pridefulness or something?"

"*Pride and Prejudice?*"

"That's it." He tapped the spine of his paperback against the table, taking another look at the front cover. "My professor is all about the author this semester. So, we could choose whatever for our first assignment, and since I watched the movie with my little sister before, I chose this. She's all about romance books, much to my mother's dismay."

She seemed like my kind of girl.

"You took biology too, right? I'm trash with research."

"Yeah. I changed my major to bio halfway through my first year. My friend Vadika thought I would make a good horticulturist."

"Your tall friend who commutes? The one with the dark hair?"

I nodded, still confused how he knew all this.

"Did you like it?"

"What?"

"Biology."

"I liked the horticulture part," I admitted, though that part was few and far between.

Some of my happiest times in class had come when I ended up drawing leaves and other herbs in my journal during the spring for "research."

"Like botany—plants and their uses. Vadika was right about that. The rest of the coursework and the premed students I could live without."

"It sucks that you can't just study what you want. You could be, like, an expert then. It's kind of like your crystals, right? Learning different plants and how they can help things?"

"Yeah, sort of."

"You could always switch back," suggested Ryan.

The idea of going backward wasn't something I liked to ruminate on, but this point was something I considered. I really didn't know what kind of use horticulture was going to get me in life after my final year in school came to a close, however. Tests completed and honor cords perhaps hung around my neck.

No one seemed to talk about such practicalities in university. It was all about getting a degree at school and less about if you cared about it or would be able to live off the piece of paper after graduation.

"Maybe," I conceded, confused about where this conversation had taken us.

He smiled again, as if I had given him the moon. "I used to want to be a scientist as a kid. Crazy hair and bubbling potions and all that."

"Really?"

"Until they started using random squiggles in math, yeah," said Ryan. "It made me more confident that I wanted to teach. I'm hoping I'll be able to up until the fifth-or-sixth-grade level. Anything beyond that, and I'm pretty sure I would fail out right along with whoever I was teaching."

"Good call then."

"I wouldn't want to teach in middle school anyway."

I raised my eyebrows. "Why not?"

"Middle school is terrifying." He scrunched his nose. "Did anyone really have a good time in middle school? I don't want to have any part in that sort of future trauma."

Good point.

Glancing down at my own things still laid out on the table, I reached, setting my laptop's screen alive with light once more. At some point, it had fallen asleep during Ryan's conversation. "If you are going to sit here, you should at least try to work."

"So, you're going to help me?"

"I didn't say that." Not yet. "Just …"

I gestured toward his things. He at least had to give me some sort of hope that this wasn't a ploy to get me to do all the work for him. *If* I was going to help.

Clicking his pen, he grinned as he checked something off the top of his notebook.

It'd better not have been a task about me.

I rolled my eyes and checked my email first and foremost. I double-checked my own due dates and other reminders that I had until the end of this semester, constantly reminding me of how I needed to declare a major. If, of course, I did plan on graduating.

Quickly clicking out, I moved on to my next pressing assignment I had started the night before during my last solo library session. Vadika's busy schedule to start the year was keeping even me busy and ahead of deadlines.

A blessing and a curse now that I had nearly nothing else to do.

I glanced over the edge of my screen back at Ryan.

He lifted his eyes up to meet mine from where he had been glowering down at a set of very messy notes in an equally messy composition book.

"Tell me about this thing of yours you had to go to the dean's office for," Ryan said.

I turned my attention back to my work, typing the first sentence of my conclusion paragraph. "That sounds like I did something wrong."

He only shrugged, as if to ask, *Did you?*

"No," I said seriously. "It's honestly kind of stupid, the more I think about it."

"I doubt it's stupid."

At least, that was one person. Vadika had basically said it was a waste of energy to begin with.

"I had an idea when I started the year that needed approval from the school. Really, I started the whole thing to keep myself busy." To keep my entire mind busy and everyone thinking I was busy with it. I wasn't proud enough not to admit it or turn anyone away who wanted to figure out my mishmash of a life for me. "I wanted to have a big campus party of sorts. A Samhain celebration."

"Sow-een?" Ryan tried to repeat.

"Samhain. It's Halloween." I shook my head at his rough pronunciation, giving the more known title for October 31. "I made all the plans and had everything ready, but it looks like it's a no-go."

"Why do you say that?"

I shrugged.

"Did the dean tell you no?"

"He told me I needed to get it approved by the student council, " I explained.

"Is that a bad thing?"

"Not for everyone." I stared straight ahead at him.

If it were him going to the student council with the idea, I had no doubt they would barely even glance at the proposal or the kind of work that had gone into it before ushering it through the academic popularity contest with a striking yes.

"I doubt they will ever actually get back to me about my

proposal, let alone consider it."

"I'm sorry."

"Don't be. Like I said, it was ridiculous to begin with." I glared down at the table.

"I don't think so," said Ryan. "I think it would be fun. Different than the normal stuff that goes on every year."

"You don't even know what I planned on doing."

"Fine then. Tell me," he demanded, though it came out soft and self-assured rather than assertive.

"You actually care to know?"

"I wouldn't be asking otherwise."

"Not to make me feel like you're a good person who deserves my help to pass your classes?"

He shrugged, not answering.

Pausing, I guessed I shouldn't have expected him to.

"All right then," I began. "I planned on having a small fire in one of the pits on the quad. Nothing huge, nothing fancy."

"Good start."

"Thank you." I'd take the compliment where I could get it. Even if it was from Ryan Gardner. "I figured that people could roast marshmallows or throw in a piece of paper that said what you hoped to manifest for yourself in the coming year. There would be caramel apples and basic spell-making canisters and paper lanterns to send up into the sky …" I let myself drift off, thinking of my multicolored pages in the binder I'd handed over this morning.

I doubted I would ever get it all back, and I was already low on printing credits.

"Sounds like a better version than the fall festival."

"I thought so."

"You don't know. There is still a chance that it could happen, though to me, it sounds like a lot of work."

That was sort of the point.

I hummed in agreement. I reached back down toward my bag,

grabbing my travel container out of the side pocket. Moving away from the table, I walked through the slowly disappearing groups of people scattered through the second floor of the library. No one sat near the water dispenser around the counter. Turning the handle to hot, I ripped open the paper packet of tea with my long, dark-purple fingernails. I dropped it inside my mug as water flowed over the top until the liquid turned from clear to a murky-gray-peppermint shade.

When I returned to the table, my cup was still steaming, and Ryan remained where he had been. He sat upright, rather like a defeated puppy, eyes wide as he stared at me to sit back down. The very beat-up copy of *Pride and Prejudice* was still flung in front of him.

"I thought you said you only saw the film?" I inquired, reaching forward to pick at the worn cover's edge.

"I skimmed."

Or more, it appeared. Narrowing my eyes, I sat back down, swirling my tea bag around clockwise twice, counter once, and then clockwise again before taking a sip.

I winced. Too hot.

"You just keep a bunch of tea bags in your bag all the time?" Ryan asked suddenly.

"Yep."

Ryan raised his eyebrows. He actually looked pretty impressed by this strange habit I'd developed.

Not that I cared what Ryan thought of me.

Lifting my cup, I tried again to take a sip without scalding myself. My tongue didn't flinch in protest. The temperature this time was much more palatable. "You never know when you are going to get kicked out of your own dorm for the weekend after all. Having everything you need with you at all times is actually a good plan then."

"What do you mean?" The space between his eyebrows creased, the book next to him completely forgotten.

"My roommate and I don't have the most ... ideal of roomie relationships," I said. That was putting it mildly.

"Ah."

Yes, *ah*.

I reached for his copy of *Pride and Prejudice* once more, looking to see if there were any notes in the margins. If I had to guess, I would say that Ryan did a lot more than just skim. Which, of course, made no sense if he was here with me, asking for help on a book he chose yet also insisted he knew little about.

"She and her boyfriend will be there, and frankly, I'd rather not be."

"Gotcha. That sucks. If it were me, it wouldn't be the first time I had been thrown out of my room for a night," commiserated Ryan. "Only made me gladder when I got my single. It's like a dream."

I could only imagine.

"I live down in the sports house," he went on.

Figured. I turned my gaze back down to the book, continuing to let the tea bag steep in the hot water in my cup off to the side.

"Can I try it?"

I peered up through the shag of my bangs to where his finger pointed. "My tea?"

"Yeah," said Ryan, leaning back, however, as if it were an awful thing to ask. "Unless you don't want me to."

I shook my head slowly, nudging the cup toward him.

As he took a careful sip, the steam curled around his chin. His face immediately wrinkled.

"Not a fan?"

Ryan shook his head. "No. I'll stick to overpriced coffee, thanks."

I almost wanted to laugh at the unnerved expression on his face. Instead, I looped my hand around the rim of my tea, bringing it back closer. "What do you drink, caramel mocha frappés?"

"They are a perfectly good source of energy."

"From sugar," I granted.

He laughed. "I didn't say that wasn't the case. Delicious though. So," he said, "you're really just going to hang out here for the next two days instead of going back to your dorm room?"

I was about to answer with what my plans were, but I paused. I hadn't thought about staying here in the library. In theory, technically, I could do that. I wasn't sure I'd ever heard of someone abusing the library hours like that before, but I had been here long enough to know that they never locked the doors with the alarm from the inside. I'd been the last one in the library as the night turned back into day before. Why not extend those late-night cramming hours?

Slowly, I dipped my head, lips pursed. That was exactly what I was going to do. Hiding out here sure beat sleeping on a lumpy common room couch where who knew what acts people had committed on it.

"We can stay here for as long as we want, but once the door shuts behind us after midnight?" I clicked my tongue. Then, we'd be locked out.

"We?"

I rolled my eyes. I had said that.

"So, you're really going to help me?" He grinned wide. "Like, really, it wasn't a joke before. For a minute there, even though you had left your stuff here, I did have the thought that you weren't coming back from your tea expedition."

Tea expedition? If I didn't have any other knowledge of Ryan, I would classify him as a nerd.

Still, I held my uninterested stare. "Against my better judgment."

"You won't regret this," Ryan assured. "Tonight and whenever else. It's going to be great. This is going to be the most amazing yet weird sleepover ever."

4

"Seriously, this is the best. Lu, my partner, helping me pass my classes and graduate. I love it," Ryan continued to muse with elation.

That made one of us.

Leaning back in his chair, Ryan looked around. I took the time to as well. In the past half hour, the library had cleared out. The lights had dimmed from the last of the librarians leaving for the weekend.

Was I really going to spend the entire weekend here? Campus security could pass by and find us and then … what? Kick us out? It wasn't so bad when I thought about it like that. Then, I would just be right back to sleeping on a gross campus couch, bolted down to the floor in case anyone wanted to steal ugly blue polyester.

I took a deep breath, turning back to the matter at hand as I met Ryan's eyes, already situated on me.

"I think we need to order a pizza," Ryan said seriously.

"I think we need to order two if you think I'm helping you write your whole essay and who knows what else," I said, shaking my head at the rest of what was going on inside my head.

His grin never faltered. Reaching for his phone, he scrolled through what looked to be his contacts. "Benny's or Atajio's?"

"You're serious?"

He nodded. "I don't joke about pizza."

"Atajio's. Half pepperoni."

"Good choice." He dipped his chin in approval. "I always took you to be vegetarian or something."

"I am. Sometimes," I conceded.

Ryan cocked his head to the side. "Sometimes?"

"Mostly, I disagree with the entire meat and production industry, but then"—I sighed—"I really get the hankering for a good cheeseburger with mayo."

"Mayo?"

"Yes, it's a perfectly good condiment," I argued. "And it's been a rough day."

Ryan lifted his hands in surrender before he leaned over the side of his chair to grasp his crutches. He adjusted them one at a time under his arms before he stood to head in the other direction. "Hey, you aren't going to hear any complaints from me. We'll get one of each in case your conscience gets to you."

Probably for the best.

I watched as he moved back toward the other side of the library, where I knew the service was better. I wouldn't have thought Ryan frequented this place that often to know. I realized I was staring. I forced myself to pull my eyes away from Ryan's retreating form and flipped the lid of my laptop.

I started to jot down a few of the call numbers for generic books that might help Ryan with what I assumed was the standard three to five sources minimum he didn't yet have. That way, at least he wouldn't have to be here all night with me.

The image alone of him with tired eyes glaring at my attention to detail from across the table caused me to spell a title incorrectly from the database as I wrote it down on the paper.

By the time Ryan returned, I was done, kicking my own legs up on the other chair he wasn't using next to me.

"Pizza is on its way."

"And you need to get started on that paper if you plan on ever getting it finished." I pointed with the back end of my pen. "I already got started on a few sources I think will help."

His shoulders slumped. "Didn't forget about that, huh?"

"Did that hit on the field take out more than your leg and you're forgetting about why you are hanging out with me at all in the library on a Friday night? No. I didn't forget unless you don't want me to help you get through this essay anymore."

"Please?"

I was a sucker for a good *please*.

Plus, I had already said yes. "What do you have so far?"

"A topic."

"I thought you already said you were doing *Pride and Prejudice*?" I asked, not understanding what he meant. Was that really all he had?

"Right. I mean, a thesis," he corrected, seeing the horror on my face. "We already had to get them approved."

I waved for him to go on, hoping that he had one to share.

"I'm going to talk about the courting practices and the house parties that are thrown at the fancy guys' houses is basically the eighteenth-century version of online speed dating. You know, swipe right, swipe left?"

I stared at him. I wanted to make a joke, and yet, somehow, it was oddly accurate. Creative even. "Have a lot of online dating experience then?"

Ryan shrugged, a little bashful. "Enough to have some good stories."

"A slightly anecdotal paper it is then," I offered, glancing back down at my list of resources.

I wanted to ask more questions but held back. Though Ryan certainly had a popular reputation, I never heard of any dating mishaps. That kind of thing was sure to go around a school as small and tightly knit as Barnett like wildfire if it was amusing enough.

"Good. Now, we can find some sources."

"Where? Online in the database thing?"

"Well, we are in a library, so let's start with books, Ryan. You know, the things on the shelves?"

He looked at me without humor. "I know what a book is, Luella."

My eyes flared at the name, and I knew he saw it the moment his lips pressed back together in a humorous challenge. Oh, now, he wanted to tease the moment he got what he wanted?

"We'll find sources on the book as well as on the historical consequences of regency seasons. You're right after all. As well as bragging rights to a good party, they were created to make suitable matches, though they usually took place in higher concentrated places. London, for instance, compared to the smaller villages where Elizabeth and Darcy met more coincidentally than actively, like your thesis says. Perhaps that means you could also go into how the two of them caused a break of what was proper and expected based on their status."

Ryan blinked. "Wow."

I raised an eyebrow, pushing my chair back to stand. "Am I overwhelming you?"

"No. I just had no idea you could find things like that here. See, you're helping me already," Ryan encouraged. "Let's do it."

Ryan's eyes followed me until I rounded the table, standing in front of him.

"Are you going to make me get them all for you by myself too? It's going to take a whole lot more than you picking up the phone and ordering a pizza to make this worthwhile."

"What you're saying is that you do have a price to do my essay for me?"

"You should be ashamed as a future educator."

Laughing again, Ryan made a little noise of effort as he hoisted himself back up to standing and stretching his leg out, as if it was tight. He took my lead as we headed past the stairs to the other set of bookshelves.

Holding up my piece of scrap paper, I split it in half. I held out the other piece in front of him. He took it with little more than a snatch, as if he thought I'd taunt it in front of him like a cat. The thought had occurred to me.

"All right. First person to find their books on the list wins," I explained. "Fair?"

"What's the prize?"

"I don't know," I said. "Bragging rights?"

"Lame, but all right." Ryan twisted the piece of paper around until it was right side up.

"What, you have something better?"

"Winner gets to choose."

I narrowed my eyes at him. I could only imagine what he would have me do if he won. Not, of course, that he would. I knew this library like the back of my hand after spending so many hours inside of it, with or without being coerced into helping Faith with whatever her latest project was. Witch to witch.

Which basically just meant Faith batted her purple eyelashes a few extra times after being told she couldn't require such hard labor, stacking and restacking, from any of the other students sitting at the desk for work study.

"Fine," I agreed.

"Fantastic."

"On your mark, get set—"

"Hey!" Ryan yelled before quickly settling into a whisper, clearly forgetting that we were more or less alone in the nearly empty library. His head whipped back and forth for any angry librarians.

I curved around the side of one of the bookcases, paying his concern no heed. Still, Ryan managed to be close behind.

"You didn't say go."

"And?"

"Obviously, you don't know what sportsmanship is." He hustled after me, using more of his leg than was probably wise.

It wasn't only me who had a competitive edge.

I turned down another shelf, lifting myself up onto my toes to see on the shelf above my head. My finger slid down the spines of books.

I snatched my first oversized reference book down from the shelf at nearly the same time Ryan found his first. I tucked the book under my arm before skimming the next row over. I knew that it was somewhere. I, myself, had taken the same class that Ryan was now in, though that professor had had much more of a preoccupation for the Brontë sisters at the time.

The section of eighteenth through nineteenth-century women writers was sadly small, right next to the monstrosity of the school's Shakespeare and romance collection.

Another book was yanked down off the shelf, and I went for the final one. I found it easily, the edge sticking out, likely from someone else who was also using the library for a similar project. I jogged my way around to the bookend, where Ryan was already. I lifted the book up in front of him. He still had to go to the aisle I had just been in to get his last one. Maybe I should've made it a little fairer. I should've only given him two compared to my three.

"Aha! Beat that."

When he pressed his lips together, it almost looked like he was forcing himself not to smile at his devastating loss. It didn't last long before he exposed his pearly teeth and pulled out the final book at his side.

I stared at it. My eyes widened. "How …"

"Guess this means I won, huh?" asked Ryan smugly.

I said nothing as I turned back toward our table.

"Don't worry. I'm still trying to think of the perfect thing I want as a reward for my exceptional win."

He could keep thinking all he wanted, for as long as he wanted. I shrugged, as if it were nothing. His smugness could only continue, however, for so long.

"Seriously, how did you get that one? I didn't see you in the shelves there."

"Can't give away my secrets," he said simply.

"Maybe then you'll be able to find all your own books."

"Nah, that would be a whole lot less interesting without you here to beat."

My lips parted for another comeback. I wasn't sure exactly what to say. Talking with Ryan was easy, and I didn't know how I felt about it. Then, add in the compliments.

If I didn't know any better, I would've assumed Ryan was trying to get into my pants. Of course, in this scenario, he was much more likely trying to get into my brain than my pants.

Sweatpants.

I tuned myself out as I gestured down to the books spread out on the table.

We were both back at a respectable distance from one another.

"Well, you definitely have your five sources here, and we can probably look up another on the school database if you need an electronic one too. Like you said before, an extra will also take up some more page space if you decide to quote directly."

"Probably smart. One more thing checked off." Ryan grinned, much less out of breath than I felt. He swiped his blue pen over what was clearly a previously empty box.

"You use a planner?" I tried not to sound surprised.

"Yeah," Ryan said. "I might not get things in on time, but at least I know that I have to do them. You don't use one?"

"I have everything online. I run my coven's calendar, so it seemed easier to have everything in one place."

"Coven."

Shutting my mouth, I paused before letting myself sink back into my seat. Right, I had just said that. It wasn't a secret of coven extracurriculars, but for a minute, it was easy to forget the Ryan from three years ago.

The crazy soul-stealing witch.

"Is that what they call your church?"

Slowly, I nodded. "Kind of. More like a church group if you think of it like that. Less chanting, more chatting."

"Who else is in your coven then?"

"It's me and about five other ladies. There's Gertrude, Celeste, Essie, Ana, Faith—"

"Faith, the librarian?"

I stared at him, surprised he'd put that together, let alone knew who any of the librarians at Barnett were. Librarians were almost always witches. I didn't need to open that conversation right now, however.

"A few of them tote along their kids too. I usually drag along Vadika a few times each year."

Ryan snickered. He didn't look upset or anything other than interested.

"It used to be more structured. Nowadays, we end up just eating snacks and talking about the ways of life." As well as possible solutions that didn't come from the charmed snack cake or cinnamon bread for lively abundance and luck.

"The ways of life?"

I nodded.

"Have you figured that out yet?"

I snorted. I couldn't believe I was laughing with Ryan Gardner now. "Not in the slightest."

"So, you don't really, like, cast spells and do magic then?"

"No, we do," I said. "Just not like the movies."

"What do you mean?"

"Magic is in the intention, which is then transformed through manifestation, an understanding of the physical and metaphysical world."

"I have no idea what you just said."

"You honestly want to know?"

He nodded.

"Okay, then think of it like ..." I narrowed my eyes, thinking. "You are a kitchen witch, and you want to create happiness or joy."

"There are different types of witches?"

"Depends on how label-y you want to be, but of course. Anyway—"

"What type of witch are you?"

Wow. We were really getting into this.

Taking a deep breath, I set my laptop to the side.

"I consider myself an eclectic witch." Like all things, I couldn't make up my mind. "Before school, when I was fully able to embrace myself and all of it, I was a solitary practitioner. It was magic in an odd sense, which I found comfort in when I was alone more than any other time, I think. I kept hoping for a better next."

"A better next," he repeated.

"I have to remind myself how grateful and happy I am not to have to learn and talk about magic by myself. Not since I gained my coven. They took me in. A family. Back in high school, this, right here, was my better next. Anyway ..."

I waited for him to cut me off again.

He waited in case I had anything else to say, a softness to his eyes.

Of course, they always looked that way.

"For example, with the magic question. A kitchen witch might use witchcraft or magic by baking. She might decide to create little cakes for happiness. She'll put corresponding ingredients in and make sure her intention while baking them is her end goal. What you want hard enough, already is."

"I like that. What you want, already is."

"I'm sure there is a better way to phrase it. Anyway, that's mainly the thing. Desire and manifestation for a witch, like a kitchen witch making her cakes mindfully is bringing her goal for happiness in others around her to life."

"Huh," said Ryan. A hint of confusion clouded his expression. It was the same sound he had made when I explained my crystal necklace in the dean's office. "I think I need some of those cakes."

Didn't we all?

His phone chimed.

I forced myself not to lean over the table to see who was messaging him.

He only grinned, grabbing his crutches to stand again. "I guess we'll have to settle. Pizza's here."

Pizza. The thought of pizza caused any talk of happiness cake to disappear. Outside the wide second-floor window, a nondescript white car with a dent in the bumper pulled up to the curb.

"I didn't realize it was so late," Ryan whispered, looking around the empty library as they made their way downstairs.

Like them, however, there was likely at least one other person still hiding in a corner somewhere. The steady tapping of a keyboard echoed through the empty lengths of space, pausing with the occasional hum, as if someone were writing to music and couldn't help but sing along to their study playlist.

They likely thought they were the only ones inside the library at this point too.

"What? Have somewhere to be?" I asked at a normal volume, watching from the bottom step as Ryan made his way down the final few stairs.

He stumbled on the second to last. I flinched, as if to catch the large buffoon of a man.

He cocked his head. "You going to try and save me, Lu?"

"Don't even."

All I needed was to be a headline in the school newspaper next week after they ran out of anything interesting to report on.

Campus witch causes collapse of Barnett football star in after-hours library squatting.

Ryan shook his head, still smiling. "It's nice to know you have my best interests at heart."

"Only your bodily ones."

He cocked his head to the side, the picture of delight.

"You're bodily well-being—just stop." Best to put myself out of my misery. I shook my head, turning away from him toward the front double library doors.

"Whatever you say, Luella. I'm already starting to have the feeling that you don't hate me as much as we both thought you did," said Ryan.

"Think again."

Ryan continued to hold the same smug expression.

He could look however he wanted as long as he listened closely.

"Now, we cannot let the door close or else we will be locked out for the rest of the night. Got it?" I asked, waiting for some sort of nod.

"Got it. If I shut this door while you are going to get the pizza, you'll be locked out."

Very amusing. "And I'll sit by the door and eat two whole pizzas while you watch."

"Cruel."

I threw the door open a little wider before it was grasped back in Ryan's hands. "Hold the door. And make sure no one sees you."

"Why do you say that?"

"I'm not saying that this is against the rules or anything..."

"Only it is, isn't it?"

"We just don't want to give campus security any more fun on a Friday night."

He waved me off. "Hurry then."

The south end of campus was surprisingly vacant, save for the loud voices echoing through the trees toward University Row. Leaning against the door, Ryan shouted at me quietly the farther I got away down the straight pathway where the pizza boy was looking between the two of us with both intrigue and humor.

"Go! Go! GO," called Ryan.

Unable to help myself at the immediate tone of voice, all fun, I grinned as I raced out the darkly lit doors of the library, looking back to make sure that he hadn't accidentally locked us both out.

As I fished in my back pocket, the young delivery boy shook his head the moment I got close enough.

He extended the pizzas out to me with a smile. "Already paid for."

"Oh?" I narrowed my eyes, taking the two pizza boxes from his hands.

He waved over my shoulder, going up on his toes. "Hey, Ryan!"

"Hey, Lucas!" he called back in his whisper-yell. "How's it going?"

The boy shrugged as he fell back on flat feet. I'd never seen him before. At least, I didn't think I had. Not apparently like Ryan had.

"Have a good night."

"You too."

I walked back to Ryan with the pizzas, and the doors shut behind us with a heavy click. Once more, we were sealed inside. No alarm went off, and no one yelled after us to condemn our Friday night literary exploits.

"Regular customer?" I asked Ryan. I yanked the pizzas away from him as he reached out toward one, as if to carry it the rest of the way. "Nuh-uh. I'm not letting you drop these. I'd rather let you be the one who falls down the stairs."

He glanced back down at the crutches he was leaning on a little less than before. I hoped he wasn't pushing himself for no reason.

"Fair. And I gave Lucas, the pizza boy, lessons last spring. Most of the team did it for our volunteer hours. Plus, it was good to have the high school on my résumé," explained Ryan with another goofy smile. "But also, yes, it's really good pizza."

"Was he any good?"

"Who? Lucas?" Ryan asked as he started to climb the stairs two at a time. "Not in the slightest."

I laughed.

His head turned around to me. "I wondered if you could do that."

"Do what?"

"Laugh."

Slowly, whatever delight snuck its way onto my face dissipated. My lips closed again. They pressed together the rest of the way back to our table. The overhead light was still on above the table, staying on dimly all night. Another reason it was the perfect spot even if I never intended on sharing.

Before I could even drop the pizza down on the edge, ignoring the *please no food* sign, Ryan lifted the lid and grabbed a slice. The cheese oozed off the side along with a slice of pepperoni.

I reached for my own.

"Do you ever think you smile at people too much?" I asked.

"No." Ryan shook his head as if the thought were utterly preposterous. "It doesn't cost anything."

"But it's dishonest."

"A smile?"

"False happiness. False hope."

"Aren't you just a bundle of joy?" he teased.

I was pretty sure we'd already gone over that. I dipped my head back down to take a bite of the pizza, still warm. I could've moaned at the taste. My face must've said enough.

"Good, huh?"

"Really good. I see why you risk your football physique for such magnificence."

He rolled his eyes. "Keep denying it all you like, Lu. You've been checking me out, haven't you?"

"Be quiet."

"I'm eating," he excused. He still couldn't stop laughing.

"Then, eat more." Anything to get him to stop talking. "Or get started with your essay. You're never going to finish at this rate."

He kept smiling as he took an obnoxiously large bite and reached to lift the screen of his computer. Immediately, it burst to life. He opened a preformatted document. He was right. He did have more than nothing.

He had the thesis right there in the title.

And his name.

"At least you can check off one more thing on your list," I said. "Started essay."

"Don't joke about my lists. They're super helpful." He took another bite of pizza, straight from the crust. He chewed, and it piled in his cheeks like a chipmunk. A pleased glimmer shone in his eyes. "And I already marked that off yesterday."

Of course he had.

"To be honest, I haven't spent too much time in the library since I got here," said Ryan. "Not for actual work anyway. It's nicer than I thought it would be."

I didn't say anything, and he seemed to understand why.

"Don't judge."

"I didn't say a word."

"Exactly."

I shrugged and continued to eat from the second plain cheese pizza. It looked better than the first one, whether or not it was going to give me a stomachache.

"I always hated to do my work in the library," he explained. "Too quiet and studious."

"Things you aren't?" I asked.

"So much pressure to get things done. I don't do well with pressure."

"Says the star football player."

"That's different. I'm playing then." He paused, running his tongue along his teeth as he took stock of his words. "*Was* playing."

"How long did you play?"

A crease formed between Ryan's eyebrows. "Maybe since I was thirteen or so? We had flag football before, which I used to do after school."

"Devoted," I commented.

"It's just something I did," Ryan said as if it were the easiest thing in the world. "My friends played, and so I played. It was a small town."

"Where everyone knew everyone?"

"Pretty much." He shrugged. "You know how it is?"

"No. I lived in a suburb on the edge of the city for most of my life. I would be lucky if I knew our next-door neighbor at any given point to let them know what kind of cardboard was allowed in the recycling bin."

"You and your family lived in an apartment?"

I hesitated, wondering just how much I was about to hand over to Ryan. "A condo. You were in a little house with a picket fence?" By his face, I could tell I wasn't far off. "The perfect nuclear family?"

"Kind of actually," he admitted.

"I'm sorry. That's not bad." I tried to correct myself. He was right; I was the opposite of a bundle of joy. "It's a good thing."

"Sometimes. Everyone knew my dad. My teachers knew him.

The whole town did. I was constantly trying to be more like him, though I wasn't. The only things we had in common was that we both played football and were liked." He paused, as if he didn't want to say something. He cleared his throat. "I got to be me when I got here. No one made fun of me or judged me based on my family. You get that?"

I stared at him. "Sort of."

"What do you mean?"

"I'm just saying, I think our college experiences might be a little different." I said.

"In what ways? Didn't you say you found your best friends and family here?"

"Yes," I admitted. "But that doesn't mean I didn't feel as if I'd left one high school who looked at me like I was some sort of *other* for another the moment I stepped on campus. For you, Barnett was a relief. For me, it was another test."

Each new week was another for things to possibly form into something better. They never just arrived pretty and perfect, wrapped up in a bow. At least, not for me.

"Explain."

"You," I said.

"Me?"

"You made fun of me."

His jaw clenched. "When?"

"It's stupid." To think I had been holding on to it for this long felt like it meant a lot more to me than I wanted it to.

Ryan's words didn't have any effect on me. At least, not more than I'd let on.

He didn't even remember, clearly. I was insignificant to him.

"No, it's not. I think it's stupid that I don't remember better," he said, shaking his head down at himself. "Tell me."

"It was during that first week of orientation at the SUB. All the first-years met together after a day full of those stupid community-building activities. Everything was new, and people were already forming groups. I was still not in one of those groups. But you noticed me."

"I did?"

"You did. You noticed me—who had been, at the time, shy and terribly uneasy with her body over the past few years—and you and your friends on the football team ruined whatever shred of confidence I managed to get to Barnett in less than thirty seconds. Instead of saying hi, you smiled that ever-present smile of yours and made a joke."

Ryan's smile slowly faded into something painful as I went on.

"You said that I looked like a gothic freak show or Satan coming to steal innocent virgin souls—I don't remember the specifics. I do remember all of them staring at me and laughing." I waved a hand, as if it were all of a fleeting memory I shouldn't have brought up.

"Oh."

"You certainly got a good laugh," I added quickly. "Anyway, maybe I should thank you. Vadika, my friend, overheard and promptly adopted me, which has been one of the best things to ever happen to me. She pieced me into the person I really was even if it is still unconventional."

"I think you're beautiful, Lu."

My head whipped up to stare at him before I could avert my eyes back down to my book.

He nodded once. "I'm sorry I said those things. Honest. Back then, well, I wanted to be liked."

I slowly nodded. *Didn't we all?*

At least one of us had succeeded.

"Anyway, if it makes you feel better, I was basically just trying not to let the rest of the world know that I was included in that statement."

"What?"

"An innocent virgin soul to steal," Ryan joked with a shrug.

A moment passed before understanding swept over me. I

blinked and pointed back to his laptop that, at some point, had fallen asleep.

"You need to focus on your paper, or we aren't going to ever get done before the weekend is over, let alone before the sun makes a reappearance."

"I'm working; I'm working."

"So you say." I raised my eyebrows, reaching back toward my half-eaten second slice of pizza again. "So, go on now. Tell me more about your online dating escapades. For the paper, of course."

He barked a short laugh. "Not that you want to get another laugh out of me."

"Not at all."

"Not at all," he repeated with a shake of his head, swiping over his touchpad before his essay lit back up on the screen.

5

Ryan and I maintained a steady stream of conversation over the next few hours as he wrote his examination of regency dating as detailed within *Pride and Prejudice* and further explored in their historical sources. I marked each particularly helpful passage I found within the first few chapters with a sticky note before passing it across the table.

He talked more about football and high school in a small town, where his parents still lived in a close-knit development. He talked about wanting to travel for study abroad, but at this rate, he'd never get to. He talked about favorite colors since there couldn't just be one and foods and how much he hated night classes—almost more than *eight in the morning* lectures, but at least you could show up to those in your sweatpants.

I could only agree, mostly because in the late evenings, I much preferred to be exactly where we were then, if not running off to accompany Vadika to her lab or sneak off to see Gertie in town, which Ryan was surprised to realize was so close.

"Who knew that a whole plethora of witches lived in Barnett?"

"Just the ones who need to," I answered. *At the very least.* Much like how many of them had found witchcraft and believed in the world and all of its unknowns to begin with. *We needed to.*

As well as a conversationalist, Ryan was surprisingly well written.

When he was engaged, he fell into a typing frenzy. He had to pause and go back to make sure he had put spaces in the right place between words, as if he could not keep up with his thoughts fast enough.

That, or he just wanted to be done.

He was typing his final few words of the conclusion by the time I put on a movie. I set it up on the edge of the table, where I could still see from the couch next to us, and let it play as my eyes dropped. I shifted to prop my feet up.

I glanced over his essay. It could've been better put in the middle sections. In Ryan's words, it was good enough. I fixed some minor citations and quotation marks before handing it back. If his professor wasn't impressed, I was.

Not that I'd ever say that.

In fact, I was close to being shocked at how well formed his unique argument was in only a few painstaking hours, however modern. I'd read worse clickbait articles that came through my email daily. Even more so, I was shocked the moment he shut his computer lid and collapsed on the couch next to me.

"Freedom," Ryan sighed, stretching his arms overhead.

He shut his warm eyes for a moment before he opened them again, getting comfortable in the dark corner we had found ourselves in without the bright screens of computers lighting up our faces.

"Congratulations. One paper down."

"And about a half dozen more to go before the end of the semester," he added.

Well, that was one way to think about it. "Now, who's the pessimist?"

I turned my attention back toward the movie I'd put on. I had seen it more than a few times. Ever since I'd first arrived at Barnett, it had become sort of a tradition when I needed to settle myself.

I didn't want to come back to campus not long after arriving and hesitantly heading off campus to meet the small coven with a sad, yet somewhat active social media page Faith maintained when she was in the mood to mark meetings. The rest of the ladies stuck to a more ancient, yet easier, phone call when they needed to cancel. An incident which had only happened once two years ago during a rainstorm that flooded the river and Gertie's cellar.

When I had shown up, I pushed past the white picket fence to the large, slightly sloped backyard of Gertrude's home. It looked like something out of a fairy tale. Her yard was adorned with raspberry vines and a small, smoldering firepit in the center with women around it. And they acted as if I had always been there.

When I didn't want to go back to campus, a few of the ladies simply shrugged, taking me inside the sunroom, where they laid blankets on the daybed and watched Audrey Hepburn films until I fell asleep. I woke up to tea and a promise that I was allowed to come back to the meetings whenever I needed.

I'd never felt more at home.

I slouched into the cushions and indirectly into Ryan, mind lost from the sound of nonsensical dancing on-screen.

"You seem sad."

"Just thinking."

"I get that," Ryan said softly. "You still worried about that party you wanted to host?"

I shrugged. I'd forgotten about that for the moment. "Kind of. For the longest time, moving on in life, I kept telling myself that things would get better. They'd get better when I was in middle school—"

Ryan scoffed.

I lifted a hand in agreement. "Then, I said it would get better in high school, and then I said it would get better in college."

"And it didn't?"

"No," I said, "it did. Not right away, but it did. But I don't know what to look forward to. I don't know what I'm going to do afterward. It's all finally better, and I feel good here, just kind of hiding out and living and spending time with my friends." *My family.*

"That's hard."

I sighed. "It's fine. It's late. I'm thinking too much."

"Nah. But it will be," he said. Without pretense, he wrapped an arm around my shoulders.

I stiffened at the movement but did not move away. It was nice to be held. Plus, I was too tired to move.

"See? Something to look forward to in the future again."

"What is?"

"The *will be*," he repeated the two words from before. "Doesn't have to take place during a monumental moment, like everyone else, right? It just happens."

"Maybe."

"It will be. You're too interesting for great things not to happen to you."

I looked up at Ryan, though there was no hint of a joke.

"Thanks for helping me. I owe you," he said. One side of his mouth curved into a short smile as he glanced at the film on my laptop again. His eyes flickered back and forth between it and me, as if he expected me to say something great.

Movie. Me. Movie...

"I think I know what I want my reward to be," Ryan whispered.

His lips tilted over mine in a breath of a second. It was barely a kiss, and yet our mouths touched all the same, as if sharing air, sharing this moment and everything we were with me in Ryan's arms.

Ryan Gardner's arms. The boy who had made fun of me right when I thought my life was turning around.

He kissed me softly, carefully, as if I were priceless glass before he pulled away. His eyes were still closed, as if he was afraid to open them again and find me staring up at him with a heavy-lidded gaze.

Eventually, his eyes did open, and there didn't appear to be any fright or regret as he leaned back. But there was also nothing else. There was not another kiss. There was barely a breath, let alone a single word.

The movie played on, and at some point, I was the one to shut my eyes and let myself drift back into content darkness.

6

My gods, my back.

A vacuum cleaner rumbled in my ear from across the room, scraping over something hard and clacking, like a paper clip.

I groaned as I sat up. Hunched over, I rubbed my hands against my eyes before I opened them, stiff and butt numb. Behind me, or rather collapsed against my shoulder, Ryan stretched out.

He grunted as he leaned into his bad knee.

"Ugh, I'm so ready to get this brace off along with being done with my crutches soon," he complained. His eyes were still closed as he took another deep breath, as if considering never moving from his spot where he laid, half on top of me. Every inch from his head to his waist was curved into mine.

For someone so large as him, I didn't understand how this strange little spoon situation would have ever worked, and yet ...

Only when he glanced over his shoulder and saw his head against my thigh did Ryan smile and hoist himself off the couch, as if he wasn't at all surprised where he had ended up.

"Not gonna lie," he said. "The whole *sleeping in the library* thing sounded a lot better in theory."

"You could've gone home."

"I could've." He shrugged. His hair was more haphazard than usual while he reached for his things, shoving them all into the largest pocket of his backpack. "It'll probably be worse to go back to the sports house now. They are all probably hungover or worse."

I slowly followed suit, letting my legs drop down from the couch. My laptop had long since turned dark. The film flickered on, paused past the halfway mark. Had Ryan stopped it?

If he had and then laid back down with me, that made a whole lot less sense.

Yet I didn't ask.

"Worse?"

"Didn't you know? Football players are all about the drama," Ryan chuckles, garnering the attention of a few other hungover, early rising university students who started to wander around us. Large coffee cups from the cart down on the first floor were set up beside their books or on the surrounding square tables with curved backs for privacy.

A few of those same eyes cared a lot less about my own privacy as they landed on me. Or rather, Ryan. Then, they landed on me.

Ryan and me.

The phrase really didn't sound right. Too simple.

The only person who wasn't looking at me right now was Ryan. I glanced up at him as he threw a tired smile over his shoulder, quickly turning his gaze back in the other direction again. "I need to head off to meet the team for the fundraiser they are hosting, if they make it out of bed. You know, whether or not I'm still on the team."

"Good luck." I nodded dumbly. "Have fun."

"We'll see if that's possible when I tell everyone the news

about me and my good old leg here. See you later, right?" Ryan asked, pointing back at me.

"Yeah, see you."

With a twist of his crutches, Ryan moved back toward the steps without looking back. I stared at him until I could no longer see him over the brass railing.

A few more stares stuck to me as I finished putting the rest of my things back into my bag and grabbed my boots. Interest lingered there, yet I rolled my eyes at one of them. If they didn't have the confidence to ask me what it was that I had done, staying the night, they did not deserve the answer in return.

Then again, what *had* happened last night?

I felt my fingers drift up toward my lips, as if I could tell if the kiss was a dream by touch. Shaking my own head, I stopped myself, slipping back down the stairs and out the heavy front doors of the library, not confident I wanted any answer.

* * *

"You look absolutely dreadful."

"Thank you." That was exactly what I needed to hear.

Stepping through the door, I kicked off my boots and padded my way down the frame-lined hallway of Gertrude Maison's— also known as Gertie—opulently eclectic home.

The moment the heavy door shut behind me, a weight dripped down from where it had been sitting on my shoulders, like the rain outside sliding down the old-fashioned paned windows. The pressure I'd been putting on myself drained past my elbows and through my legs, escaping through each step of my feet toward the sharp pitch of voices from my coven members. The light from the crescent moon stained glass window high above illuminated the way to the kitchen.

So did the smell of warm baked apples drifting through the air.

"That's exactly what I always hope to hear," I added with a heavy glaze of sarcasm to Gertie trailing behind me, taking in my slouched gait. Though truly, I never expected to get any compliment other than honesty from the eldest coven member and our high priestess for all intents and purposes.

Being high priestess was a symbol of honor. Gertie had created this space for all of us to live and practice together. Thus, she became our gratifying leader of a sort and would be until she could or would no longer.

"I'm merely stating the truth. I still don't understand. If you didn't have anywhere to stay for a proper sleep last night, why didn't you just come down here?" she asked. "You know where the key is."

Under the very inconspicuous frog lawn ornament?

Yes, I did.

I gave Gertrude a deceptively sweet smile. "Because I already planned on staying tonight to bother you after everyone else leaves."

With a roll of her eyes that made me see the young woman who had lived the bold and heart-wrenching stories Gertie now told when needed, she waved me off, as if I had given her an unreasonable answer.

Still, she gave up on constantly reminding me that I was not a bother. After so many times, it was clear that she was never going to get such a thing through my thick skull. After all, one could only say so many times that I was more than welcome to call Gertie's home mine. She'd never correct me.

Many of the coven members, past and present, at some point lived in the house until they were able to move on. Still, I didn't want to overstay my welcome, if that was possible.

When I did spend more than a few hours at a time here for shelter or just good company, I was also put to work. When the berries blossomed, I picked them. When the garden needed tending to, I learned the proper way of assisting the plants so as not to stifle growth. I weeded every week or two, so no one would have to hear Gertie complaining about her old-lady hips during the days after, like she usually did.

It was no hardship. I loved the garden that sprawled through the backyard. You could see a piece of it through every window, especially in the kitchen. Trees were already beginning to drop their jeweled leaves, as were the thick vines up the side of the house, next to the flower beds. The earth was slowly drifting to sleep for the next season, light and dark colliding with splotches of rich and hardy green visible in the clean rain.

I dropped my overstuffed bag onto the floor, jostling the small table in the breakfast nook. The noise caused heads to turn midconversation as I hopped up on the empty section of the wood countertop, crossing my legs over one another. I still wore the same sweatpants from last night.

"My gods. You look terrible." Ana's dark eyes took me in, glancing up and down.

"Thank you, Ana. Everyone is full of compliments today."

"Are you sick?" another asked.

"No, just homeless for the next twenty-four hours," I explained to them all, using a tiny voice. "Take pity on me."

Ana snorted. She, if no one else, was appeased by my answer. She moved back to rinsing the dishes, shaking out each plate in the sink before she set it on the beveled drying rack.

Her smile was one she shied away from sharing most days, like a hidden secret. I couldn't help but try and tease her to bring it out. It was all too easy. When Ana did grin, it was genuine and bright, both things I appreciated, and a stark contrast to her sleek, dark-brown hair and row of industrial piercings that lined each ear.

I wondered what Ryan would say about Ana if he ever saw her. I might have been Satan's gothic mistress a few years ago, but Ana would be a glamorous succubus or vampire coming to seduce your soul for me.

I pursed my lips to the side, smirking at my own humor.

Celeste peeked into the oven to check in on whatever her creation was this week that she always made at Gertie's house instead of at her own. For some reason, we were all quite positive Gertie's oven had its own bit of magic inside, making flavors pop and bread rise to new levels.

Whatever beautiful creation was made here, it was always promptly demolished by the hungry witches who made it.

Celeste's short ashy-blonde hair stuck perfectly out on one side as she gave a small shake of her head, letting the oven door shut once more. "A few more minutes."

"I thought Essie would be coming tonight since we don't plan on wreaking havoc on the world," said Ana, before glancing back at me once more. "Unless that's necessary, by the looks of you?"

I shook my head, resting my elbows on my knees—the perfect opening for her to hand me a towel to start drying the many bowls. Carefully, I ran the worn cloth over the edges of each dish I pulled from the basin before setting them safely on the other side of the counter.

Celeste slouched against the counter. "Estrella decided to spend the night with a new friend she'd met at school. He recently moved to the area. She and he are both back home."

The only one who called the poor girl her full name was her own mother. Besides her name, Essie was a sweet girl, set to be inducted into the coven as a witch in her own right on her sixteenth birthday this November, though she often attended meetings since she was old enough to walk.

"Alone?"

"I don't figure they can get in much trouble yet. Brenson's there." Celeste shrugged, referring to her eldest son.

"How lovely," commented Faith from where she leaned, perched on the edge of the windowsill, completely out of reach of doing any grunt work before the evening meal, unlike me and Ana. "It's good that Essie is getting out there in the world before she ends up stuck here, hanging out with us more often than not."

"You mean she hasn't been that way already?" Faith asked, truly interested in the answer as she sipped her wide cup of tea.

"That poor, corrupted girl." I nodded gravely.

Celeste narrowed her eyes at me with little humor at my plainly amused tone.

"So?" Faith's voice intoned from across the room.

I set my tea towel aside, finished with the final dish. I reached into the berry bowl next to Celeste. This week, it wasn't holding any berries. Instead sat a bundle of plump purple grapes. Popping one into my mouth, I chewed slowly as Ana turned the water off and dried her hands on the other fall print towel hanging off the stove.

I realized that Faith was still staring at me.

"So?" I stared back at Faith, waiting to see what kind of comical punch line this had to lead to by the way she swayed her loose skirts back and forth before letting her temple lean against the rounded window arch.

Gertie reached for the bowls still sitting on the other side of me to put them back on the shelf. She took a glance once at me, as if waiting for me to say something as well.

I could, however, only handle one inquiry at a time.

"So," Faith repeated, "how was it?"

"How was what?" I asked.

"Your Friday night escapades at the library."

I shrugged. Faith never did check on me before she headed out for the night.

"It was fine. Got a few things done."

"They said they saw you with a boy," said Gertie, her voice hushed to fill me in on whatever was happening, but not so quiet that everyone couldn't also hear.

My head whipped toward her.

"A handsome boy!" Faith intoned louder, nearly squealing.

Everyone's head lifted along with my own.

Another three pairs of eyes flew toward me as I dropped another grape into my mouth. I took my time chewing until I could think of the correct possible thing to say to a bunch of bored busybody ladies who had a preoccupation with anything that could even hint at love.

They all brewed their fair share of love potions for kicks and giggles every year to sell at the markets come spring along with handcrafted soap and salves. But this was not one of those silly moments, such as talking about Essie and how this young boy she was spending the night with—under the not-so-watchful eye of her brother, Brenson—could possibly be her prepubescent soul mate, drawn to town.

I narrowed my eyes at Faith. "I thought you didn't work this morning."

If anything, my response made everyone lean in closer.

"I didn't. That doesn't mean the faculty I can actually stand doesn't like to hand out a little piece of gossip here and there."

"Gossip?" I repeated.

I was gossip? Ryan and I were the latest weekend scoop?

"Well, not gossip exactly. Apparently, some of the student workers stumbled upon the two of you." Faith pointed with both hands toward me, like accusing finger guns. "They were all curled up on the second-floor couch. Looked like someone had pulled an all-nighter."

I shook my head. "That didn't happen."

"You didn't spend the night in the library with a boy?"

"Well, yes, I did," I admitted.

"Now I see why you didn't come here to stay the night," murmured Gertie.

I stared at her, hoping that my eyes would stop her from continuing whatever it was she was about to insinuate. "We were not curled up."

"My sources tell me otherwise," Faith singsonged.

"It wasn't like that."

"Then, what was it like?" Celeste asked, pausing as she took a tray out of the oven with tiny firefly-print oven mitts.

Goo-filled pink floral Pyrex never looked less appealing as my stomach churned.

"He was in my spot," I said, exasperated.

It had been my mistake, telling him where I was going when I was pretty sure at the time he was going to root himself in the cemetery, like the living dead, but he was the one who had sought me out.

Not the other way around.

"What are you talking about?" Ana raised an eyebrow, clearly lost in this conversation.

Faith waved her hand, as if it was ridiculous. "She sits in the same spot in the library every day."

"And this boy, he was in your spot?" Gertie rephrased for us all once more, as if I hadn't said it clear enough.

"Yes."

Gertie and Celeste looked between themselves with renewed interest.

I needed to put a stop to whatever those looks were. I never liked that look, especially not on them. "No, stop it right now. It isn't like that. I was helping him with an essay. He'd basically guilted me into it."

"All night?" Celeste questioned.

"He's … terribly wordy."

Faith snorted. "I bet he is."

"Stop," I warned.

The women put up their hands in surrender, but it wouldn't last for long. It never lasted long enough.

"Do we know the guy's name?"

"Ana!" I scolded. I figured that at least she, out of all of them, with her consistent relationship drama, would have the decency and understanding to stay out of it.

Faith only grinned, looking at everyone like she'd struck gold. "His name is Ryan."

"Ryan," Gertrude repeated with a terse tilt of her chin. "A kingly name. Strong. Even keeled."

"Since when has there ever been a king named Ryan?" I snapped.

They were beyond listening to me as they went on, debating as if he were standing there in front of them right now.

"He has the funniest strawberry-blond hair," Faith continued to describe. "He was the star of the football team."

"Faith!" I scolded, knowing it was all too late at this point, but trying nonetheless to stop this.

"Was?"

"He got the stuffing knocked out of him a month or so ago," Faith further informed everyone.

"A jock?" Celeste asked, making a tiny sound. "I don't think I've ever pictured you with someone like that, Lu. You should've brought him along for the evening."

I would not be bringing him to Gertie's for any meeting. There was no reason to.

Nothing had happened.

I'd tried not to feel oddly confused by that fact after he looked down and leaned into my lips—

"Can we seriously not?" I cried. "There is no reason to be talking about him. Honestly, it was nothing. He knew that I had taken the class he was in and practically guilted me into helping him last night. I felt bad and fell asleep on the couch because I had been kicked out of my room by my heinous roommate. Leave it at that."

They all paused.

"All right," Gertrude conceded.

"Thank you."

"Then, I do expect you to come to us next time there is something to be told," Gertie said. "Us ladies need to get our kicks somewhere."

I rolled my eyes. "Oh, please."

"Something entertaining this year at least. Last spring was such a snooze," Gertie complained.

Faith pursed her lips in consideration. "The summer was pleasant."

"Another word for boring, darling."

"Fine," I agreed. "But it was nothing. He got up and left this morning, barely looking at me. He got what he needed from me. Now, I'm back to exactly who I am."

"And one day, someone will see just how wonderful that someone is," Gertie said gently, as if only now noting my extreme discomfort.

Sure, sure. "Are those turnovers, Celeste?"

"Apple blossoms actually."

Of course they were. The message of love had practically been stacked in their many layers.

"I am testing the apples before I share my recipe with you all next week on Mabon, so come early if you care to learn it. Care for one?"

I picked up a plate from the drying rack next to me. Depositing one out of the tin, Celeste waited for me to say anything else. I only stared down at the crisp-covered apple rose.

Faith was still staring at me, wagging her eyebrows as she leaned against the counter beside me.

"I heard you two looked cute together. Opposites attract and all that. I wish I had been there to see," Faith whispered in my ear. Her tiny radish earrings clanged together.

"You would've seen nothing."

"Defensive over your future mate—I like it."

Mate. Like we were animals in one of her fantasy novels.

"You're so weird, Faith."

She grinned. "Thank you."

"Stop."

"You're only going to make me tell you *I told you so*, you know."

"You'll be saving that one for a long time."

"We'll see."

7

The final patters of rain gently clanged as they slipped down the brass gutters. I curled my legs in toward my chest, and my eyes shut as I let the sound envelop me like the thick blanket tucked under my chin.

For once, after so many days, I was at peace. My hair was washed and combed. My body smelled like black-lavender soap. The air was fresh, fresh and not stained with a hint of air freshener and body odor the residence halls constantly had the tang of.

The screen door slid open to the sunroom, built on a deck overlooking the backyard and swirling river. Gertie made her way out, wrapped in her own thick shawl. Once all the others had left, the house had turned soft and easy after bursting with so much energy.

Reaching up, I took the round mug from Gertie's ring-lined fingers. I looked down into the cup, knowing that it was a perfectly steeped chamomile tea, made from fresh ingredients instead of the bags I carried along with me.

I could never get my tea just right when I made it without Gertie. Either too weak or too strong, but good enough. One day,

I figured I'd be able to perfect it as much as Gertie managed without her looking over my shoulder or simply making a cup for the two of us.

"Thank you," I whispered.

"You're welcome."

I sighed, holding my cup up high near my chest so I could feel the comforting heat soak into my bones. "I love this house."

"I know you do." Gertie grunted with effort as she sat down beside me, curling her legs up like the two of us were twins. "You never did say how your meeting went at school," Gertie said. "I figured after so many weeks of planning Samhain on campus for everyone, you'd let us know tonight."

I shook my head. "It didn't go great."

"That's a shame."

I didn't say anything else, holding in that it was a shame. It also wasn't. I didn't know anymore.

"Of course, we all know exactly why you decided to put your energy into something you doubted would be possible to begin with," Gertie said, looking out toward the yard. "Unless I am wrong yet?"

My head lolled to the side, I was completely transparent. If to no one else, then to Gertie. "Maybe."

"I'm not going to tell you to do anything. It wouldn't be right of me," said Gertie.

She herself had lived a more adventurous life than most—from the few stories she'd let slip to me over the past few years. Trouble and strange whimsy were never far behind. Her life was not simple—not like mine was—but still she managed to create some sort of magic out of it all.

A piece of perfect, even when life wasn't.

It was hard to think that I would ever manage to be as strong as Gertie, let alone make something out of my life as much as she had. Not when it was plain as day that I could barely figure out a simple choice, such as a major. I was too afraid to decide at all these days, lest it be the wrong decision, sending me right back into a life I'd struggled to get through before I arrived at Barnett and found her and the rest of the coven.

If I could, I would stay right here forever.

I told Gertie so more than a few times, and it still held true. I was more productive at her house anyway. I baked and tended to the plants and lived.

Why couldn't I just live? Why did it feel so hard?

"Don't retreat." Gertie reached over and squeezed my knee.

"I'm not."

"You are. I can see you withering before my eyes, and I am not going to let it happen. So, you look at me," she insisted, though her tone never rose harshly. Another way I wished I could be more like Gertie. "You can do anything you set your mind to. It's a trait not all have, no matter how easy it is to say."

"You're just trying to make me feel better about myself."

"Since when have I ever done that when it wasn't due?"

I lifted a single shoulder.

"Oh, Lu."

I snorted. Now, that was the more correct reaction I expected from her—exhausted with me.

Reaching over, she gave my leg a small smack. "Stop it. You really don't see it yet, but you will. You care so much about everything. It's another reason I can only ever imagine you taking over this place. When that time comes, of course."

I blinked, turning my gaze away from the screened-in porch, and narrowed my eyes at Gertie. Gertie always joked that I was the one who appreciated her and the house the most out of everyone, but never like that.

"You find little pieces of magic in everyone, whether or not they see it in themselves quite yet. I like to think I do too—most of the time anyway, when they aren't arguing with me," she teased.

"I thought that Celeste … Essie …" I tried to find my words in case Gertie was trying to pull something over on me. Or more likely, this was some sort of test, and Celeste was watching on a secret camera somewhere.

Gertie waved the names off. "Don't worry about them. You worry about you right now. You deserve to. More than that, you deserve anything you want and that comes to you. You're listening now, correct?"

"To you? Always."

Gertie rolled her eyes again. And she wondered where I had gotten it from. Still, my voice was now far less joking than it had been a moment ago, tea forgotten in my hands.

"Oh, girl, you have a piece of soul that I couldn't place in anyone else, I don't think, if I tried these days."

"What do you mean?"

"I mean …" Gertie sighed, gathering herself. "I mean—let me try to explain. Do you know why I have this house, Luella?"

I shrugged. I assumed she had bought or inherited it at some point, and it was perfect for a coven to gather. Picture perfect as well as charitable to lost souls, like my own.

"A very long time ago, when I first ever trusted that the world held a little more magic in it than anyone else thought, my life was also not so great for a bit when I was young, like you. I've told you about that."

I nodded.

"I had nothing and didn't know what to do when I was your age and even older," Gertie said simply.

"I know. I should be grateful."

"That's not what I'm trying to tell you. Not at all. You get to be who you are and feel how you feel, no matter how anyone else does. I'm telling you a story. Not a good one, mind you, but a story of when I was nothing. But somehow, I was pulled away to a house of women, run by a single woman and usually her daughter."

"Like a cult?"

"Not at all." Gertie smiled fondly. "More like a haven."

"A safe haven," I provided.

"Better. More than just that. I looked up one night, and suddenly, I was there. A home full of women in similar situations as me and women who still had a bit of hope. All of us had magic tucked away inside of us that we didn't realize we'd been searching for all this time until we were able to get back on our feet. How we all found it, I don't know. I doubt I would ever be able to find it again if I tried. We all had the same story, however. We had all been lost, in pain, and in upside-down situations. So, we'd followed the stars, and we'd stumbled upon a home with an open door and tea always on the stove."

"Like magic."

"Exactly—magic. That house and that place found me, tucked away somewhere in the world. When I left, I still had little clue what I was going to do," admitted Gertie. "But I knew who I was. I created this house similarly—for anyone who needed to find this coven here, where people least expected. That house was a place that I believe was meant for women like us when there was literally nowhere else to go but downward. Only ... you looked up one night."

I remained silent as I listened, looking up at our own dark sky. I couldn't see any stars.

"Here, this house, is another place. You get to choose. You did choose," said Gertie.

She was right. I had chosen this house. I had chosen her and the rest of the coven the moment I came to Barnett, searching for them. Following my own metaphorical stars perhaps.

"You have the power to change lives however you decide to. Whichever way life turns you. Here or otherwise."

"Sounds like a lot when you put it like that."

"It is." She nodded thoughtfully. Her eyes glittered with delight when she turned to face me straight on. "It's also a lot of fun."

A small smile puckered the corner of my mouth.

"I've always had a feeling that maybe this house needed you as much as you needed this space since you arrived. You might not have noticed it, but our meetings have developed, as have our members, since you came in and encouraged them to find their magic in whatever form they pleased without guidelines. This place has blossomed with you even if you seem intent on making yourself wilt these days."

"I am not—"

Gertie stopped me, putting a hand to her chest. "I'm just telling you. You want this? I can think of no better person, nor would I want to. Perfection is boring after all, especially in people."

Well, at least I could live up to that statement. Imperfection was my middle name. In all things. Still, I couldn't quite wrap my head around all this. The idea of staying here forever had crossed my mind. I would spend mornings with tea on the porch, afternoons in the garden, evenings with the coven, drinking rose hip wine and sitting right where I was now, staring at the moon through the trees and listening to the full river roar as it passed. I thought about it all like a vision more than a few times and yet …

Gods, I was really trying to talk myself out of this, just like everything else.

How couldn't I? It was Essie, after all, who was supposed to be sitting here, bonding with Gertie to walk in her footsteps. Essie was the perfect age to take over under Gertie's not-so-strict tutelage. Not me, no matter how often the way Celeste bragged about her daughter had made me jealous. Envious. It all didn't make sense in the grand scheme of things.

I made no sense.

Yet here we were. Witches talking about stars and magic leading us to where we were meant to be. Now, that made no sense.

It also made all the sense in the universe.

"Take your time. There's plenty of it, I sure hope, before I'm up among the stars and looking down. It's your decision. But I made mine," said Gertie with certain conviction.

To be that sure of anything made me stare at her.

She glanced down at my cup. "Are you really going to let that get cold?"

I huffed a laugh, taking another large sip, gulping most of it down in one go. Then, I took a deep breath.

Now Gertie was the amused one. "Relax. Life isn't all that serious."

She was the only one telling me that.

"Sleep well, Lu. Tomorrow is yet another day." Gertie patted me one last time before standing.

Leaving the door cracked open, she retreated into the house. The light dimmed as she blew out each lit candle in her wake.

I stayed out in the sunroom for a while longer until the night took over fully. I could hear the birdhouses swaying in the brisk wind, and the screen door clicked shut before I turned the knob back inside.

I never thought of Gertie's house as a gift to anyone who found it, though it certainly had been to me. From the moment I'd stepped inside the chaotic wonderland of a home, it'd called out and wrapped me up in a warmth that made me feel … at ease. Wanted. I didn't want to leave.

Now, Gertie didn't want me to either.

With careful footfalls, I trailed up the stairs, careful not to step where they creaked. I glanced once more back at the crescent moon–shaped stained glass above the front door, brighter in the darkness. I always saw it as ironic, the moon there. But Gertie had followed the stars.

This house was the moon. Steady. Always there to be seen when you looked up to the sky.

Nearing the end of the hall, I slipped inside the room I always used when I stayed at Gertie's. The iron bed frame curved like vines. A thick patchwork quilt was folded on the bottom half of the sheets, which I slid into without switching on the light. Dim light from the night itself was enough to light my way. It passed through the sheer curtains that pooled around the curved window seat, which was what had first made me choose the space as mine.

Growing up, I'd always wanted a window seat. Like a damsel peering out onto her kingdom when she pulled her attention away from whatever book or challenge she had been working on inside. Deliberating.

Always deliberating.

Perhaps it was the exhaustion. Perhaps it was the knowledge in the very back of my mind that everything could be solved if I simply trusted myself for once in my life. Trusted Gertie and everyone else.

But even they could be wrong. And they didn't have to stick around to see the wreckage.

8

"Well?"

I froze as I continued digging through my never-ending bag. It would be better called a pit. I really needed to get a different one that wasn't falling apart from the inside out. The tiny holes in the lining created new dimensions. I glanced up at Vadika eating her small bag of salt and vinegar kettle chips across the table.

"Well?"

"You need to spill. Right now."

I sighed. For some reason, I'd figured if there was anyone spared from the rumor mill, it would be my friend.

Then again, I'd thought I'd be spared from the rumor mill entirely, never as interesting. And technically, I still wasn't until my name was attached to the great Ryan Gardner.

"Vadika."

"Since when did you become besties with Ryan Gardner?"

"It isn't—"

"It's not like that?" My friend was unconvinced as she filled in my all-too-obvious retort. I raised my eyebrows, unamused.

"Was this a hookup? In the library?" Vadika rambled with

renewed excitement, clutching her bag of chips to her chest. "I mean, I always figured you were kinkier than you let on, but wow. That's a whole new level. I don't think I could do it without panicking about the cameras or some weird janitor stumbling across me and whoever. Like, what if he got off on that and just —ew. No."

"Vadika." I repeated her name once more. This time slowly.

She slumped. "Yes?"

"Are you ready to hear me now?"

"More than. Tell me everything."

"All right," I said slowly, taking a deep breath as she literally sat on the edge of her seat. "Nothing happened."

"Liar."

"I'm not lying."

"Doubtful. I thought you didn't like Ryan. Didn't he say something rude to you before? That's what it was, wasn't it? Or have you two been having some sort of affair I haven't noticed all this time because I've been stuck in a sterile wonderland?" Vadika glanced around, slouching back in her plastic seat as she reached for another bite of her lunch.

"There is not and never has been any affair. Ever."

"Promise?"

"Promise," I assured her.

She sighed, pushing up her protective glasses. "I'm not going to lie, Lu. I'm a little disappointed."

I chuckled with a shake of my head.

"So, what *has* been going on with everything I've been hearing? It isn't every day I hear that the football star and weird, witchy girl were getting it on in the library. Or did all that *library companion* gossip not happen either?"

"That's really what they've been saying?"

"In so many words," she admitted.

I had a feeling I knew which.

Oh gods. "It really was nothing. I bumped into Ryan when I was at the dean's office and then again when I was walking. He was the one who showed up in my spot in the library. Apparently, my reputation wasn't only as a witchy chick, but also as a major failure who's taken over half of the Barnett course catalog."

"That's not true."

I raised my eyebrows. We both knew it was true enough.

"And?" My friend waved her hand for me to keep going. She was unwilling to let us get off track.

"And he wanted me to basically walk him step by step through an essay for the British literature professor he's taking this year."

"The one with the Brontë obsession last year?"

That was the one.

"What's his major anyway?"

"Elementary education," I said.

Her well-glossed lips pouted. "That's kind of cute."

"That the children of our future are going to be getting an education from Ryan Gardner?" I asked. "I'm not sure I'd call it cute."

"It is though. Imagine having a big man walk into your classroom, and it turns out to be Ryan. He looks like the kind of guy who would totally host a few caterpillar funerals at recess."

"Since when do you know much about him?" I asked.

"He's a well-liked guy, Lu. I just don't like him because you don't. We ladies stick together."

I looked down to my bag again before turning my attention back to Vadika. For some reason, the thought had never occurred to me before. Vadika was just not friends with someone because of me. She always wanted to do all the fun, traditional college things even though she lived off campus, which made it more difficult.

My eyebrows creased. "Do you resent me at all?"

"What are you talking about?"

"About me holding you back," I tried to elaborate.

"I still don't understand what you're talking about. You don't hold me back."

"It isn't like you couldn't have also been well liked in the way that Ryan is. I know you commute, but still. You're gorgeous and intelligent—"

"Though I love the compliments to stroke my ego, I'm going to stop you right there," Vadika interrupted finally. "You're gorgeous, and you're intelligent, first off. Also, there's literally no one else I'd rather have my college experience with than you. Who else would I drag to the theme parties on the Row, who would also let me leave after fifteen minutes when we both realized what a mistake it was? Who else would sit here in the lab with me while I worked until ungodly hours of the night after I made the mistake of declaring myself exactly what my parents always wanted me to be?"

I snorted. I still easily remembered the Vadika I'd first met after stepping on campus.

Vadika had rushed to the admissions office to change her major to something drastic. In her case, that meant anthropology. She promptly changed back to biochemistry a week later after the all-consuming fear that her parents would find out she was rebelling by no longer being a woman in STEM. The title was one she took on rather proudly at the top of her class.

"You're my college soul mate, Lu. Sorry, it's been decided."

Warmth spread through my chest at the words. I slouched farther down in my chair as I looked at my friend. "Thanks, Vad."

"Seriously, I still can't believe you spent the night with Ryan. And you didn't call me!"

Ugh, for a moment, I thought we'd moved on from this. "Nothing happened. I told you, I was there because I had been kicked out of my room, and I helped him with classwork. That's it."

"I know." She sighed, a devious smile still playing on her lips. "But that doesn't mean nothing won't happen."

"It won't."

"Oh, well … is that your library lover over there?"

Trying not to whip around, I glanced over my shoulder toward the hallway where none other than Ryan Gardner was coming out alongside another guy, talking loud enough about his weekend dirt biking. I could hear him across the room. A few other people looked up toward him, too, before going back to their own lunches.

"You should say hi."

I stared at Vadika. "Why would I do that?"

"Why wouldn't you do that?"

I said nothing.

Without a glance in my direction, he crutched toward the door with his friend and walked out into the greenway. As he was talking, his eyes flicked in my direction, meeting my eyes without a word as he continued on his way.

It felt like the door shutting behind him hit me in the chest.

I cleared my throat and reached over to take another one of Vadika's chips, cringing at the pungent taste.

"Well then, I believe you now," Vadika said. Lips pouting, she gave a little nod of disappointment.

"Nice to know it isn't just on my word," I mumbled, tilting my chin down in case anyone was still staring in our direction.

"Is that hurt I hear in your voice, Luella Pierce?"

"Of course not."

"Uh-huh. I can only imagine what the Gertie crew will think about all this."

"Oh, they had their thoughts," I agreed. Many, many thoughts.

The wide-eyed expression I gave her must've said enough.

Vadika laughed. "Of course they knew before me."

I shrugged. It was the way of things.

"Essie also found her soul mate this weekend," I said, changing the subject once more.

"Again?"

I laughed.

"Seriously, how can a thirteen-year-old have more soul mates in her life than I ever will? I don't understand."

"She's almost sixteen."

"Still," Vadika insisted. "Life isn't some sort of sweet young adult novel. At least, not that I am aware."

"Now, it's your turn."

"My turn?" Vadika's eyes flew up to mine.

"The wedding," I said. "How did it go? Did you end up finding an amazing boy your grandmother set you up with?"

"Oh, please. Spare me."

My eyes widened. "That wasn't a no."

The door leading outside opened again. Cool air skittered across my exposed ankles. I couldn't help myself but turn around to look back at it. I hated the small part of my mind that wondered if it was Ryan and his friend coming back inside.

Vadika noticed the movement. "Is there something you're not telling me?"

"Is there something you're not telling me about a likely suave mystery man you met at your cousin's wedding?"

Vadika sighed and looked away, as if that didn't just give us both our answers. Brow furrowing, I watched as Vadika turned back to her open computer. She typed a few more notes in the corner of her screen, evading the conversation she'd started. We both seemed to have enough we didn't want to talk about.

"There is definitely something you're not telling me."

I remembered the way Ryan's lips had angled over mine in the darkness of the library, subdued lamps lighting the space. For some reason, I wasn't ready to admit that to Vadika or anyone just yet. It wasn't a long kiss or a spectacular kiss, yet it almost felt unreal, and it was only for me right now.

Even if Ryan didn't remember it or care. He had gotten what he wanted, so maybe after that, he forgot altogether, just like he had with me before.

***

"Don't stare too hard."

I narrowed my eyes at someone I clearly had never met before. I stood up from my seat. Vadika had left a bit ago, leaving me with sending off the last section of a group project before packing up and throwing away the trash she left behind on the table. "Excuse me?"

The girl didn't say a word. Shoving a piece of light-brown hair behind her ear, she nudged past me.

Behind me, I could still hear her though. "Looks like yet another person falling into the Ryan trap."

"Didn't you hear? Sounds like she did a little more than just falling. She practically laid down and spread her legs the moment he said so. Ryan might not be the shiny boy next door any longer now that he's off the team."

"Seriously?"

"In the library, no less."

The other person started to laugh. "That's so disgusting."

I rolled my eyes as I headed toward the exit. So much for gossip fading quickly. By next weekend, hopefully something else more interesting would come along. There had to be a first-year set to make an embarrassing legacy for themselves on campus soon enough.

Still, who could've possibly started the rumor? The two of us spending the night in the library had been obvious to those who came in early the next morning. These things had a way of twisting and turning out of control, and yet I couldn't help but think about the words I had heard about me the last time people on campus looked at me strange.

Could Ryan have done this for some reason?

I wanted it to sound ridiculous, and yet it didn't, burning a flush to my face with consideration. This was Ryan after all. However sweet he might have been, he'd said cruel things about me before. This was Ryan, who a half hour ago, had passed by like I was a complete stranger to him.

It wasn't as if I'd expected him to have a parade in my honor after helping him with his essay or anything, but a simple hello would've sufficed. It would've at least been enough for me not to spend otherwise perfectly good time thinking about him in a very unflattering way.

What else had I pictured from him though? Along with being a rude jokester for the football team, he should try out for theater.

I might have been making more out of this than there was, and yet I shook my head at myself, continuing the path of my normal schedule to the library.

This time, my area, per usual, was empty.

The scratched mahogany was cleared of random sheets of paper and cardboard pizza boxes, like it'd had the last time I sat. Everyone else surrounding me was going on with their own business. Some leaned back in their chairs with headphones in while others sipped thick smoothies through tiny straws and typed one letter at a time with the other hand on their computers. There were, thankfully, fewer glances my way.

I dug into my backpack to the back compartment until I found what I was looking for. I might have gotten down most of my work for the week, let alone for today, but it was still too early to head back to my dorm even if comfortable sweatpants were calling my name.

If I went back now, I would likely have to face another chance encounter with Natalie. I would also have to pretend not to be bothered—no, infuriated—by how loudly Natalie slammed the door into the wall whenever she entered.

Taking a deep breath, I refocused my energy away from Ryan and Natalie.

The list of people sending my blood pressure through the roof was growing, and I knew one way to fix that.

Carefully, I slipped out the bent composition notebook from the compartment of my book bag that it shared with my laptop. The edges were faded, and when I opened to the first page, I faced the loopy handwriting of my high school self. I declared the sad ninety-nine-cent notebook my personal book of shadows. The binding was frayed. Tiny pieces of string stuck out from pages I ripped out and stapled back together as I found a better organization method.

Beside the old, I laid out the new leather-bound journal I had purchased especially online. After looking at it for approximately three months, I'd finally convinced myself it was absolutely worth the money. From the tight embroidery on the outside of the leaves and a strap that wrapped around so that I could add as many pages as I wanted or needed in the future, it took me a bit to get over the fear of accidentally ruining it and writing inside, but it might have been the most beautiful thing I'd ever bought for myself.

I'd been slowly transcribing all the information from my past dingy notebook into my new journal, much more magical artifact than middle school diary—though it had served me well for long enough.

My book of shadows was getting a face-lift, and it was stunning.

If I did say so myself. And I was the only one who would ever see it, so I did.

The pages were slowly coming together with careful line drawings and pictures I'd previously been too nervous to draw, less of them looking amateurish. I took my time on each page, careful that nothing would smear. This way, I would be able to refer to all my herbs and their meanings as well as all the recipes and spells I'd been taught since I'd arrived at Barnett, and I planned to keep it with me for the rest of my life.

I had gotten to the second paragraph of a motivation jar charm, getting into an almost-meditative state of careful work, by the time a very different sort of shadow floated across my page.

"I figured you'd be here."

I shut my eyes, and my body took over before I could think of whatever sort of condescending words I wanted to say to this wide-set block of a person in front of me. They'd surely be something good rather than the pitiful-sounding things I'd said to Vadika.

A girl was upset that the popular boy wasn't talking to her.

That was what everyone thought of me as now, wasn't it?

As if that had ever troubled me before.

Shutting my book, I grabbed my bag off the floor and began to shove my supplies inside. I barely paused to close the sticky zipper of my pencil case, contents clattering against each other inside.

"Hey, Lu, wait up. Where are you going?"

I continued to pack. I forced myself not to glance toward the voice across the table, laced with confusion.

Why should I act like he was even there?

He certainly hadn't looked back at me today. Who knew what else he was doing behind my back after I took a chance to think he could be a good human being?

Ugh. There was the pitiful hurt again. I could hear it lacing my own traitorous thoughts. I shouldn't care, yet I did.

I cared. One night with Ryan, and it'd sent three years of hate-filled walls crashing down.

"Luella."

My full name made my eyes turn upward of their own accord. "Oh, Ryan, right?"

"Funny." He looked me up and down.

I huffed. My hands braced on either side of my final two notebooks.

My one pen was still stuck between the pages of my book of

shadows. I had to pause to carefully take it out so that ink wouldn't get everywhere, slowing my retreat.

"I don't get why you're acting like this toward me." Ryan stepped around the table.

I raised my eyebrows, finally getting my pen free and everything stacked up in a nice pile. "You're kidding, right?"

"No."

"Then, maybe you do need more than a tutor."

He scoffed. "Can't you just tell me what I did wrong?"

"You …"

It was going to sound so outrageous, coming out of my mouth, and I knew it. I'd told myself this for the past five minutes. Yet here we were. Another hysterical woman with her feelings hurt.

So be it.

"Have you been the one spreading the rumors?" I asked.

Understanding dawned on him. "Is that what's bothering you?"

That wasn't an answer.

"No, Lu. I'm not spreading rumors about you. People saw us, but I didn't think that you'd care so much."

"You didn't say hello," I said.

"I didn't say …" Ryan cocked his head.

"You looked right at me today in the science building. I was with Vadika," I reminded him, as if he'd forgotten that as well. "It was as if you had no idea who I was."

"I didn't think you'd want me to."

Why wouldn't I want that? A few good reasons popped to my mind immediately. Like the fact that I never talked to anyone in class unless there was a group project or I needed the notes from a day I'd missed. That was a reason. Still, it didn't matter.

I didn't like people bothering me when I calmly sat alone in the library either.

But Ryan had done that without pause.

"Was it because you were with your friends? I get it if you don't think I'm cool enough to say a polite hello to on any given day when I'm not saving your academic career out of the goodness of my own heart—"

"Goodness of your own heart?" Ryan smirked, as if I were making a joke.

Was he seriously going to laugh right now?

"Yes. Maybe you haven't heard of it since everyone else bends over backward for you."

"Ouch." He put a hand to his chest.

"Would you rather I lied to make you feel all warm and fuzzy inside?"

"I'd prefer if you didn't look like you would rather be anywhere else but in front of me right now," he offered. His humor turned solemn. "Look, I'm sorry that I ignored you earlier. I didn't give it much thought, to be honest. You could've said hi too, y'know."

Could I have? I wasn't so sure.

My opinion of Ryan Gardner was changing, but not that much. Not yet.

There were still a few bricks of animosity standing between him and me.

The slant of my eyes as I stared at him said as much.

"Do you need me to apologize again?"

"No," I said.

Still, he waited for more.

I glared out the window before facing him again. "So, you didn't have some vendetta against me. Why are you here? To get a few more essay writing tips?"

"Well, y'know"—Ryan shrugged—"I do still have some biology to work on, and the whole footnotes thing is messing me up. I figured you would be here. For company, of course, nothing more."

I stared at him.

He raised one hand in the air, nearly setting him off balance on his crutches. "Scout's honor."

"You were a Boy Scout?"

"No, but that always feels so official."

I rolled my eyes.

"Can I sit?"

I waved at the seat. "Sit."

"Why, thank you." Slowly, Ryan arranged himself in the same seat he sat in the other night, making himself at home. Opening his laptop, he clicked on his document.

Reaching across the table, I automatically turned his screen toward me. All his sources were crowded together at the bottom of the first page. I raised an eyebrow at him. I knew for a fact that though Ryan might not be the most studious, he knew that he didn't need to have his whole works cited page within the actual report. Nonetheless, I copied and pasted over to the next few pages, where they were actually referenced and labeled correctly.

He could've gotten anyone to tell him he was being a dumbass.

Instead, he had come here. To sit across from me.

"Whatcha got there?"

Blinking, I lifted my attention up. He pointed down to my book of shadows perched on top of my pile that I had moments ago been ready to shove into my bag and rush across campus with to get away from him.

I didn't answer. My lips parted while my fingers remained on his keyboard to fix the mess he'd made of a perfectly good lab report. A minor mess, but a mess nonetheless.

I knew there was some way to explain that it was basically a more accessible and prettier version of a witch's grimoire you saw in movies around Halloween, and yet I couldn't find one. The looseness I felt in Ryan's presence was still tightly wound around my throat.

As he reached out to grab it, my hands, however, didn't pause. They slapped down against the smooth cover to keep it shut.

"See, this is where you are supposed to say *nunya*. Like none of ya business. Not in the joking mood today just yet? Gotcha." Ryan sat himself back down comfortably in his seat before I could point him back toward the door. "Sorry. Not supposed to touch?"

"It's personal." Sort of.

"Like a diary?"

My expression twisted to one side. "Like a life manual. I'm rewriting from a past version to this one. It's not done yet."

"Still a lot of life yet to live to fit into such a tiny book," commented Ryan.

That was also true.

I took a deep breath. "It has different things, like my plants and their meanings, and everything inside I've learned since I got to Barnett and met my coven."

"Oh, so it's like a witchy diary."

Well, when he put it that way, I couldn't help but roll my eyes at him again. This time, I had to resist the small smile forming on my lips.

A tiny voice in the back of my head piped up, *At least he is trying*.

"Yeah, in a way."

"But I can't read it?"

"Not yet," I said.

"But I can in the future?"

"I didn't say that either."

"Now I'm just confused."

I pushed his laptop back around to face him. "Reread your lab report and turn it in, so you can check it off in your planner. I'm surprised you got it done so quickly."

"My Sunday didn't have a lot going on at the house. Not with my leg and everything." He flicked one of his crutches that was leaning against the table, as if in evidence.

I nodded slowly, unable to hide my gaze that traveled downward. "You took the brace off."

"Thanks for noticing. Everything is nearly as good as new again." He grinned. "Nearly. I go to my doctor and then the physical trainer tomorrow, who is going to give me a final therapy schedule before he signs me off the team roster for good. Then, I'm a free, injury-less bird."

"You don't need to do that."

"What?"

"Joke about it," I said, trying not to show how pitiful the laughs he gave himself were whenever he referenced his leg or football. "I might not get what it is like to be a part of a football team—or any team really. You're allowed to be sad about it even if it's your decision to leave. It's the right decision. If you ask me, that is, which I know you're not."

"I sort of am."

"Well, you're allowed to not make everyone else feel better about something that concerns you. It sucks," I said.

He snorted once and nodded. "It does. Thanks. I have to keep thinking positively."

"Why do you say that?"

"Why do you keep hoping for a better next *whatever is going to happen* in life?"

He had a point.

"Plus, I like to make others happy. It's why I like kids. They are an easy crowd. Worst critics though," he joked with a shake of his head. "Just brutal."

"What could they possibly have to tease the running back of Barnett University about?"

"Mainly that I'm old."

"You're kidding."

"No. I must look not only huge, but also ancient," said Ryan.

"One kid asked why I was playing football when I was in college. Why didn't I have a real job or get married, like his parents who were in their late twenties? Humbling."

"Maybe you have found the job you were fated for."

"I'd like to think so. I can't wait to have my student teaching semester, but we'll see when I'm actually set loose in the *real world*, as my dad says." His tone took a sour note.

I paused, unsure if I should ask. "You don't have a good relationship with your father?"

"No. We do. My family has always been pretty close compared to others I've met. We had dinner every night and all that. I think we talked about this, right? My dad and I have just always been sort of at odds. My mom says we're a lot alike and that's why." Ryan shook his head. "Not sure I like that reason though either."

I didn't press. There had been nothing but fondness in Ryan's voice, sure, but there had also been an edge.

"You know," Ryan went on, "you can go back to whatever it is you were working on now while I read through this one more time. I have a few other things I should probably not push to the last minute."

"Seriously?" I looked between him and the mountain of books slipping out from his book bag. The thing probably weighed half of me. Half of him.

"I do know how to finish work on my own sometimes, Lu," said Ryan. "I did manage to get this far. I told you, I didn't come just for your smarts today. Library companionship."

That was true, and yet I still stared at him, unsure of what else to do. "Library companionship."

"Is it so hard to think that I want to spend time with you, Lu?"

I watched as he turned his attention back to his planner, marking off something else before turning to his next task.

Slowly, once I was sure that he wasn't going to pull something or simply sit there and watch, I reached back for my book of shadows, old and new. I lifted the ribbon of the page I had been working on. I was careful to keep the one piece of paper on the other side of the page. I didn't want it to smudge as I took care to finish my detailed paragraph about using the charm. Then, I slowly went over each line of my illustration, careful to capture each penciled stroke and previously blended watercolor.

It was easy to get back into the groove as I went on. It was almost calming to remember the first time I'd actually made the charm, burning myself with melting candle wax for the seal. Red clumps hardened over my knuckles before the drips stuck to the wood table of the house. Gertie had tried not to laugh at me as I cursed behind clenched lips so as not to mess up any outwardly said intention.

My lips curved at the memory. The two of us in the house.

The house that Gertie had asked me to take over out of everyone else. The thought came back to me unbidden and clenched inside my chest.

I still didn't understand why. Why me? Was it because I was clearly flailing around, trying to figure out what other sort of purpose I had in life, and Gertie was taking pity on me, whether Celeste and her daughter cared or not? I loved Gertie, and I knew that she saw me as family, but to think she would see me as her daughter, enough to take over the space and the coven along with the drama and incense-scented carpets and wax-covered altar tops, it was more than I could comprehend.

"That's amazing."

I didn't realize I'd paused until I glanced up to find Ryan leaning farther over the table. He stared at the lines I was just finishing working on. I resisted the urge to yank the pages away, hiding them toward my center.

"I told you not to look."

"How couldn't I? It's eye catching."

Sure it was. Glancing down, however, I was truly proud of the page. It looked exactly how I'd wanted it to, better than expected, even with all the extra captions and labels needed for ingredients.

"Thank you," I whispered.

"You're seriously talented. And you haven't taken your chance at being an art major yet?" He cocked his head to get a better look at the other page.

"Not that talented." Plus, it was for practical use more than to be art.

A book of shadows wasn't only meant to be stared at and judged and picked apart for meaning. A book of shadows was a piece of the witch and the culmination of their practice. I wanted to make sure mine represented me at least somewhat after all the years of hiding in a fuzzy black-and-white composition notebook.

"And then I wouldn't have time to do what I wanted."

"I don't mean this in a bad way, Lu, but why did you come to college?"

I blinked. That was frank.

"I just mean, if you don't want to do anything ... or is it the opposite?" He tried to make himself sound better. "You want to do too much?"

"More the second one, I think. Most of the time," I admitted. "I don't know. The experience drew me. I always wanted to get away and meet other people and live. Next step in life was college. I certainly didn't have the means to jet set off on some grand expedition around Europe for a gap year or something."

The idea had crossed my mind more than a few times throughout the years. Run away. Find my own magic.

Instead, I had come to Barnett and found a different sort.

"That would've been great. Huh?"

"You would've put off your grand football scholarship opportunity to become a nomad for a while?" I tried to imagine Ryan with a heavy backpack on his shoulders and sleeping under the stars.

"Maybe?" Ryan shrugged. "Maybe not. Still sounds nice."

It did.

"Ah, yes. Lu. There you are," Faith exclaimed.

She dropped a heavy book down on my table, letting it slam. A few looks turned in our direction. A few specks of dust spattered into the air.

Across from me, Ryan looked delighted at the sudden turn of events.

Faith's attention went back and forth between the two of us, as if she just now realized we were not alone for likely another one of her projects she needed help with. "Hello."

"Hi," said Ryan. He lifted a hand up in greeting.

"Oh! Are you looking at Lu's book? She has a talent, doesn't she?" asked Faith, a whimsical expression on her face as she leaned farther over the table with us, getting comfortable.

Her long necklace, full of charms, grazed the table with the noisy clatter of a wind chime. How she passed whatever mandatory quiet course for librarians, I'd never know.

"I never knew she was an artist," said Ryan, restating his previous comment.

"Because I'm not," I said, hearing the grumpiness in my tone toward her interrupting. I didn't know if it had been premeditated or not, but then again, I'd also known I couldn't manage to stay unscathed from Faith for long. "Did you say you needed help with something, Faith?"

"I did." She reoriented herself, looking down at the massive text in the center of us. She strummed her fingers along it. "Only now, I'm not positive what that was. It was either that I needed help finding more of this kind of book or that I wanted to tell you about my latest endeavor into how Nordic culture continues to prove the possibility of a true Arthurian era, hiding right under our noses."

Silence hung as she pondered the blatant lie I had heard similar versions of multiple times before. The detail and overall flighty nature of Faith's brain played well, making it a crowd-pleaser.

I plastered a smile on my face as I pushed to my feet. I picked up the book; it was much heavier than expected. "How about I assist you with this one?"

"That could also be helpful."

* * *

When I walked into her office, it was immediately apparent where the large gap was on her personal shelf and where the obnoxiously heavy book was meant to be. By the time I slid it back into place, Faith's hands excitedly cupped either side of her face.

"Are you two really?" Faith inhaled with intrigue. Any sense of calm and collected she'd had moments ago was lost. "You said before you weren't, but here you are—"

"Don't," I warned, stepping away. Not that it did any good.

"I feel gifted to see this boy before anyone else you know. You have a boy." Faith gripped hard on my arm.

I swatted her. Still, she did not let go as I hushed her. "I do not have a boy."

"A man really. I mean, look at him. I always thought he had funny hair, but now that I'm looking at him, I rescind my previous comment. It suits him."

"Faith."

"Lu?" She raised her eyebrows in an oddly similar yet menacing way.

"Stop it. He's here as a …"

Her eyes glittered.

"I'm helping him with a report."

"Seems like that's becoming quite the habit."

"Can you act at all natural?" I asked.

"I'm all natural," Faith said, genuinely confused from her chunky footwear all the way up to her fluffy hair.

"Right."

"Just give me a chance. I'll be perfectly good. I'm always good to your friends." She meant Vadika, and that was true.

I nodded, turning back around to head back to Ryan.

Only he was now behind us, peeking his head in.

"Hey, sorry. I actually have to head out," Ryan said slowly, shifting his backpack higher up on his shoulders. "I didn't realize the time. I promised one of my housemates I'd get an early dinner with him before he went to train."

"Oh, of course," I said. It was more than perfect to get him out of here. I could only picture Faith following me back upstairs. "I'll see you."

"Sorry about that before. Lu didn't want me to embarrass her," said Faith. Because, of course, she did.

Ryan grinned, getting more comfortable where he stood in the doorway of the glass office. "That's too bad. She didn't properly introduce us."

I sighed, waving a hand between the two of them. Now, there was no turning back. "Faith—she's a part of my coven actually."

His eyes widened before they turned back to Faith. "The librarian, right? Neat."

"He thinks we're neat, Lu." Faith spread her glossed lips.

"I heard."

"It's nice to meet you, Ryan. Lu told us all about you the other day."

"Oh, did she?" His gaze cut back to me as I stood with my arms crossed. "Were you talking about me, Lu?"

"All terrible things."

He put a hand to his chest in mock sadness.

Faith snorted. "It was nice that you kept her company in the library. She really needs to get herself a new roommate, don't you think?"

"I don't know her roommate, but Lu was actually helping me out, I think, more than the other way around. I've been slacking up until now." He nodded down toward his leg, which he threw out with the help of balancing on his crutch. "Lu set me straight."

"Our Lu certainly does that."

Our Lu?

"I'm still right here, you know," I reminded the two of them before they went any further.

"Don't mind her. You know, I have a crystal somewhere around here that could probably help with some healing," Faith said immediately. "I think I have one on me actually."

"Of course you do," I said dully as I tried to step forward and stop whatever insanity was happening in front of me as Faith dug through her oddly deep pockets.

Immediately, in the palm of her hand, she produced a smooth piece of lapis lazuli. It was a powerful stone, helping to relieve inflammation as well as anger or negative thoughts.

"Take this one too." She plucked out rose quartz from the other side of her trousers. "You look like you might need it."

Faith met my burning glare.

What was with these women and their passive-aggressive crystal pushing, laced with not-so-hidden meaning? First Celeste, who honestly couldn't care less about the celestial witchcraft practice most days, and now Faith?

Ryan beamed down at the smooth stones in appreciation and awe. He carefully pocketed them. "Thank you."

"Anytime. Soon, I'm sure, Luella will have you lathered in her tonics as well."

"Tonics?" asked Ryan, intrigued.

"Why else do you think she always smells like herbs?"

"Because only strange people who invade others' space take it upon themselves to smell them, Faith," I insisted. My latest concoction included a mixture of hyacinth and lemon balm, mixed with water and a light oil, like any perfume. Mine, however, was handmade and specifically formulated for one reason specifically other than smelling good.

I resisted the urge to lean down and see if its aroma was really that potent.

"You should come to our meeting tomorrow. Big holiday, you know."

"I didn't know," said Ryan, glancing toward me.

Once again, I turned to make sure Faith saw my displeasure.

"It's the equinox. First day of fall." I quickly filled him in.

"You didn't invite him?"

"Faith," I warned.

"What? It's not overstepping," she insisted. "He should absolutely come if he'd like. Brenson will be there, I think. So, he won't be the only boy. It isn't like we plan on doing some necromancy and raising the dead tomorrow."

Ryan's eyes widened.

Faith grinned wickedly at his reaction. "We should save that for Samhain. Need to gather the supplies. Sage, charcoal, the necessary sacrificial virgin."

I rolled my eyes.

After another pause, Ryan chuckled, as if he finally was getting the joke.

"Don't mind her. She's not very funny," I assured him.

He shrugged. "She's kind of funny."

"Why, thank you. Ryan, was it?"

Ryan raised his eyebrows toward me, the picture of delight toward this entire exchange. "You've really been talking about me, Lu?"

I stared at Faith. "No. I just have snooping friends who have yet to learn to mind their own business."

Faith was not deterred. "You should absolutely come to the meeting tomorrow. Especially if you like pie."

"Pie?"

I sighed. "Another member is teaching us her recipe before the meeting tomorrow."

"Well, I do like pie," said Ryan kindheartedly.

"He'll think about it," I insisted.

Faith shrugged. "Let me know if I can help you with anything in the library too."

Waiting until Ryan turned away toward the entrance of the library, I twisted back on Faith. "Oh, I think you've helped enough."

"Don't be mad."

"I'm not."

"Then stop talking to me and go with your cute little boy toy there." Her hands fluttered in his direction.

"He's not—goodbye, Faith."

"Blessed day, my dearest."

She gave a single salute before disappearing back somewhere in the mess of her office, but not before I called out, "You're just as bad as Celeste."

She nearly gasped with a hand perched on her collarbone. "Take that back. I'm far cooler."

That was true. I stared at her and shrugged. She could take that as she liked.

I caught up with Ryan near the edge of the checkout desk. He seemed to be taking his time, unsurprised as I came up next to him, walking outside, where the air was humid but cool.

"Sorry about that."

"Don't be. I'd always seen Faith around this part of campus, but I had never met her before. She seems nice."

"She is," I agreed. "Most of the time."

"I also didn't know you guys had so many holidays."

"Some are bigger than others, but yeah. We like to mark time. Magical moments not to be taken for granted and all that," I mumbled, looking down. Picking at my nail polish. Most of it had already fallen off in flecks.

"So, when are you picking me up?"

My head popped back up to meet his round eyes. "Picking you up?"

"Yeah. For tomorrow."

"You actually want to go?"

"It is one of my New Year's resolutions—to learn how to cook," said Ryan. "I have a feeling I'd be good at it, especially if the end result is pie."

I worried my lip.

"What? Do you not want me to go with you to celebrate …"

"Mabon. The equinox," I filled in.

"The equinox?" he repeated, finishing his question.

I sighed. "I mean, no. Yes."

"Oh."

"No, it's not that." Then again, it also was. Though Ryan was nice enough, it wasn't as if I had been hanging around with him a lot. Just a lot recently. It had taken me months before I considered letting Vadika meet the coven, let alone join us on a holiday. "You just need to understand what you are getting into. They are going to pick and poke at you like you're some strange insect."

Or worse, a guy I'd been seen spending the night with in the library after having all of them insisting I needed to liven up my life more.

It sounded like a travesty of a night waiting to happen, the indication swirling in my stomach.

"I know you are suddenly open to whatever this is." I pointed between us. "Talking and getting to know me and sitting in other people's library spots. But you coming to a coven meeting—my coven's equinox celebration—it's sort of a big deal."

At least, it was to me.

"You shouldn't come just because you feel like you should," I said.

"Lu, take a deep breath."

I stared at him.

He mimed taking a deep breath in and out.

I took a deep breath in and out. It helped.

I sort of wished it hadn't as I listened to him.

"I know it's a big deal," said Ryan. "I also know that I have been a royal ass in the past. I can't change that. But I think you're cool. I've always thought you were cool, Luella Pierce. So, if you let me and only if you want me there, I totally want to go to a witch coven meeting or celebration. I will arrive with the utmost respect and understanding that walking in there with you means I might be up for some sort of sacrificial purpose."

I shook my head at him.

"I want to experience nature turning into fall." He nodded once, decision made.

"Fine. Okay then," I said slowly. I wasn't going to be able to talk him out of it then. "I will see you tomorrow."

"Looking forward to it, Luella."

"Please behave."

"It makes me smile that you have to say that to me."

It made me feel like I'd made a very bad decision.

Turning around, I didn't make it another step before Ryan called back after me, "Hey, Lu."

I turned back to face him.

"Why do you always smell like spring flowers and lemon? You said they had meaning, right?"

I inhaled, taking a step back to return to the library. He remembered what Faith had said to him about my tinctures. Had he just noticed?

"Self-love."

Seeming to consider this, Ryan dipped his head once.

"I might still be your villain, Lu. But I'm also hoping to be your friend."

9

Alone and sitting on the bed with her hair looped into a messy bun, Natalie had her work spread out around her on her amoeba-patterned bedspread. Her eyes stuck on me.

"Finally back to take a shower?" Natalie commented.

I rolled my eyes as I beelined toward the door.

"I do think there is a hygienic clause in the whole roommate agreement crap they make us sign at the beginning of the year."

"I stayed with family," I said. "Very good water system. Very good soap. Eucalyptus to exfoliate my pores. It was basically like a spa. Would you like me to bring you some next time?"

"No, thanks. I'm good."

"Do you really think I'm that disgusting, or are we just projecting? I expected the room to smell a bit more like a brothel, so I'm glad we are still on the same page there," I threw right back. I was impressed with myself tonight, minding my own business.

She huffed as she leaned back over her binder, clicking her pen shut. "He didn't stay."

"Excuse me?"

"My boyfriend. He didn't stay," Natalie enunciated, staring at me.

I paused, reaching for my towel on the back of the wardrobe door. "Oh."

"Yeah," she said stiffly. "Oh."

I turned back around, dropping my backpack and things against my desk with a heavy thud. Would've been nice to know that. However, I never gave Natalie my phone number, or vice versa. Friends did that sort of thing. And we weren't friends. It almost hurt that I did still want to get a shower.

I reached for my shower caddy, sure to flash the black soap that I'd brought a fresh batch of from Gertie's before I turned back around toward the bathroom.

"I saw that you put in a funding request for some sort of project on campus," said Natalie suddenly before I could make it home free. Or rather, private bathroom free.

I paused, holding on to the old doorframe that rocked in my hand. "I did."

"I guess we'll see what happens with that."

A heaviness settled on my chest as I huffed out a breath of air. "Yeah. Guess so, Nat."

"I'm going to bed soon, so don't be loud, coming back in."

"No other interesting things going on around campus tonight?" I ask, surprised to see her already in her pajamas so soon.

Her eyes tore away from mine. She shut her books. "I'm going to bed."

I walked down the hall to the bathroom.

"Sleep tight," I murmured to myself.

Stepping under the water, I made sure the curtain was closed before I took a deep sigh, feeling the tension of my muscles and in my shoulders from the day. It had been a long day—a long year already, and we weren't even in the throes of fall yet.

And yet it still wasn't enough time for me to figure out what stupid major I needed to be approved by the registrar or to contemplate and sort out exactly what Gertie had offered up the other day.

Because for that one, I knew what I wanted my answer to be.

Just like Gertie knew exactly who I was when no one else seemed to get it.

Except maybe Ryan. I still couldn't stop running his words through my head. So simple as he'd asked me when I was going to think I was enough to let him hang out with me. I still couldn't quite figure that out either. Because I was enough.

I knew I was enough.

Now. Always. Even when it seemed I'd forgotten.

I let the water run down my back with the slightest smell of chlorine, standing under the shower bare and eyes shut with one image left flirting through my mind.

Ryan Gardner was going to accompany me to the fall equinox tomorrow night.

* * *

If Ryan Gardner had cold feet about going to Gertie's for Mabon and was hiding from me, he'd better be prepared. In another minute, I was prepared to make my way inside the never-before-entered sports house and rip him out from under whatever bed or closet he was hiding inside of because I was not going to be stood up. Though, of course, this evening wasn't a date.

Standing up someone didn't only have to deal with dates, right?

I hadn't wanted him to come along to Mabon to begin with, and now, I was pacing back and forth over the uneven, cracked sidewalk in front of an equally dilapidated house on the Row, like a gentleman, waiting for him to sneak out of the house.

Me. I was the gentleman.

Soon, I was going to be a mad-ass bitch.

"Lu!"

My feet twisted around before the rest of me. I let out a rush of air. "You are so lucky you showed up before I knocked on that door."

Ryan shut the door of a blue car before he carefully made his way up the path toward the front door. He walked without crutches or his brace.

My eyes widened as he extended his arms on either side, as if he were walking a tightrope or a very narrow runway.

"I know, right? Freedom."

"You're crutch-free."

"Somehow, it feels better every time. I'm sorry. There was traffic, and my doctor's appointment ran late," explained Ryan. "I just need to change my shirt quickly, and then we can go. Are we late?"

We were going to be.

"Not yet."

"Good. I can work with not yet." Pulling open the unlocked front door, Ryan waved me in after him, immediately trailing up the stairs. Slowly yet with a smile with each step he didn't fall over on.

Glancing around the space, I wasn't surprised to see the house in disarray with sports bags swung over the railing and random pillows lumped over equally lumpy couches—which had likely been dragged inside from the stoop by whoever lived here in the last few years—in the living room. Still, it didn't smell like BO, so that was something. As was the silence. No one appeared to be inside other than us.

"Sweet, sweet freedom," Ryan exhaled at the top of the staircase.

"Can you hurry up? Please?"

"And hurt my sweet, recently healed tendons?" Ryan pushed open the door to his room, also as unlocked as the front door.

This one, however, was also hanging open by old, unscrewed hinges.

Any updates the school had made to the theme housing must've been only on an external level. Otherwise, the walls didn't look like they had been painted since the late '70s. The floors were nicked and watermarked, much like the ceiling.

A speedy scuttle came from the space next to me.

I took a hasty step back from where I stood. The floor creaked, but still, that was much less concerning as I pointed a finger toward the spotty walls. "What the hell was that?"

"What?"

The scuttling in the walls echoed through the room again in Ryan's momentary silence.

"Oh." He dipped his chin in understanding. He waved toward the haunted wall. "Don't mind that. That's probably just Potato."

"Potato?"

"You know, these old buildings. Potato is our mouse," Ryan said.

My eyes widened. "You have mice?"

"I don't. The house does."

"And this doesn't concern you?"

He shrugged. "At first, but they mostly leave us alone."

"Mostly?"

"Well, we can't leave the good cereal out anymore," he conceded ironically. "But Potato is more or less a communal pet now."

My gods.

"So, you feed him potatoes?" I asked, trying to make sense of all this.

"Nah. He just sort of looks like one. My teammate thought he was literally the vegetable one morning when he didn't have his glasses on. The name stuck," explained Ryan. "Honestly, we think there might be two mice in the walls, so they aren't lonely. We can't tell them apart though, so both of them are named Potato. Potato, potahto, y'know?"

I stared at Ryan for a long moment as he ruffled through the center drawer of his dresser. Once more, I turned around, looking around the walls, which had now quieted. "Interesting."

"Haven't you ever had a mouse as an unintentional roommate?"

Luckily, no. Gertie also had cats.

The moment I turned back around to tell him as much, Ryan still stood with his back to me. Shirtless.

My eyes caught on his bare skin—from his well-carved shoulders all the way down to where his jeans hung loosely over his hips. His defined muscles flexed with the everyday movement as he yanked a deep-green shirt overhead.

Ryan wasn't one of the largest players on the team. In fact, he was almost slim from all the running he did, yet for some reason, I never expected him to be so fit. Not that I spent time imagining him without clothes on at all.

His shirt hugged the roundness of his biceps as he pulled it lower over his abdomen. When he turned back around to face me, I noticed the hem graze the copper button of his jeans.

"Does this look okay?"

"What?" I started to nod as I processed his question. "Oh, yeah. You look great."

"Not really sure what equinox attire looks like."

"You're fine." I still stared, blinking as I brought myself back to the present moment. My eyes back toward Ryan's face rather than the rest of him.

He pressed his lips together to hide his never-fading smirk. He didn't say a word if he noticed my momentary stroke. "Ready?"

"I was ready a half hour ago. I don't take as long to primp as you apparently do."

"Be quiet." Ryan nudged me with an elbow as he stumbled back down the stairs.

I followed close behind, biting back a giggle at the sudden race to the front door we'd started.

At this rate, maybe we wouldn't be so late after all, so long as Ryan didn't accidentally trip me down the stairs. Then, we would have someone else in crutches.

And someone would have a lot of explaining to do.

"Hey!"

Ryan froze in his pace toward the door. Unlike when we had entered, there was another person stretched out on the couch, one leg up over the top. His laptop was open in front of him, playing some sort of show while he fed himself another few chips at a time. They crunched loudly with each bite, crumbs scattering onto his sweatshirt.

"Hey, Trevor," said Ryan.

"How's the leg, man?"

At that, Ryan smiled proudly. He stuck his cleared leg out in front of him, as if his friend could see through his loose sports pants. "Good so far!"

"Good stuff. Who's this?"

"This?" Ryan glanced back at me with my hand reaching for the doorknob. He took a deep breath. "This is Lu."

His friend blinked tiredly, sticking his hand back into the family-sized chip bag. "Oh. Hey … Lu?"

"Hi. That would be my name, yep." I stared at Ryan. "We're going to be late. You do not want to meet the wrath of overly involved witches when you are late."

"Good point. See ya, Trev."

"See you whenever, I guess." Trevor raised a fluorescent-orange cheese-stained hand, still watching the two of us before we made it out the door.

Ryan tugged it shut behind by the brass handle.

"Trevor's a pretty good guy," Ryan said nonchalantly. He reached out, however, before I made it to the sidewalk, taking a right toward town. "I heard it might rain later tonight, so I figured we could drive if we're out that long before getting back to campus."

For some reason, I wasn't thinking about getting back to campus. Usually, when I had a meeting at Gertie's, I automatically stayed the night with her afterward, not wanting to traverse back to campus alone. Only I wasn't going to be alone this time around. Ryan was going to be with me.

Another strange, uncomfortable feeling rose through my stomach and toward my chest at the re-realization of just exactly what I was doing. I was bringing Ryan directly into the hellfire of Gertie and the rest of the nosy coven. We were falling directly into their clutches. They were going to make much more of it than it was. Ryan and I were … friends.

Sort of friends?

Whatever we were, all I needed was for them to mess up whatever it might be. He was coming not only to a coven meeting, but also a holiday. Even Vadika had only come to May Day my first year and made an oath to never again after we all got a little too rowdy with dancing around our makeshift pole and the dandelion wine that Ana and Faith had had the bright idea of trying to make and succeeding all too well.

It had been a good night. Like with Vadika though, I wasn't sure what Ryan would think if things got a tad out of hand, if I sank into my true colors—if I could manage to relax enough at the sudden understanding weighing on my shoulders. I felt like I was bringing Ryan home to meet the parents.

Gods, I was giving myself a headache.

"You all right there? You look nervous."

Instead of lying, I didn't say anything at all. Ryan led me to his car, still parked up along the curb. He opened the passenger door and waved an extravagant arm for me to get in.

Wrinkling my forehead, I ducked down into the seat and

pulled the door shut behind me by the time he made it around to the driver's side. With a flick of his key, he revved the engine to life and smiled, getting himself situated.

"Ah, how long it has been since I've driven without feeling like I was squished in here with that awful brace and those stupid crutches." Ryan smiled again with boyish pleasure. He strummed his fingers on the wheel. "You'll have to give me directions. I have no clue where I'm going."

I shook my head as if I should've realized. "You can just go straight from here into town and across the Riverwalk Bridge."

The old Riverwalk Bridge, of course, wasn't much of a bridge. It was really just a rusted blue-green metal crossing that led toward what everyone considered the isle. The bridge also made new drivers swerve, for fear of being too close to the shallow edge when sharing what should truly be a one-way lane.

When it was dark and rainy out, going toward the isle also gave the appearance of doom and gloom. Heavy cloud cover formed a thick haze, as if a river monster was bound to make an appearance tonight under the bright moon. The lunar light peeked out between dark-gray swaths.

Ryan made it across the bridge with ease. No one else was out on the small-town roads as I directed him to keep going straight before making a single right until we were at the end of the road, in front of the looming Victorian.

I unbuckled, waiting for Ryan to cut the engine. "Coming with or deciding against it?"

He seemed to understand then. "This is it?"

"This is it."

"Whoa. I mean, I've passed this place before, but for some reason, I never thought anyone actually lived in it," said Ryan, pulling the key out of the ignition and unbuckling himself by the time I was already waiting outside the car in the damp air. He carefully shut the car door behind him, as if apprehensive about disturbing anyone on this side of Barnett with the noise.

"Just wait until you get inside," I said, pushing past the front iron gate and up the path to the front door.

Voices were already teeming inside the house. They echoed gleefully through the hallway, where I could glance into the living space, where the altar was already lit. The space was draped in offerings from coffee to apples and pine cones to still partially green leaves, kept far from any tiny flames, captured in mason jars for extra safety.

"We were wondering when you'd ever get here!" cried Estrella from behind the front door. "I said I would stand watch. Faith said you were bringing a boy for some reason. She wasn't lying, which I find exceptionally out of character, but here we are."

Here we were.

"Hi," Ryan said, looking down at Estrella from his considerable height in comparison, even with Essie being rather tall. "I'm Ryan."

Looking him up and down with her piercing eyes, she nodded once and smiled back. "I'm Essie. Welcome."

With a twist on her heel, she turned around back down the hall, a flare of her long blonde hair guiding us with her.

Ryan looked at me, leaning his head close so as not to be overheard. "Does she live here or something?"

"No." Or, at least, not yet.

A heaviness settled in my stomach as we followed her back.

"Since when has Lu ever not been the first one here?" Faith asked by the time we were just outside the cozy kitchen. Her voice held a tinge of pride. "I feel like I should earn some sort of prize."

"Because you are usually always the last."

"Turning over a new leaf," Faith said.

"Right before they fall." Ana snorted.

Her head lolled over her shoulder as she watched us enter.

Ryan, for the first time, remained a step behind, as if prepared to use me as a sort of makeshift shield as we came across the group of women looping aprons around their bodies with limp bows hanging in the back.

The kitchen was lit still by the sun cresting in the wide windows that showed off the backyard. Plants draped from the tops of cabinets. The glass windows showed the many different thrifted items inside. Today, however, what was most notable were the carefully allotted ingredients laid out in front of each of them, along with the plethora of Pyrex bowls, which Gertie had accumulated in all colors and patterns.

"Look who's arrived."

"I would've been earlier," I muttered, glancing back toward Ryan. I took a step to the side, as if to present him and his reddening cheeks while also heading toward the peg that held the aprons. Mine that I always wore—a classic '50s number with yellow ruffles—was still there. "Someone made me late."

Ryan lifted a hand in greeting as he glanced toward Faith. "Hi again."

"Hi there." Faith's gaze pulled away from him and back toward me. Her voice turned a bit quieter, as if no one could hear her quite clearly. "You actually brought him."

I nearly scoffed. "After you invited him, you mean? Yes, I did."

Flipping my apron over my head, I reached for one of the final few. Blue-and-white checkerboard, it was embroidered at the bottom with springtime pastel flowers.

"Do I look pretty?" asked Ryan, holding on to the two ties on either side.

"Absolutely dashing." Reaching out, I took the ties from him, letting them loose around his hips before I tied it in a perfect, fluffy bow in the back. "Still ready for this?"

"More than."

"Oh, so Ryan is going to be crafting today?" Ana asked, her voice low, as if we couldn't all hear her anyway. "*Très* interesting."

I rolled my eyes.

"How are the stones working for you from yesterday?" Faith

piped in, standing as she approached the counter with the rest of us.

Everyone—except for Gertie, who slipped inside like she had always been there—sat at the small table against the wall.

"So far, so good," Ryan admitted. "I don't feel anything yet though."

Faith tied her own apron in a prim knot in the center of her back. "You'll know when you know."

Celeste paused in the doorway. Lips parted, as if she was about to say something, she raised her light eyebrows instead. Her silence lasted long enough that Essie squeezed by and took her place at the end of the long worktable.

"Looks like we have an extra," she finally managed.

"*Faith* invited him," Ana informed her.

"Well, Lu certainly wasn't going to," Faith said.

Not looking up at Celeste, much like myself, Ana never really did pay much attention to the mother figure. She picked at the skin around her nails.

"The more, the merrier," Gertie spoke up, settling herself in a chair at the tiny table and kicking her legs out. The ideal view to watch the chaos that was about to take place in the kitchen any moment now, if the ingredients lined up had anything to say about it.

Celeste nodded sensibly, as if she would never consider otherwise. "We already set up for tonight. You two will have to share."

"Not a problem, Celeste," I said blandly. Not that it looked like she was searching for my reaction.

Her eyes were much more focused on Ryan.

He cast a glance over the pile of apples set up in the center of the butcher block.

"I think my son might be on his way if he doesn't get caught up in schoolwork again," Celeste said. "He was never really interested in the craft like the rest of us ladies, but don't worry, dear. You won't be the only male in the house by the end of tonight."

"I wasn't really worried," Ryan said with a smile, eyes immediately greeting her politely.

Was it just me, or was there a twang of a nervous church-boy accent I heard?

He cleared his throat. "Happy to be here."

I looked behind me toward where Gertie continued to watch the exchange, her eyebrows raised, as if she was curious what I could possibly have to say. I had nothing. I'd just expected her to have more.

I'd brought a boy. I brought an outsider boy, who had no idea that magic was a possibility that existed out of the realm of storybooks, into her home and into the coven of women who found some semblance of love and safety inside of each meeting together.

Not that one of those women hadn't invited him herself.

Maybe it was only me who was nervous about him being here. It was a ticking time bomb for him to do or say something stupid. Everyone else acted as if he had always been here. No stranger to crafting kitchen magic as a very male nonpractitioner who had once teased me about the stereotypes that now made me roll my eyes.

I cleared my throat and took a deep breath. I forced the bubbling nerves to subside alongside the seemingly nonexistent judgment around me. Down the line from Faith to Ana to Essie, they were staring at Celeste intently. It made no sense compared to how much they had all been ready to tease me the other night after the tiniest bit of gossip Faith brought with her.

Celeste was already talking about something, fanning her hands over the arrangement of things—from the apple peelers to the wooden spoons. "All right then. I think we are ready."

"I've been ready and starving," joked Ana, already reaching for her first apple and sharp knife.

"Let's begin."

Handing Ryan the knife, I set to peeling, passing him the apple when it was done to chop.

"We do the apples first so that the fruit and sugars have time to break down. Apples, after all, are very important, especially this time of year." Celeste spoke, going over each piece of the whole. "Apples are often associated with the spiritual realm. They are wonderful offerings to send to your ancestors or other spirits we choose to work with, as you might've noticed from our altar. Protection is another correspondence of the apple, making it a great form for protection workings, as we come together, in this case, to share in this holiday when the realm between physical and spiritual gets thinner at this time of year."

I continued to work, Ryan and I finding a steady rhythm of peeling and cutting into perfectly square shapes before he dumped them one clump at a time into the glass bowl. Ana hummed to herself from the other end of the counter.

"Apples are also a symbol of love. Cut an apple in half, and you can share with another to ensure happiness. A simple form of love—or more so if the core forms the shape of a heart in some cases." Celeste cut open an apple and displayed the inside, more of a fine circle around the seeds than any other shape.

Next to me, Ana snorted as she chopped her apple open in one fine motion. Looking inside, she turned her apple heart to show from her chest with a chuckle and handed over the other half to Faith to put in her pie.

Faith handed hers over to Anna.

Holding the peeled apple in hand, I sliced it. Inside were a few lines, slightly inverted at the crest, sort of like a heart. When I lifted my gaze, Ryan had already extended his other half to me.

I took the delicate piece of apple from him and traded back mine with a hesitant smile of my own. He lifted the piece of apple up, as if a toast between us.

After a second, I mimicked the motion.

"Happiness," he said simply.

I stared down at the slice of apple before moving on with the process. I couldn't help but look over at him as we ended up placing both pieces of that apple in our pie together while the rest were coated in a thick goo of cinnamon and sugar, breaking down the apples.

Since when had my life turned into a witchy Hallmark card?

I refocused back on what I was doing. Otherwise, it was seriously getting a little too touchy-feely in here. Not acceptable for any holiday in my books, let alone Mabon, where things were literally supposed to be coming to die.

"Does Celeste do a lot of these sorts of in-person cooking shows?" Ryan leaned over my shoulder to whisper.

I shook my head. "Occasionally. We all were rooting for her pie."

"Why?"

I stared down at his bowl of crystallized apples. "It's a *really* good pie. Plus, it fits well with the holiday. Both physical apples and the metaphysical are in season."

"Now I really can't wait to eat this."

"It's so freaking good, Ryan," said Faith, overhearing. She leaned over her bowl she was adding more nutmeg into to see down the line. "Unless you count her chamomile buns or raspberry strudel in the spring. Those are life changing."

Celeste peeked over each shoulder while she directed. "Once you start to have enough apples in your bowl, add your spices. We want cinnamon and nutmeg for prosperity. Ground clove for protection and kinship. And a pinch of salt along with our brown sugar. Fold it in gently. Remember to start thinking now of what this pie brings for us. The time we spend together making it and future positive feelings we hope to gain from those we share our energy with."

I nodded for Ryan to begin mixing while I finished the final few apples, letting them all have time to meld together before going into the oven.

Sprinkling the spices over the top of the apples, Ryan stared down at the fruit, rather serious for a moment before he grabbed the wooden spoon. Carefully, he stirred, making sure the slices were evenly coated.

"Like this?"

"Perfect," praised Celeste.

Ryan grinned as he folded more. He looked like such a dork. I couldn't help but shake my head and turn away, so he couldn't see my own smile begin to overtake my lips.

"See, Lu, I'm cooking."

"Baking," I corrected him, reaching over to sprinkle some leftover sugar over his head.

He wrinkled his nose, shaking out his head to send the sugar right back at me. "Semantics."

I squealed at the pellets hitting the side of my cheek.

He reached back for the last apple I wasn't already on, taking it in his hand to add to the bowl.

Unable to help himself, Ryan swept his fingers alongside the bowl, tasting.

I swatted his hand. "Stop that."

"In my belief, it's basically bad luck not to taste the batter."

I rolled my eyes but couldn't help but continue one direction at a time as we began the arduous process of trying to complete Celeste's legendary prosperity apple pie, which usually took her two days, in a matter of a few hours with a few minor adjustments, such as pie crust dough already laid out from the fridge.

I fit myself in line for the next bit, tightly squeezed next to Ryan as he rolled out the dough. Using both of our hands, we carefully lined the pie dish and dumped our apples inside. Then, all that was left were the extra dough pieces we had trimmed.

"Get creative. Decorate the top of your pie by weaving in your intentions further or displaying what you are working toward," said Celeste. "Feel free to add crumble if you prefer."

"Oh," Ryan said, hushed, as if the word brought him pleasure. "Crumble."

I snorted, shaking my head. This pie was going to look like a mess.

"You do your side, and I'll do mine," I insisted.

Ryan snorted. "Like that's going to help anything."

He was right. By the end, the one side of our pie had gentle crust braids and puckered leaves around the edge while Ryan's took on a more abstract quality, looking like a partially completed game of Chutes and Ladders.

Honestly, I'd thought it would look worse than it did.

"See, you did wonderfully."

"Sure I did. You are just trying to make me feel like not a complete loser in front of your family."

"A masterpiece," I assured, giving a swift pat on his back.

I let my hand rest there, near the back of his neck, for a second. I gave it a squeeze, like I'd do to Vadika when she was stressed in the lab to ease her nervous system. Midway, I realized what I had done. Ryan and I hadn't really touched before besides the occasional nudge or yank to make sure the other was following in the right direction.

Trying not to make it weird, I let my hand slide off his shoulder, and I went back to staring down at our Frankenstein pie.

"Hey, Lu."

Turning my head up, I was immediately speckled with flour in the face. It wasn't much, but just enough to know my freckles were coated in white spots, much like Ryan's fingertips. I sputtered my lips to make sure they were clear.

"Very mature."

"To purity and sweet beginnings," Gertie toasted from behind the two of us. "Flour and sugar. A wonderful companionship, especially at this time of year when endings are all around us."

Gertie raised her eyebrows at me.

Celeste's attention also snapped to Ryan and me. Her fingers paused as she helped pinch the edges of Essie's awardworthy-looking pie into perfect crinkles.

I went back down to our pie, straightening out one of my lopsided crust leaves.

"We now put them into the oven," Celeste said as she stepped in front of us all. She wiped her hands off on her simple white apron. "And it's time to clean up."

A round of moans echoed through the kitchen.

* * *

Little giggles went up when Ryan was splashed with a fresh coating of soap bubbles. One of them was himself, laughing at the mess he had made as he helped clean up each tiny bowl and wide sugarcoated dish.

Essie dropped the last of the dirty dishes on one side of Ryan, who was still at work, dipping his hands into the bubbly water.

"It's not like I'm leaving for no reason, Mom," Essie argued casually, glancing back in Celeste's direction.

"It's Mabon," was all Celeste said.

"I know. I know it is, but my new friend, the guy from school I have been showing around, is still going out tonight with the rest of the group I introduced him to." Essie traveled around the kitchen as she spoke. She leaned over her mother's shoulder to make sure that she heard.

Celeste hummed good-naturedly as she wiped up the mess on the table. "You said that earlier, didn't you?"

"I might have mentioned it," said Essie.

"It won't harm anyone if she's not here, Celeste," Gertie spoke up, keeping her voice mellow so it didn't sound as if she were intruding.

Still, Celeste glanced over at the high priestess, considering her words. She shut her eyes. "Where are they going?"

"I think they are going to that fundraiser at the roller rink. I'm terrible at it."

"You sprained your wrist the last time."

Essie smiled, as if it was a fond memory. "Can I go? If I leave now, they can pick me up. I can still make it."

"You knew today was a holiday. You missed the last meeting on Saturday."

"Please? I know I said that I would be here. But I am in my heart and soul, and I feel bad, but I feel like I will also feel terrible for my friend if I back out on this."

"But not for your coven?"

At that, Essie paused, silent in her plea.

Celeste sighed. "Go. But I expect you to know better when it comes to Samhain."

"Yes, Mother. Of course, Mother," said Essie with a hint of humor. She brushed her hands off on her apron, pulling it off to hang up on the hook. She ruffled her pin-straight hair around her shoulders and brushed the flour from her jeans.

"How is your new little boy toy, Essie?" Ana asked from where she tried to whip her with the edge of a towel.

She gracefully evaded, turning toward me to make sure someone else had seen that. If only I wasn't equally amused by Ana's sense of humor.

"He is not a boy toy, Ana, for one thing," Essie said severely. "He's a friend who doesn't have many others right now."

"How kind and up front of you."

"Have a good time and be careful!" Celeste called out as her daughter darted toward the door.

"You don't worry about her running away with that boy? Essie's becoming a little woman," Faith said with a hint of a joke.

All of us knew that Essie was more attuned to the world than most her age. She was a quiet soul, but we all knew never to underestimate such. It was another reason that Essie would be the ideal high priestess candidate when she got older.

"Oh, she knows better. I have nothing to worry about with her yet. And she has the rest of you ladies teaching her things far before her time anyway." Celeste brushed off.

We all snickered, even Gertie, who never stopped a bit of well-intended life talk when it took a saucy turn.

"And that's okay?" Ryan asked. His words hesitant from where he soaped up the next bowl and listened to the rest of the coven giggle. He dumped the watery contents before starting on the next dish.

Celeste raised her eyebrows with a gentle nod as the noise died down. "In most pagan culture or in magic, relationships aren't seen the way many others view them. If that is what you are intrigued about."

"Sort of. What do you mean?"

"She means, we are all much bigger whores," Ana proclaimed.

Now, it was Celeste's turn as she swatted Ana with her tea towel.

Ana strummed her fingertips against her amused lips as she hopped out of the way, taking off her apron and hanging it back up on the hook. The fabric was still covered in a healthy spatter of white flour, which floated down toward the tiles.

"The world has a very strange view on innocence and purity, usually in women. That brings us to a whole other topic I have always felt strongly about," explained Celeste. "But when it comes down to it, love is love in whatever form or kind of relationship it finds us in. Sharing our own energy is perhaps the most potent understanding of true magic we have. So, we celebrate it. If that means spending time, so be it. If it means tender kisses—"

"Or tender lovemaking," said Faith wistfully.

Celeste didn't swat her for the comment, only looked upward toward the ceiling, stained with other kitchen experiments. She shrugged. "So be it. It's a natural thing we were made to do and are called to it. It isn't shameful or taboo. It is bravery and strength and beauty. It's magic."

My gaze was stuck on Celeste as she went on with her tidbit into the life of being a modern witch. So easily prepossessing.

And it was to me. When I'd first realized that witchcraft wasn't something that belonged in fantasy worlds, it'd struck me, just like the idea that all the flowers I'd loved in the garden my mother grew while I was a little girl held more meaning and life than just to be beautiful.

Right now, I could see the beauty too. I saw it in the way Faith laughed and Ana pressed her lips closed at whatever was being said, trying to maintain her well-kept composure. I could see it in the way Gertie looked upon us all with fondness. I could see it even in Ryan.

It looked like—he looked like he fit.

It was as if he belonged right there with me with the rest of the ladies with no other judgment as he worked along their side. This was not the Ryan Gardner I'd assumed I knew, and something tingling swept up my center. That was becoming abundantly clear.

"Of course, you probably know that as Lu's boyfriend," Faith teased with a heavy layer of tongue in cheek.

"Ooh," both Faith and Ana intoned as they watched his face flush an endearing red.

My lips curled up in the corners before I looked away from the scene of them all. Of him with his messy hair and bright eyes that were as stunning as a clear day.

I was getting ahead of myself.

I gave my hesitant smile to Gertie, who had been watching me closely. "I'll be right back."

Her hand reached out, drifting over my arm. "It's getting dark. Be careful and don't wander too close to the water."

"I won't."

10

The sprinkle of impending rain tickled my shoulders. I stared into the flowing river. Tiny waves jumped over rocks. The bark of the tree that lived half in water and half on earth, unable to make up its mind, scratched against my back. I was feeling similarly as I glanced back toward the house through the thinning raspberry vines and sections of garden. I was one step into something. My other foot was ready to take me away and run from whatever it was happening inside.

A now familiar figure didn't take long before they arrived next to me.

"Hey," Ryan said softly, sticking his hands in his pockets.

"I'm sorry about all that."

"About what?"

"Them," I said, though I wasn't sure if that was what I meant. "They are all slightly out of their minds. That's why they're calling you my boyfriend and everything."

He shrugged, looking down at his shoes. "It's all right."

"It is not. You don't have to say that."

"I'm not just saying that," Ryan insisted quietly. "There are a lot worse things to be called than your boyfriend."

When I looked up, our eyes caught for a moment. I let mine linger there, looking at the deep-blue color his eyes turned in the darkness that was slowly drifting over the river. The river that I quickly turned my attention back to. "Oh."

"It's kind of nice actually," said Ryan. "It's nice here. I can see why you like it so much. The house. The people."

I glanced at him, peering through my eyelashes.

"The feeling," he added.

"The feeling?"

"Yeah." He smiled. "There are memories all over that place. There are pictures of you all on the fridge and old notes. It feels like a home. My home didn't feel like that exactly. It was much more … clean. Less lived in."

"That's one thing that Gertie never held true to."

They had spring cleaning, but Gertie never proclaimed her house was anything close to minimalist. The rocks Essie and Brenson used to collect and gift to her when they were little, which Celeste brought to all of the coven meetings years ago, still lined bookshelves and windowsills. Dozens of them.

"If you look in the living room, you'll notice the dark ring from the time that Celeste's son, Brenson, knocked some of the candles over around Yule when we were playing cards. They lit the carpet on fire."

"You're kidding."

"Nope," I said, remembering. "It's a reason Gertie always has a bowl of water among the offerings as well. Still, he screamed like a little girl."

After that, he rarely came back to any meetings of his own volition.

"Now I regret him not showing up," said Ryan.

Maybe next time, I thought before I could stop myself.

"It's like you all are a family."

"We are," I said, feeling the correction in the words as the wind kicked up lightly, brushing my hair to the side. I gave a small chuckle at the memories I'd heard of and the ones I'd managed to experience over the past two years.

It didn't feel like much time, but it was more than I could've ever hoped for.

And now, Ryan stood in front of me, eyes catching as something grazed the top of my head. I reached up for it, but his hand caught mine before I could.

"Wait." He chuckled, pulling a dried leaf out of my hair, fallen from above. He held it up between us. "For you."

It wasn't flowers, but for some reason, it stopped the air in my lungs. I took the stem from his fingers. I twisted it back and forth, staring down at it with warmth flaring in my chest.

What was happening to me?

"What else are you thinking about?" Ryan stepped up next to me, looking into the river.

I shrugged. "Life?"

"That's all?" he teased.

Like earlier in the house, he nudged me. This time, he leaned a little easier, lingering his heavy weight against my frame. Uneven, I almost reached out to hold on to him, to stay steady and to keep him right there, grounding me.

"You'll figure it out."

"You seem to be about the only person who thinks so."

"Is there anything specific going on?"

"It's a long story," I sigh.

He shrugged. "Well, Gertrude said we have about fifteen minutes until they are out by the firepit for whatever else you all have planned tonight."

The Mabon rituals. I shut my eyes, not attempting to hide my amusement at his contentment, having absolutely no clue what was going on this evening.

"So, Gertrude," I started, saying her full name so he wouldn't get confused, "she's sort of the leader of our coven, you understand?"

He nodded. "I figured. She reminds me a lot of you."

"She does?"

"In a weird way," he said. "She has a certain vibe."

Well then, this was going to go over easily for him.

"Yeah, well, she knows I've been struggling, and the other day, she basically offered me her position. The high priestess-ship when she's done, the house … all of it."

"I'm sure it's not because she thinks you're struggling."

The thought had occurred to me that she pitied me, though I knew that was very un-Gertie-like. Ryan was right about that. I shrugged.

"And you don't want that?"

"It's not just that. I never thought it would be an option when I can barely figure out a single major at school, Ryan," I heard myself complain.

He seemed to consider this very factual information. "Maybe you weren't supposed to."

He'd already spent too much time here if he was getting all fateful.

"That's not the only issue anyway."

"What else is there?"

"The job is already taken."

"By who?"

"Essie."

It was always supposed to be Essie. She had basically been born in this house. Celeste's water literally broke in the entryway like some sort of prodigal daughter of whatever gods ruled over the house that day.

She had come into the world in this house.

I'd just walked through the door.

"Celeste's daughter who is, like, fourteen?" Ryan asked.

"She's fifteen right now, and it isn't like Gertie's set to keel over anytime soon, Ryan," I said.

"The family drama here is unbearable." He put his hands up, as if it were almost too much.

"Now you're making fun of me."

He pressed his lips together. "Not intentionally. Promise."

His endearing nature was almost making me smile with him. Instead, my shoulders slumped with a sigh. I needed to pull myself back together before everyone else wandered out here and dragged the two of us back toward the firepit. I could already hear someone shuffling around, likely also spying.

"I think," Ryan stated, considerate, "sometimes you need to stop worrying about what is right and wrong. It just is. When that happens, it's more about what you want. It doesn't always have to be about anyone else."

I let his words sink in, looking at him carefully to see if there was anything but earnestness there.

I patted his arm. "Maybe you will be a good elementary school teacher."

"I doubt I'll be giving a lot of motivational speeches," he said. "And that's just what I've been telling myself lately."

I shook my head. "You're able to tell things how they are."

It was a power I certainly had never been able to gain. Another reason perhaps I shouldn't accept Gertie's confidence in me to take over all of this. Whether or not it needed a lot of monitoring these days.

All these decisions might have been my wants, sure, and yet I always hated fallout. And with Celeste, there certainly would be a confrontation once she heard.

If she heard, I corrected myself.

My brain already didn't seem to understand the difference.

"So, what else do I have to look forward to for the rest of this equinox?" asked Ryan, glancing back over his shoulder.

The others were already starting to drift outside of the house with preparations and a much less traditional lighter to start the small pit for warmth. I must've been out here longer than I'd thought. The air was colder than I remembered before, sweeping across my shoulders with a fine mist from the river before Ryan put his own arm there.

I didn't push him away as he turned us around back toward all the action and bickering voices.

"A few things. Unless Faith and Ana get carried away again."

* * *

Ryan took his seat next to me around the small yet slowly building fire. Ana let a blanket drift between us over our shoulders. Sharing, Ryan stretched the blanket over my back before pulling the other corner around himself.

We were certainly snug.

I adjusted myself, careful not to tug on the tasseled quilt.

"The equinox, Mabon, brings balance to us and the world," said Gertie. "We think of the things we are grateful for as well as the things we wish to cast aside from our lives and from ourselves. So, now, we can write on a piece of paper and cast those things we are grateful for into our hearts and that which no longer serves us up and into the flames. The cold washes them away and grants us the power to be renewed as the new year approaches."

Gertie settled in her seat, nodding to herself as everyone took a moment.

Celeste took the longest, and we passed along the pen until it made it back to Gertie, who flung her scrap of paper into the pit first.

"I cast aside that and the many lives I have lived that are no longer serving me."

"Chasing solitude," Faith intoned, staring into the flames.

"Heartbreak," added Ana.

"Perfection," said Celeste.

"Loneliness."

I blinked at Ryan's simple word, brow furrowing, yet I didn't break our circle made of words, strong and true like any incantation should be.

When no one said anything, I realized they were waiting for me. It was a rule that you need not say anything aloud. All that mattered was that your intention was in your soul.

I stared at the fire, flicking another few inches higher before flattening out again. Taking a deep breath, I let my own simple word roll off my tongue before I realized it was there as I tossed my piece of parchment into the flames.

"Uncertainty."

Gertie's soft eyes found mine with a gentle sense of approval. She must've thought I'd made some sort of decision based on her words the other night. But sadly, I didn't cast aside my indecisiveness.

Not yet, with or without wholehearted intention.

Still, a sort of lightness seemed to drift over the group of us as we took a deep breath.

"Finally, I will pass the metaphorical wand to Faith and Ana, who will introduce the next ritual of our practice." Gertie waved a hand toward the two women, as if lending the stage.

"I'll be right back," Faith said. Jumping up, she ran into the house. Quickly, she returned with a small bowl in the palms of her hands. "The rite of the pomegranate."

The small fire of mostly embers, besides a few sparks, caught almost as bright as the color of Ryan's hair.

He quickly cupped the tiny bowl that Faith passed around, looking down into its dark contents, fishing his seven seeds out. "I've never had pomegranate before."

"Really?" I asked.

"Not that I know of." He remained unsure. "Is it sweet or sour?"

I shook my head, taking the bowl away. He'd find out soon enough.

"The seeds of Persephone are very relevant as well as magically involved within the natural cycle of the seasons," Faith informed, her voice giddy with knowledge we'd all heard more than once.

Ryan hadn't, however, and that was all the encouragement Faith needed.

"Historically, eating at another's home showed trust. It was a sort of truce or an agreement for protection for as long as you remained in the other's land or under their roof. In Persephone's case, it was a bit different. In the traditional story after all, after Persephone was perhaps torn away—"

"Perhaps?" Ryan's brow furrowed.

Ana shrugged a single shoulder. "I like to think that she had a taste for the darker things in life."

"Ana is our resident worker with the goddess Hecate," Gertie explained across the fire, as if that would make perfect sense to Ryan. "The guardian of Persephone, who in a sense, bridged worlds."

"Anyway," Faith cut back into her lecture, "when Persephone was taken from this realm and into the underworld under Hades's rule, what kept her there might have surely been her own will, but the thing that sealed the deal so no one could come after her was the seven pomegranate seeds she ate while in Hades's care. Thus, she remained. For half of the year, we are plunged into darkness, where things lie dormant while the goddess of the underworld reigns below. When the next equinox returns—Imbolc—so does the goddess of spring to this realm. In simple terms anyway."

Faith paused to look at Ryan, who hastily nodded with a smile, taking it all in with good humor as well as interest.

"So, we celebrate as well as mourn Persephone's return to the underworld today."

"And her return to uninterrupted time with her dark, forbidden love," Ana added wistfully.

Gertie smiled with a shake of her head. "To brightness, even when the nights turn long and dark. We welcome the change of season and the changes happening within ourselves. Blessed be."

"To the mother, the maiden, and the crone," Celeste added within her practice.

I looked around at the rest of my little coven, repeating the simple send-off. I watched each of their lips as they spoke the well-known trio that had made up the world.

The mother. The maiden. The crone. Life represented by each cycle of the moon.

I spoke each on silent lips as my eyes met Gertie's, who spoke more than just the words with her eyes as we echoed each other.

"Now, turn and help your partner share this feast with you. Take their pomegranate as they move forward into their life, leaving what is no longer serving them in this world or in the ether behind." Faith turned toward Gertie to carefully pass each of the seven seeds past her lips. And her in reciprocation.

Slowly, I turned to my right, facing Ryan with our own little bowl still settled between us.

"Too weird?" I asked.

"Not at all," Ryan responded. His voice had, however, turned a bit shaky and breathless as he lifted his gathered pomegranate seeds.

I could feel the energy vibrate between us.

"I'll go first," I said, my words but a hushed sound as I lifted the tiny seeds up to Ryan.

He ran his tongue over his lips before parting them, pulling back after another second. "Take turns instead?"

After a second, I nodded. Of course.

I let the seed drift right outside his mouth, touching his lip before he pulled it in, tasting the burst of flavor. He shut his eyes at the taste. When he opened them again, a striking blue staring back at me, he lifted the next seed up.

Carefully, I parted my lips and opened my mouth to him.

His fingers grazed up past my chin as he stared between my eyes and mouth, similar to the way he had that night in the library. Only now, there was trust and concentration as we traded gentle touches and fruit back and forth until all I could taste was honeyed desire.

The slightest bit of tart pomegranate juice ran down my lips the same way it caked the corners of Ryan's mouth. Our fingers were stained the deep-red color as they froze between our bodies. I couldn't pull my gaze away from his lips. His eyes, in the low, flickering light, were hooded as he looked back at me, stuck, as if we, too, were being pulled down.

Down.

Down. Drawn into the underworld, like Persephone, where every hidden desire would never see the light of day or anything else other than how Ryan's mouth gleefully took each sweet, juicy bite of pomegranate, like he'd never tasted anything better. I wanted to prove him wrong. And I'd stay right there for eternity to do so.

I blinked.

Inhaling, I turned my head back to the flames. No one else seemed to have noticed that anything had just happened or changed.

Gertie stared in my direction, swiping her fingers back over her tongue once more to get the final taste of summer. She dried each off on her gladiolus-embroidered lace handkerchief.

"Did you have a moment over there, Lu?" Ana asked. Her head cocked to the side in study.

Swallowing, I shook my head. "I'm good."

Her dark eyebrows rose. "You sure?"

"Mmhmm." I nodded once more.

Out of the corner of my eye, I noticed Ryan still slightly twisted in my direction, blinking back to himself. The corner of his lips tentatively curved up. Soft and mellow.

"Sweet," he whispered.

11

"You two can stay the night here if you'd like," said Gertie, motioning at me once the pitiful fire burned low and everyone made their way back inside.

It was getting cold early this year, and though things were rather cozy between me and Ryan under our shared quilt, which neither of us commented on, everyone was ready to make their way back home or into the house with their lack of layers.

"Guests are always welcome. Not that you're a guest, darling," Gertie made sure to add. She waved me off as she focused on Ryan, who was still making sure he didn't have any apple crumbles left on his face.

It was honestly shocking how easily he had been able to consume nearly half of a pie.

I wrapped my arms around the woman, shaking my head for the two of us. Ryan had managed to do well. He had somehow been able to win over most of the ladies with his boyish humor and constant smile, which I was beginning to realize seemed to be always genuine.

"No, we're good tonight. Thanks, Gertie."

"If you're sure."

"I'll check in tomorrow."

"You'd better." She leaned and poked me in the chest. "More of this."

"More of what?"

"Less of this." She shoved the entire palm of her hand against my forehead before leaning in close. "Don't think I didn't see what happened out there."

Very nice. Not knowing which part she was referring to, however, I rolled my eyes.

"I did," she insisted quietly so that only I could hear. "You might not listen to me. But you should listen to what the goddess and the stars were reaching out to tell you."

"You're telling me that the goddess thinks with her dick?"

Gertie laughed, loud and proud.

The final few people left in the house turned their heads at the sound, including Ryan. His eyes widened between the two of us from a few steps away.

"Then think with yours, Lu, if that's what it takes." She gave me a squeeze before she looked back at Ryan. "I hope you have a wonderful rest of the week if I don't see you, Ryan. Please know this home is open to you whenever you'd like to come back. I have a feeling this old place likes you."

"The house likes me?"

"It compliments a few people I know. It makes its opinions on who walks inside rather clear, I think," she agreed, looking up and around.

"Well, okay then." Ryan smiled as if it was the best of compliments. "Thanks so much for having me."

"Yes, thanks," I repeated with much less gratitude as I headed out the door, shutting it behind us.

Ryan was quiet in the car. The two of us both were. We drove the road back up to campus. A few cars were out, and their bright headlights flashed as they turned down the side streets to home. The parking spot along the curb Ryan had left was still open, and he slid in before pulling out the key. Then, it was just us, shutting the car doors to the murmured sounds of others in the distance, the air on campus never fully settled or without noise, especially not on the Row.

Ryan took an easy step up onto the sidewalk in front of the sports house. I watched the way he had one leg flexed, still used to taking the weight of the other.

"You doing all right there?"

Ryan looked down to where my eyes were, a slight concern in his own eyes until he seemed to realize what I meant. "Oh, yeah. It's a mind thing for a while, getting used to having two fully functioning knees to hold me up. It was nice to get out. Good thing Mabon wasn't more strenuous."

I pressed my lips together, trying not to smile as I tipped my head. "Sometimes, we run around the fire and scream out our impositions of life instead of writing them down on paper. You got the calm version."

"Oh?" he said, pleased and disappointed, all at the same time. "Maybe next time."

Next time.

"It was really cool to hang out with you more. I like hanging out with you," he added, giving a little shrug.

I couldn't help the heat that pooled in my cheeks. Luckily, it was dark enough out here as we stood in front of each other, not much distance between as we took deep breaths. The light flickered on the front porch, wavering to the hum of mosquitoes.

"Being in that house, everything felt like a dream," Ryan admitted after another moment.

"That's part of the magic." It created a home that you didn't want to leave, and where it didn't want you to leave so soon.

"I can't believe that I'm twenty-two and only now starting to believe in that."

His eyes turned down from where they'd held on to my eyes, looking over my lips for a split second, and once more, I couldn't help but be transported back to the library, in the dark with his head angled over my shoulder.

"Magic?"

"Yeah."

I huffed a laugh. "Magic might be the only real thing. How else would you explain you and me?"

"What do you mean?" His brow wrinkled.

"The boy next door all the school fawns over. The freak he teases." I meandered around the subject. "Have you never seen an '80s movie?"

"Lu, when are you going to accept that I—" He took a deep breath. "I always thought you were stunning. In every way. Your independence. Your confidence."

I was none of those things. Not really. I was constantly leaning on Vadika when I got lonely, hanging around the lab for hours at a time, even when I knew she would be busy.

"You have a control and pride over your life that you worked for, and that … that seems pretty extraordinary to me. It's me who has been the stupid one up until the other day when I felt like my life was falling apart, and then there was you. Like you were meant to stitch me back together. I've admired you, even when I was some asshole first-year who didn't care about anything other than being liked."

Ryan, I started to see now, he was a people pleaser. A *keep quiet, hold tight, share a little more of yourself, afraid to make a decision if it affected others—affected his team—*people pleaser.

At some point, we had stepped closer to one another as we talked. I could feel each word that he spoke toward me. He was so determined to make others in the world happy with him. Since when had anyone last pleased him?

Tilting my head upward and on my toes, I brushed my lips over his, just like before, only this time, it was me who was starting this. The world held its breath. Ryan returned a gentle kiss. His mouth softly pressed against mine, a whisper of something more to come, yet that tiny spark lingered like a tingle.

Excitement flooded my chest as I waited for more, waited for him to lift his hands up to cup my face so that I could grip the extra fabric of his forest-green T-shirt and hold on tight as we tilted and kissed under the equinox moon, hearing our prayers from earlier.

Indecision be gone.

Loneliness be gone.

Ryan pulled away, as if he'd startled himself.

He blinked and took a step back away from me. My hands were so prepared to hold on. Quickly, I dropped them to my sides. I stared into his eyes, wide and dilated.

"I'm sorry. I mean, I—" he cut himself off.

My heart hitched at his unsteady words. The tingle that had ignited something within me fizzled and withered. Trying not to show the range of emotions crossing my face, I took a step back.

Right. He hadn't meant to do that. Of course he hadn't meant to almost kiss me back.

The moon was wide, and the air was catching the sort of chill that made you want to curl up against someone, and yet we stood farther apart than ever tonight, hands awkward and mouths hesitating for the first time.

I shook my head, feeling whatever softness that had calmed my body turn back to heavy stone. I swallowed it down, rejection clogging my throat. "That can be a dream too, if you want."

Ryan still didn't say anything, unable to find his words as he licked his lips, still stained from pomegranate juice. From the sugar and spices lacing apples of promise and prosperity. From me. "I..."

I tried to smile, as if that alone would prove to the ever-smiling boy that it was all right. Still, I couldn't quite get it right, my mouth blustered and bruised with the utmost dismissal I'd never thought I would receive. Me and Ryan.

How could I have been so blind? How could I have had hope for the world to give me more? The universe had led me to Barnett. It gave me my coven and magic. It'd even given me Gertie. Gertie, a woman who had become my dearest family and who was ready to offer the last thing my younger self ever wished on the stars for.

Purpose.

I'd never wished for Ryan. I'd never wished for love—any piece of it.

I ran my teeth over my chapped bottom lip as I turned back toward the main campus.

"I'll see you tomorrow," he finally said to my back. "Okay?"

I turned back with a short nod. "See you, Ryan."

* * *

AFTER BEING at Gertie's for most of the week so far, I still didn't miss the slight smell of mold and dust that permeated the west residence hallway. It stuck to me as I came in from the outside air, letting the heavy metal doors swing shut behind me as I made my way toward my door, unlocked.

Had I completely misread that whole situation from the time we left Gertie's to standing outside the sports house? If anyone had seen us, I'd probably looked like the most foolish witch of Barnett. I was sure that would be the next rumor flying through the mill come tomorrow. Another pain.

That had to be it though. After so long alone, myself as my only companion most days, I had taken the simple act of someone spending time with me as it meaning that they liked me. Like, like me, *like me*. But how could I not? I could still feel his fingers against my lips as he fed me each tiny pomegranate seed. I could still see as I looked down at my own hands how the juice stained the pads with dark sweetness. Emotion clenched within me with startling clarity. But I guess that was only my feelings. Not Ryan's.

Even if he had looked at me. He barely blinked. Soft and caring and like …

He'd wanted to kiss me, hadn't he?

I screwed up everything kissing him. I didn't even ask! Not that asking would've made me look like less of a fool.

I shook my head at myself as I pulled open my dresser drawer and changed into a large, comfortable shirt. I shouldn't have taken him to Gertie's.

That had been my mistake, though it also wasn't. I hadn't invited him.

Then again, I'd also insisted that I didn't like Ryan.

Lie. Lie. *Lie.*

Climbing into bed, I doubted that the creak of the mattress would cover the sound of my anguished groan. It certainly didn't negate the fact that my roommate across from me seemed to have smothered herself in a mountain of blankets, crying.

I could hear that well enough. The pitiful noises had paused once when I opened the door to come in. The steady drone of hushed sorrow now, however, continued its flood.

Shutting my eyes, I tried to ignore the sound. It could be like a white noise machine maybe, lulling me and my terribly overwrought internal debate to sleep.

The tiny cries continued, this time muffled into another blanket, and pitched an octave higher than before. I wasn't sure if it was better or worse.

I sighed, turning onto my back to stare at the dark ceiling. I knew I was going to regret what I was about to do. Yet here I went anyway.

"Are you okay?" I asked.

The stifled sobs went silent. It was replaced by Natalie's sharp voice, cutting through the darkness like knives. "I'm fine. Why would I want to talk about anything with you?"

Closing my eyes, I nearly rolled back over toward my side of the four beige walls we shared when she sniffed.

"My boyfriend broke up with me."

"Oh." I paused, unsure exactly what I should say. "That's rough."

"Yeah, like, what the hell?" Natalie's hands slapped the bed on either side where she laid. "We'd been dating since high school. *High school.* It isn't like we just went off to college and suddenly needed to find a way to make it work. We had been making it work for the past two years. Now, suddenly, it is different because he's been thinking about screwing some other girl? It was like he wanted my permission."

"Well," I attempted, "that's just rude."

"It's disgusting," she insisted with venom. "I couldn't get into the school he got into, but we made it work. I didn't want to stifle him, and he didn't want to come here to Barnett. It was too close to home, and I got that. But we managed. I spent money on flights to see him and everything else, and now, he just threw it all away. He didn't think it'd crossed my mind that I couldn't date when I saw all these other couples on campus? That all this wasn't hard on me? I wasted three years on him. More probably."

I wondered what she had done during the past weekend when I was gone. Had her boyfriend actually shown up at all, like she had told me he was going to, for this to happen, or had it been a quick split over the phone after getting her hopes up? Either way, I couldn't help but empathize a bit, listening.

"I don't know what to do now." Her voice quivered with another round of tears.

"I'm not sure if I'm the one to give advice," I admitted honestly. My fingers fiddled with the edge of my blankets. "Do you want options or just to wallow?"

"Like I'd ever want your opinion."

Well, okay then.

She sniffed. "Go on anyway."

I resisted the urge to snort at her pitiful-sounding voice. I took a deep breath, thinking about all the conversations I'd had with Ana. "You could ignore him, for one. You could also call him up and tell him all the things you just told me, if you haven't already."

A sigh went up, as if those were the most boring options ever.

I went on. "You could also sleep with someone else, like he is, if you have your eye on anyone. Tell him about that or not."

She snorted a short laugh, full of mucus. "For some reason, I always thought you were a prude."

"Trust me, I'm around too many crudes to be prude."

Natalie gave a little laugh, heavy with mucus as she sniffed once more.

"Or you could do something else."

"What, do you have some sort of curse to spite him?" Natalie asked, sounding somewhat intrigued.

"No," I said. This really was sounding like a conversation with Ana. Though, after a harsh breakup, it was usually Gertie or me trying to talk Ana out of doing something rash, like sending out that kind of negative energy into the world out of spite. It was basically guaranteeing that a rude awakening would eventually make its way back to you threefold. "It doesn't work that way."

"You sure?"

I forced out a tiny laugh in response. Already, the feeling in the room was growing lighter.

"I know you have those things by what I see over there on your side of the room. Do you really think you're a witch?" asked Natalie.

"I don't think," I said, not bothering to hide my distaste at her words, however laced with genuine curiosity. "I am a witch. Even if I did help you with what you're asking to get back at your boyfriend now, you wouldn't be so happy with the result.

Sending that kind of energy out into the world is asking for trouble."

Natalie hummed in thought, not completely convinced. "This doesn't mean we are friends."

"Of course not," I agreed simply, letting the conversation fade away and turning around to shut my eyes again.

12
―――――

"Why do you look like that?"

"Like what?" I glanced up to Vadika. I leaned back in the extremely uncomfortable plastic chair across from where she stood.

She stared at me like I was one of her specimens.

"Tired and moody," she clarified. "I thought we were past this last year."

"I'm just tired," I said, which was true.

I hadn't been getting much sleep, let alone more than a good hour here and there from tossing and turning. At one point last night, Natalie had tossed one of her frilly throw pillows at my head without a word. That had been oddly nice after we seemed to make an odd turning point in our unfriendly relationship.

"It was Mabon the night before last, remember?"

"Oh. Right. You haven't taken me to that one before, have you?"

I shook my head, letting her turn back toward her project, writing fresh labels and sticking them one by one onto clear canisters. "No. And you have since been relinquished from all other coven holidays."

"Except for if you do the Secret Santa thing again with everyone. I still want to be a part of that. Faith got me the coolest notebook last year, remember? Everyone loved it during my summer program. Plus, it never got lost. Whether that be from the protective spell or the fact that it looked unlike anything ever brought into a biochem intensive. It was perfection."

"The night with the ladies went well and all."

"That doesn't sound very confident. What's the *and all*?"

I stared at her for a long moment. "You need to promise not to get weird."

"Since when do I ever get weird?"

I looked around the sterile white walls she spent most of her waking hours in. They were enough to make anyone go a little nuts after a while. In my opinion and experience at least.

"Ryan went."

"Ryan went where?" She furrowed her eyebrows, confused.

I rolled my eyes, knowing how stilted my voice sounded. "He attended the equinox celebration with me."

"You took him to the lair?" Vadika asked, astonished.

"You said you weren't going to be weird."

"This isn't weird. This is unprecedented," said Vadika, setting aside everything so she wouldn't accidentally knock something over. "How did this come about?"

"Faith invited him, and then he practically insisted when he heard we were making pie."

She still had the most mind-blown look on her face. "You're kidding."

"I'm not." I wished I were.

"He wanted to go? How did he meet Faith?"

I stared at her before I finally sighed. I had known I was going to talk to her about this. I just always underestimated her level of enthusiasm. "We ran into her the other night when we were in the library."

"You were both in the library together—again?"

"Are you going to repeat everything I say back to me? I hear how this sounds," I said.

"Those books have been seeing a lot of action recently."

"Nothing is happening."

"Right." Vadika didn't give me a hint of sincerity in that one. She marked one last thing in her notebook, erasing and rewriting with her red mechanical pencil. "Just checking because it sounds like someone likes you."

"He doesn't."

"How can you—"

"He kissed me," I finally blurted.

It was better not to let this whole thing get out of hand. Vadika might have been antilove for herself. For the rest of the world, however, she was just as bad as her aunts, setting things up and making nonexistent plans for nonexistent couples.

One of which I was not part of.

Vadika swung her head back up, leaving everything behind for sure now as she crossed the room toward me. "He kissed you?"

"Sort of?" I shrugged a shoulder, curling my leg up and into my body as I balanced on the rolling chair. "I mean, he kissed me, but it was more of a graze the first time. Then, the other night I kissed him. It doesn't matter. I don't think he wanted to kiss me. Either time."

"Either time?" It looked like Vadika's eyes were about to bug out of her head.

"There was another moment that first night in the library."

"You mean, the night where 'nothing happened,'" she quoted ironically.

"Nothing did happen."

"You and I have very different definitions then," said Vadika. "Seriously, where have I been through all this? It's like you have a secret second life all of a sudden."

I looked around the lab. "You've been a very busy girl, Vadika."

"I've been doing science. Science can be time consuming when you are being fast-tracked into life-changing research. Still, I didn't think it meant I was going to be missing out on all these strangely exciting revelations. You and Ryan Gardner?" She shook her head, as if she still couldn't quite believe the words coming out of her mouth.

Luckily, she didn't have to believe it. Vadika was getting ahead of herself. Again.

"There is no me and Ryan."

She raised her dark eyebrows. I knew what that expression said—that didn't mean that I didn't want there to be something there. Thinking of that kiss made my stomach roll, but not in a completely bad way.

What did was the way Ryan had reacted to it. He'd stumbled back like I was a nightmare that had him stuttering.

"Why not? I mean, I never pictured you two together, like, ever. Ever, *ever*."

"Thanks, Vad."

"Though of course now that I am forced to think of you and Mr. Sunshine, I'm pretty sure you could be the cutest couple I'd never thought of."

Time to break her heart then. "He pulled away."

"What do you mean?"

"Both times he pulled away. After I kissed him he kept sputtering like he had made a huge mistake." *I was a big mistake.* "It's fine. It's not a big deal. I'm making this way worse than it probably is. We were at the house for a long time, and it was late."

"Let me get this straight," said Vadika. "He kissed you and then apologized?"

I shrugged, leaning my cheek on my fist. "Basically."

"Maybe he was nervous."

"It doesn't matter anyway. I don't like Ryan Gardner."

"Sure you don't."

It even sounded like a lie to my own ears. Somehow, in the past few days, Ryan had weaseled his way into my brain. It didn't mean that he'd had to burrow. Not when it was clear that he still saw me as … well, not like the other girls he hung out with. The pretty, outgoing, startling girls who drew people toward them like flocks.

Not that I ever wanted to be that kind of person. Not really—or at least, not consistently. I was happy with Vadika and now Ryan, who had apparently forgotten to keep his distance.

I shook my head, picturing it again. I could see how his eyes trailed down from my eyes to my lips as we fed each other those pomegranate seeds to hell. He'd thought about kissing me, as if he planned to lick the last of the sweetness away.

But once again, maybe all those feelings were just on my end. I was projecting.

When I lifted my gaze, Vadika was still staring at me. "I'll beat him up if you want me to. Or there is this study some students in my lab are doing. They are looking for some willing participants. I could casually put his name down. I bet he would be too polite to say no. Then, his entire weekend would be shot."

"Much appreciated, but I'm good, thanks. How's the research going, by the way?"

"Nope. We are not getting off this topic that easily." Still, her expression exploded with delight. "But you actually want to know?"

"Of course."

"You make my soul happy. Seriously though, later. The observation I'm looking at right now is much more intriguing. I don't know what you think is going on, Lu. I don't know how it is going on," Vadika mused, pacing back and forth as she worked out all the little kinks in the nonexperiment she had developed in her head. "But this little thing between you two … the evidence shows that I think you're kidding yourself."

"What are you talking about?"

"Ryan Gardner is in love with you."

"He is not."

She shrugged, as if she had figured I would put her down like that. "Maybe not yet. But I can see the strings all coming together."

"He's not. He doesn't even know me."

"You sure about that?" Vadika asked. "I mean, he did know where to find you in the library. He knew a whole lot about you that I'm not sure you told him. Correct?"

That was oddly accurate. I hadn't thought much about it.

"Sounds like someone has had a crush on you for some time now."

A spark of hope flared in my chest. Stupid hope.

"And it looks like it isn't one sided?"

I stared at my friend. "Shut up, Vadika."

She laughed.

"His leg is better anyway," I said. "The crutches are gone, and so I'm sure he's back to his normal life with his fun, normal friends."

"Please do not tell me you just referred to yourself as a literal crutch for Ryan Gardner."

I shrugged.

She shook her head, blowing out a breath. "I'm just saying, I hear he has abs too."

He did.

"Among other things."

I narrowed my eyes. "What are you talking about?"

"Really? You don't know?"

"Know about what?"

"The rumors about Ryan," Vadika said, finally sitting down.

There were rumors about Ryan? The confusion must've shown on my face.

"What rumors?"

Vadika contemplated for a moment, kicking her feet up onto

a third seat with my bag sitting on top of it. "Two or so years ago, I think?"

"That was a while ago."

"Yeah," said Vadika. "Still, it stuck around my building here for a few months, if I remember correctly. But that was our first year, when none of these nerds were having any luck in getting laid."

Even the rumors of us getting frisky in the library had died down a bit by now—unless I just wasn't paying attention anymore. I was, however, paying close attention to Vadika now. Getting laid?

I waved her to go on, feeling a tightness along my ribs.

"Some chick—I don't remember her name. She was one of the girls who hung out with your charming roommate at the time?"

"Lauren?"

"That sounds right. Anyway, she told everyone that she and Ryan slept together after a party or something. The details are a little blurry now."

I nodded quickly. "Continue."

"Turns out, he was a rather enthusiastic lover. A little too enthusiastic. She told everyone he might have had a big package, but he barely lasted five minutes. This was after everyone thought he was rather experienced in that department after another rumor about the girls he had messed with in high school."

How many rumors was Ryan involved in? How had I missed them?

"That all has to be a lie."

Vadika shrugged, not leaning one way or the other. "Just something I remember. I kind of thought you knew. Good to know, if you plan on moving forward with your little crush on Ryan Gardner."

How she sang his name, I didn't bother correcting her.

"He's probably gotten a bit more practice by now, of course, so I wouldn't be too concerned on that front, if it bothers you."

"It doesn't."

"All right." She hesitated. "I probably shouldn't have said anything."

"I don't plan on jumping his bones, Vadika."

"The fact that you phrased it that way makes me believe otherwise." My friend stifled a smile as she stood back up. "Now, let me finish this up, and we can get dinner, okay?"

* * *

VADIKA WAS TEXTING underneath the slightly sticky cafeteria table in between bites of al dente broccoli and talking to me about going to the homecoming game or the events and cookout beforehand. Eating a burned cheeseburger and chugging a cheap and grossly warm beer in the parking lot alongside alumni attempting to relive their youth was still one thing she had to knock off her *college experience* list. Her eyes widened, and then she grabbed her things, stuffing them all back into her colorful cloth backpack.

"Oh, man, I have to go."

"You never answered my question."

"You're totally coming with me to homecoming unless you have other plans with a certain someone."

I forced myself not to roll my eyes. "That wasn't my question. Who were you texting?"

Vadika blinked. The fact that she hadn't heard me made me want to smile, but my curiosity was piqued.

"You have a secret new friend I don't know about?"

"No. It's no one important."

It certainly hadn't looked that way.

"A project partner or …"

Vadika shook her head with a soft smile, like I was telling her a funny joke.

Was Vadika talking to someone? Like someone, *someone* after she promised herself that she would never find anyone until she received her PhD, even if her aunts still tried to set her up any chance they got?

"Vadika." I tilted my chin down, studying her for any tells.

She tucked a thick strand of hair behind her ear. "I'll talk to you later, okay? I have class, and then I'll probably head to the lab for a bit if you're free then and want to stop by."

"Have fun in class." I waved her off, gathering up the rest of my own things.

"You know I will." With a blown kiss, she was off.

"I still want to know what is going on with you!" I called.

Another wave, and I was back to my routine as I headed down through the center of campus. I didn't have much left to do, but I could go to the library and work more on transcribing my book of shadows. I slowly walked past groups of others sitting at picnic tables. They chatted and kicked their feet up like the perfect photo for the college catalog.

At one table, my roommate looped her bronze hair over her shoulder. Natalie looked me up and down when she noticed me. Without a word, she turned away, back into conversation with the rest of her well-dressed group. The student council.

The student council that got together one Thursday a month.

Today was Thursday.

Over the past few days, the idea of my Samhain celebration on campus had somehow been pushed to the back of my mind. Other things had been taking up the space. There were the expected looks from my professors, as I still hadn't declared what would be written on my degree. There was Gertie offering me my dreams. Then, there was also Ryan Gardner. And since when had a guy ever infiltrated my life and thoughts this much?

Ryan Gardner, who had stepped into my life like it was no big deal after we actively avoided each other for two years. Ryan Gardner, who everyone fawned over and hyped up, whether they knew who he was or not. Ryan Gardner, who I felt like I was just beginning to fully understand, and not from rumors or judgments.

Ryan Gardner, with his messy strawberry-blond hair. Ryan Gardner, with the sharp laugh. Ryan Gardner—

I was likely going insane.

Ryan Gardner was just up ahead. He limped, exciting the athletic complex with a backpack that looked like it was about to take him down for the count.

I rushed a few steps forward to him. "Are you okay?"

"Aw, look at you. Luella Pierce, coming to my rescue." Ryan tried to smile as I grabbed his backpack from his one shoulder. He sighed with heavy gratitude. "Thank you."

"You look like you're about to fall over."

He groaned, taking another step, slightly less zombie-like than the previous. "Fine. Just sore. All over. I'm not a fan of physical therapy, and I'm pretty sure the feeling is mutual."

"What?" I asked, understanding now that this mess was intentional. "Are you a fan of it?"

"We have a love-hate relationship." Ryan corrected his previous words. "Right now, it is leaning toward the hate."

Clearly. I leaned up next to him for a bit of support, unable to hide my surprise when Ryan slung his arm around my shoulders.

"So, how are you?"

"I'm, uh," I started. "I don't know."

"You don't know?" His eyebrows flared upward.

"Lot on my mind."

"Seems like that's becoming a habit."

Unfortunately.

"No decision on the major front yet?"

I hummed, more focused on him not falling over himself than

being serious. "I'm thinking medieval studies or maybe dance. I haven't given that one a go yet."

"Good choice. Let me know when the recital is."

I snorted a laugh.

"Want to share anything actually bothering you?"

"It's …" *You*, I wanted to finish with, if I was being honest. Only I didn't.

After two nights ago, I hadn't heard from Ryan. I figured he was busy. Or maybe I really didn't ruin everything with my mouth. Literally. I took a few more steps with him.

"Not that I don't want to hear what happened in the past forty-eight hours, but I think I better sit down soon," said Ryan, interrupting my thoughts. "We could go back to my place?"

"With the Potatoes?" I thought of the two potato-look-alike mice running through the walls. They were the opposite of calming to talk with Ryan about the other night. They could be anywhere. How did anyone sleep in that house? "No, thanks."

"For some reason, I never thought you'd be afraid of a little mouse."

"You thought wrong. We can go to my dorm. Come on, big guy." I hauled him further against me.

"I'm not *that* big."

"Big enough," I said before I paused. A flush crept up the back of my neck—and not from the strenuous lifting.

* * *

I PUSHED OPEN the door of my residence hall, and Ryan walked inside behind me, one slow, pained step at a time. It was especially taxing to watch as we made our way up the twenty raised steps to the second floor.

"I didn't realize how tight my leg had gotten after babying it so much," said Ryan by the time we made it to the top.

I inexpertly hid my amusement. Ryan raised his eyebrows as I pushed open the door to my room and waved him inside.

He shrugged. "My fault really."

"It's not your fault."

"It is. I haven't been stretching like I was told to. But really, who does?" asked Ryan.

He made his way inside my room. His eyes roamed around the square box, cleaner but also darker than his room across campus.

"I thought you had a roommate," Ryan commented.

"She has a council meeting tonight."

"You mean, the one where they decide if you can get funding and permission for your Sam-am party on campus?" He asked.

I didn't bother to correct his pronunciation.

He seemed to perk up at my confirmation. "That's good. I didn't know how long they were going to make you wait."

"I know it's a lost cause."

"Nothing is a lost cause until it's over," he said. "Unless you want it to be?"

I honestly had no idea anymore. I'd poured myself into that project, but over the past week, it'd simply felt less important.

It felt like years had passed since I'd tried to distract myself with a witch-approved Halloween party.

"I don't know. Maybe?" I admit.

"Sometimes, it's easier for someone else to stop you from going after something you want than for you to stop yourself." Another point and a sage remark from him.

He wandered past the window, where a tree arched over and often scraped whenever it rained. Pausing at my desk, he looked over my notebooks and book of shadows, careful not to touch.

He wasn't so modest when he lifted the old perfume bottles I'd filled, lifting each to his nose and taking a short whiff. "Your tonics."

I turned on another lamp to brighten up the space. Already, the sun fell fast outside.

Ryan paused at the homemade candles with clipped wicks and pots of beeswax salves. "You really make all these?"

"With help," I confirmed.

All the girls at the coven usually got brought into the business of making small, everyday spells, like mason jar candles and sachets of pungent herbs, sold when spring and summer came around. Few ever realized we weren't only a part of the artisanal soap craze.

"You should really think about selling this stuff, you know," he said. "Luella's Little Shop of Spells."

I huffed a laugh, shaking my head at him.

"Be quiet and sit. Put your leg on the pillow," I commanded, watching as he finally stopped snooping before he started toward my bed.

With a tiny hop, he made himself more comfortable, where my hand had patted one side of my comforter. He scooched over to make more room. The movement looked tense and strained.

There was a boy on my bed.

Ryan Gardner was on my bed.

"You know your RICE," said Ryan, impressed. "Rest, ice, compress, elevate. Maybe you should think about going premed."

I rolled my eyes exaggeratedly at him as I pulled the ice pack that was still mostly frozen out of Ryan's bag. It had been stuffed between a textbook and his laptop, where another freshly printed assignment stuck out. Looked like he didn't need my help for that one. I dropped the pack on his leg.

He hissed at the cold. "Or not."

"Probably best. You're such a baby. RICE is for injuries." I wasn't sure if post-injury rehab counted.

"Yet you're taking care of me anyway. Practicing for when you take over for Gertrude?"

I resisted the urge to swat at his leg as I stood beside him. "Quiet."

"That was one of the rules, I remember."

I quirked a smile.

"Are you going to sit down?" he asked.

Carefully, I climbed up onto my slightly raised bed. The mattress creaked as I settled next to Ryan.

He watched me, rubbing his lips together, as if I were some sort of entertainment. Adjusting himself once more, he cleared his throat before I could ask him what in the world he was staring at.

"Can we put on one of those old movies you like? Like the one you put on in the library that first night?"

I blinked. Out of all the things I'd thought he'd ask me, that was not one of them. I found myself nodding anyway. "Why?"

"It was nice. Calming," explained Ryan.

Reaching over the far edge of the bed for my computer, I slipped it from my desk and onto the bed in front of us. I maneuvered through my downloads of Hollywood classics I always had close by after I found the same calmness settle over me whenever Gertie put one on at the house. The actors played their stories on screen as background noise. Each of their movements was big and bold as if they were on the stage. Those actors were unabashed with who they were supposed to be.

I watched as the screen turned from color to black and white.

Slowly I angled the screen before looking back at Ryan. I tried to find a good spot but couldn't seem to position myself anywhere on the narrow bed that wasn't touching him. I stiffened with each minor brush.

"Why are you acting weird?"

"Honestly, I didn't know if you were upset with me," I replied honestly.

"What do you mean?"

"After I kissed you the other night," I said at once. Sitting back from where I'd angled the laptop on the other end of the bed, I peeked at him from the corner of my eye. "I should've asked, and I'm pretty sure that basically ruined whatever sort of thing this was between us. So, I understand if you don't want to be my friend anymore—"

"I always want to be your friend, Luella," Ryan said, stopping me. "It was me who panicked, and I wasn't sure..."

"What weren't you sure about?"

If he wasn't sure if I liked him back, I was pretty positive the whole my mouth eating his said enough.

He took a deep breath as he thought about what he wanted to say.

"You weren't sure..." I led on.

Was it about me? About the kiss? Oh gods, I never even considered if Ryan liked guys. He might not have been interested in me at all this entire time, and I'd been making it all up in order to convince myself of some odd fantasy.

"I wasn't sure I'd ever seen Luella Pierce look panicked before."

"It's an occasional occurrence." Particularly around frustrating ex-football players, apparently.

Tilting his head to the side as he studied me, he finally let out a deep sigh. "I wasn't sure if I was going to mess everything up."

"What do you mean? I was the one who kissed you that time."

He blushed at the reminder. "Right."

"So you did kiss me back in the library?" I clarified.

"Of course I did."

"For a while there, I thought that I'd imagined it."

"Imagined it?" Ryan asked. The idea of me being able to brush the event off sounded as if it pained him. "Lu, the last thing I ever want is for you to think of me kissing you as unimportant. But at this point, I guess..."

I watched his mouth form the words.

It was all a lie.
I was just having fun.
I don't like you at all.

"I'm cursed."

13

My eyebrows flattened. "Cursed?"

He hissed through his teeth. Bringing a hand up to the front of his forehead, he clenched the front few waves there, forcing them to stick up. With a glance ahead, the two of us watched the beginnings of some sort of argument happening on my computer screen. Then, I felt a small tap on my leg.

"We're friends, right?"

Friends. For some reason, I didn't know if that was the right word. But friends ... that was what I'd called us a moment ago. So, I nodded.

"You think you're cursed?"

"Maybe?" he confessed. "All I know is that I have never had much luck with all this."

"All this?" I couldn't help but repeat his words. I sounded like Vadika when she was trying to make a point.

"Relationships. Dating."

The idea of us dating caught something in my chest.

"It never really goes well," he finished.

"That makes no sense. You've had girlfriends in the past." Or at least, I thought he had. "You have so many friends."

He shrugged, like that made no difference. "Right. But when it comes down to it, nothing ever happens there. I'm good at making friends, but never—I never ..."

My eyes widened. Understanding flooded my brain at the way he stammered. "You never ..."

A shy grin crossed his face, teeth clenched. A hand drifted toward the back of his neck, where it mussed his hair. "Yeah."

"You're a virgin." For some reason, I needed to clarify.

"It isn't like I haven't had the opportunity exactly—wait, that sounds bad, doesn't it?" he corrected. "It's not as if I haven't wanted to before."

I put up a hand to place it on his arm but hesitated. "Take a breath."

"Thanks." He sighed, slowing down his cadence.

"You don't have to tell me why if you don't want to," I said. "It's none of my business really."

"I know," he said. "But I do want to. I want to share it with you. You trust me. I trust you. And we'll keep trusting each other onward, right?"

I paused and looked at the sincerity on his face, the nerves lurking behind his expression. "Right."

"Right. Well, yeah ..."

"So ..." I tried to encourage, feeling the conversation stop. "Tell me about this curse."

"It started back in high school. Basically anyway. I had a girlfriend, and we almost ..." He trailed off, gathering his next words. "We were caught by her father."

"You're kidding." My jaw went slack. I tried to imagine exactly how I would feel in that moment if my father ever walked in on me, period, let alone the guy I lost my virginity to. Then again, maybe he would've just shut the door and walked away back to his permanent spot on the couch during that same week after my mother left us.

But the emotions would still be all there.

The shame. The fear.

"Yeah, it didn't leave a good taste in my mouth. She was only with me at the time, it turned out, because she was a cheerleader and everything." He winced. "I came from a very traditional sort of town. Then, I came to college, and I was far enough away from everything. That first fall, everyone seemed to be getting together with other people."

"It's like mating season the first few months of being a first-year."

"It is, isn't it?" Ryan couldn't help the curve of a smirk on one side of his mouth at my joke, and a renewed warmth settled inside of me as I leaned back into my pillows to listen to him. "It felt a little less nerve racking. I knew, obviously, that someone wasn't going to come out and scream at me for being depraved and sinful for touching someone, like back home."

"Someone said that to you?" I stared at him, knowing that there was pity on my face.

After a moment, he sighed in agreement with my disgust. "They did. If they didn't say it to me, I knew they said it to the girl I was with. That fact alone made me feel awful. It was basically my fault, I figured, though we had both been into it at the time.

"Eventually, not long after I got here, I did try going on some dates. I tried the whole dating app thing too, but I got too nervous to start conversations half the time unless one of the girls I was talking to on campus came straight up to me. I'm a sucker for a good smile."

Yet here I was right now, without one.

"It was nice to be smiled at, so I figured, why not give it all a chance? The guys on the team encouraged me and never really assumed anything until they set me up on a sort of group date thing my second year. I had a good time. We all hung out, and then there was a party after. The girl I was with at the time and I ended up alone in her bedroom. We fooled around for a bit until …" Ryan glanced away.

"What? Do you have some sort of monster penis in your pants or something?"

"What?"

Ryan couldn't help but laugh. I was glad. For a minute, I'd missed it.

"No. I don't think so anyway."

"Then, what?"

"I sort of finished without her." Ryan's face flushed red at the confession.

Still, I waited for something else. "And?"

"What else? She looked at me like I was the stupidest person on the planet."

"Because you were so turned on that you came? I don't know about you, but I'd take that as a compliment. Whether or not you had ever had a lot of experience before, she was supposed to be there to make you feel good, and she didn't."

"I tried to explain to her exactly that and everything else."

"So, she knew that she was pretty much your first? I mean, you had no need to tell her, and yet—what the hell?"

"About to be my first. It didn't happen, obviously. She pushed me away after I did tell her a version of the truth," said Ryan. "Then, she sort of told a few people *her* own version, as if that wasn't more embarrassing."

The rumor Vadika had attempted to relay rolled back through my mind.

"She's a backstabber."

"Sort of."

"That bitch." If he wasn't going to rage, I would for him.

"That's another way to put it that I won't disagree on." Ryan conceded to my snarls of irritation.

Who did this chick think she was? If I didn't know who she was already, I'd figure it out. Then, there would be some karma to pay.

"Luckily, it blew over relatively quickly—until now. I now realize it must still be sticking around to be talked about by people."

"None that care."

"You don't care that I'm a virgin?" Ryan asked.

"Not unless you care that I definitely plan on sacrificing you in some shape or form now. A twenty-some-year-old almost-virgin male is a hot commodity these days."

He laughed, knowing I was kidding.

"No," I said clearly. I flashed him a smile. "I do not care in the slightest that you are an untouched flower."

"Nearly untouched."

"She's a fool for doing that to you."

He shrugged.

I pulled his face back toward me. "I'm serious."

"Is that so?" He almost looked amused as I forced him to stare at me.

"Yes, it is. Listen to me. There's nothing that is shameful or wrong about you, your emotions, or the energy you want to share with others in whatever way. Your desires are power. They are what makes you who you are, and anyone would be lucky to witness that kind of magic."

Ryan's face softened as he stared at me for a long moment. "Ever think of giving the psychology route a go?"

I whacked him in the arm. He still didn't move away. His one hand reached back out and gave my thigh a light squeeze. I stared down at that large hand.

"You're not cursed," I said. "You just have a lot of repressed people forcing their opinions on you. You also apparently have had a touch of bad luck."

"Maybe it's turning around," Ryan said with another light

smile, looking at me for a moment before he let out the question, vulnerably poised on the tip of his tongue. "So, you've had sex before?"

Something caught in my throat. Slowly, I tried to joke. "Yeah, I have. My family was much less involved than yours. There was no breaking down doors because of a little groping."

That was for sure.

"You don't really talk about your family much."

I shook my head. No, I guessed I didn't. When I thought of my family these days, I thought of the coven. I thought of small memories I had left of my dad when I went home for the holidays and stayed on his couch in a tiny apartment he'd started to rent not long after...

"You don't have to. You said your family lives in a condo, right?"

I nodded a few times. "Yeah. My dad and I had been living in one, anyway before I came to Barnett. It's been just me and him for a while now."

"Did your parents divorce?"

"No, actually. They were pretty in love," I recounted. It wasn't hard to suddenly have images rushing through my head of the two of them dancing around the Christmas tree or him putting a dollop of icing on her nose, much to her delight and our laughter, when we were baking. Her face though, it was getting blurry. "She died while I was in high school."

"Oh." Ryan's eyes softened. "I'm so sorry, Lu."

For some reason, I shook my head, trying to stop the emotion from clogging me up like it used to. After so long, I expected it to be less, and it was, in some ways. "She was sick on and off for a long while."

"Was it cancer?"

"Mmhmm," I said. "Breast cancer. They found it not long after she had me, and she fought it for a long time. Then, it came back."

With a vengeance.

"She's at peace. I have to believe that anyway."

"I'm sure she is," Ryan said, and from his voice, it was unquestionable. "Tell me about her."

"My mom?"

He nodded. "If you don't mind."

"She was amazing. A really good mom. She let me wear crazy clothes and didn't think it was weird when I started to like plants and the idea of magic far past the time of fairy tales. Her laugh was so loud. Much louder than mine or my dad's. We'd take walks together outside all the time before, and sometimes, her voice would bounce off the trees in such an echo that I wondered if it would stay there, captured in those spots and on those trails forever."

"Is that why you like to walk up the hill?"

I didn't realize he had noticed my route around the cemetery to where the sun set. Of course, he was often there, noticing everything.

"Partly. After she passed away, everyone in my life sort of expected me to keep moving. I was supposed to be excited to graduate and go to college. But she was supposed to be there. When I went home, my dad was there, too, and he never really tried to get over it all, not that I can blame him."

"That's tough."

"Occasionally, at school, someone would come up to me. They'd eat lunch with me, probably out of pity, but then after a bit, I did start to force myself to be more outgoing, so I wouldn't be called to the guidance counselor, who only ever made me feel worse," I explained. "I met a guy then. He was nice enough, and he invited me to places. He kissed me when I'd never had that kind of relationship before. Then, I met another friend of that guy. It was a small school."

Ryan shook his head slowly, as if he understood.

"After my mom, I was sort of empty. And for a while, it made me feel decent. Good even." I'd needed that good even if it was in the back of some guy's car, who couldn't remember my actual first name most of the time. I had been fine with that. Until the end anyway. "It turned out, I was quite the commodity. They made me think that they liked me. I was different and special." I shrugged. "I was a joke to them."

Ryan was silent.

"So, yes, I have slightly more experience in that department. I don't regret it, but I also don't think it was the kind of connection I'd ever want to involve myself in again. Rumors here at Barnett are bad. But at home?"

"Worse?"

I made a face. It had been brutal.

"The whole thing was another reason I really wanted to leave home and anywhere close to it. It all felt not great there anymore. I realized what I needed to do, going forward. I needed to start over, and I knew then that I could. Nothing is permanent after all. Not school. Not my mom. Not even asshole boys thinking they were the real good guys to everyone but me," I said. "I bet you think I'm a real—"

"Don't finish that sentence," Ryan cut me off. "Because that is the last thing I could ever think of you."

I stared at Ryan. He didn't look at me up and down. He met my eyes. There was no condemnation there. There was no difference than ever before. If anything, there was a softer look that rimmed his light eyes. It was not pity; it was a strange sort of understanding. Acceptance.

Of me?

Huh. For some reason, I'd never thought that I would care. But I did. I cared how and what Ryan saw in me.

Because over the past week, I had been seeing a lot more in him. I saw a soft, strong guy who was a decent listener when he wasn't laughing or going out of his way to make others feel good. Make me feel good.

Who would've thought?

It almost made me want to laugh.

"I think you're pretty extraordinary, you know. Honest. I wish I were more like that."

"Like what?"

"Brave."

I didn't think I had ever heard that word describing me before. Or maybe only once.

I had been standing in the graveyard my mother was buried in. I vaguely remember her saying that she wanted to be cremated. Burned and sent back up to the stars.

A woman I barely knew from one of my mother's survivor groups wandered up to me and patted me on the back.

"You're being so brave," she'd said.

Brave. From that moment on, I'd only ever thought that brave felt like I was crumbling from the inside out. An avalanche of fear of endings and new beginnings I needed to force myself toward, leading me to Barnett.

But when Ryan said it, it made me feel steady. Beautiful in all my uncertainty of life.

"You mean that?"

"Always, Lu-Lu."

"Ry-Ry," I teased right back.

It didn't have quite the same effect as Ryan's grin grew, encroaching. "You're only proving to me that you don't mind me so much after all, Lu."

I'd given up on that vendetta the moment we left Gertie's house together. Maybe she and the goddess she listened to were right. I needed to think with my dick—or emotions or whatever for once.

I inhaled as I continued to take in a new sort of freedom that shone in Ryan's expression. His gaze flickered over my shaggy bangs to the bow of my lips.

I let my eyes skitter over each constellation of freckles and down to his bottom lip, plumper than the top.

Our lips hovered over one another's. Our faces and eyes held on to each other so close yet—

"Maybe it's a good thing that we don't," Ryan breathed. "Not yet anyway."

My heart withered. "Oh."

"No, I mean—I'm screwing this up. I'm really liking getting to know the true Luella..."

"Renee."

"Luella Renee Pierce." His eyebrows crinkled. "Who named you?"

I barked a laugh. "They are family names. Or a combination of them. Luella was a terrible combination of my parents' grandmothers. Lucinda and Elma. Either way, I was destined to sound like an old hag on all attendance sheets growing up."

"I think your name is pretty. Unique." *Like you.* He left the horribly cheesy words unsaid. But with Ryan, somehow, they always were hanging somewhere in the air.

My cheeks heated.

The door across the room swung open with a startled breath. Natalie also made a little "Oh," before clearing her throat, as if she were debating on whether or not to back out.

Ryan sat up straightaway, settling himself beside me, as if we hadn't been so close, face to face, a moment ago, bodies leaning comfortably into one another's, as if they had been perfectly molded that way.

I blinked, righting myself in the same casual way as I took in my roommate, carefully stepping in as her eyes narrowed between us.

"Ryan"—Natalie cocked her head to the side—"I didn't realize that you ever came over this way on campus."

"Hi, Natalie. I'm with a friend," Ryan said, still leaning against my bed frame. "I didn't know you were the roommate."

I hadn't realized Ryan knew my roommate so well. The campus, of course, wasn't a large one, clearly, and it wasn't like

Natalie wasn't well enough liked in the social pool not to have her nose in everyone's business. Still, for some reason, I'd sort of thought this piece of my life had managed to be untouched.

"Housing lotteries surprise everyone," Natalie said, unceremoniously dropping her backpack against the side of her desk with a thud.

Slowly, Ryan sat up farther, swinging his legs over the side of the bed and taking his now-melted ice pack with him. Hopping down, he did so with only a minor wince now. "I still have some work to catch up on back at my place since everyone else is probably out at practice. I'm going to head out."

"Oh," I started, turning my legs to sit up over the bed as I watched him haul his backpack over his shoulder. Reaching to the side, I folded the screen where our movie still played, nearly silent. "Okay."

"Let me know when you hear anything about your Halloween event, okay?"

Natalie perked up from across the room, leaning with her hands behind her back.

"Oh, you haven't heard then?" At neither of our replies, Natalie raised her sharp eyebrows. "I guess not. The student council had their meeting to discuss last-minute additions to the social calendar schedule, including your Halloween thing."

"They did?" I asked when she didn't continue, as if this were also new information.

Natalie turned back toward her desk to unpack her things, as if Ryan and I were no longer of interest to her after she was the one who interrupted us. "Your funding request has been denied. You'll get an email. Lauren usually writes them. She has a gentle touch with that sort of thing. I'm sure she'd also say hi to you, Ryan. She mentioned you haven't called her back or something?"

Pressing his lips together, Ryan nodded tightly in response.

I wasn't shocked by any of what Natalie had told me, and yet I still couldn't help myself. They hadn't given my event a chance, had they?

"Did they even look over my plans?"

"Just the messenger on this one. I'm only an extra on council if there's a tie."

Taking a deep breath, I tipped my head at Ryan, who was studying me. He seemed to be waiting for something. Maybe for me to bust out in anger or maybe tears.

I hated to disappoint as I sat on the edge of the bed. I glanced down at my leg, where Ryan placed a hand. He gave my knee a squeeze.

"That's too bad," he commented. "I'll talk to you tomorrow?"

My heartbeat pulsed once, hard against my chest, even once his hand disappeared. I could still feel the tingle of that stupid squeeze. I also still felt the strangeness of the rejection he had given me a moment ago. "Sure."

He grinned. "Good night. See ya, Natalie."

Not looking up, she gave a short wave. Natalie's eyes were stuck on him all the way out the door. He shut it behind him, carefully turning the knob so it would slide instead of slam.

I snapped out of whatever sort of trance that had fallen over the room. I slid off the edge of my slightly rumpled bedspread.

I rubbed some of the thick lotion Ryan had been sniffing earlier into my hands, trying not to wring them in between breaths of vanilla and chamomile. So, that was it. The planning and ideas of how I was going to dress up Barnett for Samhain were over. All the hard work and time I'd spent trying to do something worthwhile at this college for myself had been ground into the dust.

A tug nagged at me in my chest. Like Ryan perhaps, I'd expected myself to be more upset.

I glanced toward the door once more, catching Natalie's glance. She leaned across the room to switch on *my* salt lamp, casting the room in a warm glow.

"Would you like some?" I raised my hands at her, coated in lotion.

Natalie scoffed.

Thought not.

I took my time getting ready for bed. Clicking through my laptop, I made sure the film wasn't still playing, draining my battery. Still, I could feel my usually rude and resentful roommate continuing to stare at me from the moment before she flipped her hair over to twist it into a messy bun to when she stood back up to slip her feet into socks.

That was another thing about Natalie. What normal person wore socks to bed?

I yanked back the blankets on my bed, climbing into it with my book of shadows and a steadier notebook to set it on top of so my lines would still be drawn straight and clean. I wouldn't be able to fall asleep now. Not for a while anyway. It was still early as I set my phone beside me.

Natalie was still slowly wandering around the room, moving things around, only to put them back where they had started.

She glanced at me again.

"I never knew you to be speechless." I flipped open to the page I'd left off on.

"I didn't know that you and Ryan Gardner were a thing," Natalie said.

Impressed? I wanted to tease.

I shrugged, looking back down to my page, and pressed down on it, so it laid flat. I only had the outline to go. "We're not."

"You two sure looked cozy when I walked in a minute ago."

"We're friends," I said. "I thought you had those?"

"Oh, I do," said Natalie. "I just didn't assume you did."

"Now, that's just rude."

"I think I intended for it to be."

I chuckled along to the sound of Natalie's soft laughter. We were settling into a sort of relationship. It wasn't exactly warm and friendly, but it was cordial enough to be tolerated. Nice even.

"You know that he and my friend Lauren had a close relationship freshman year."

"The same Lauren who is going to be writing my touching dismissal letter from your student life popularity club?" *The same Lauren who spread the rumors and the one I basically just agreed to strike revenge against a short time ago?*

Closing her eyes, Natalie gave a dip of a nod. "The very one."

"Good to know."

"I didn't know he was seeing someone new. I didn't even know he knew you."

"What? Think I'm cooler?" I asked.

Natalie barked that soprano laugh again, short and concise. "Afraid of me actually liking you now, Witchy Lu?"

"Only of that nickname sticking."

She shook her head, giving one more glance as she climbed into bed. "Keep the bizarre to a minimum for the rest of the night, all right? I'm going to bed."

Would it be too much to wish my enemy roommate sweet dreams?

Deciding against it, I leaned closer to where the light pulsed over my workspace and took my time on each fine-tipped line. I moved on from my motivation charm to the classifications of different ingredients, remembering what Gertie had said the other night. Even simple, everyday elements had meaning.

Flour for purity and wholeness.

Sugar for sweet, new beginnings. Tiny specks that Ryan had flicked at my cheeks and scattered overhead. I drew sprinkles cascading down the edge of the crisp folio.

My phone lit up with a new message. Expecting it to be Vadika for me to run her a late-night coffee or debrief me about the rest of her day, I paused at the name. At some point, Ryan must've put his number in my phone. How, I had no idea. I glanced over at Natalie, who was facing the wall as I clicked it open.

The message was one thing.

:)

I snorted to myself.

Looked like I was getting Ryan's smiles, even before I went to sleep now. I stared at the little emoji. A spark of undeniable happiness burst to life in my chest. Biting my lip, I set my phone to the side. I closed my book of shadows and shut my eyes to a memory of the real thing, sitting next to me as he called me brave.

What was I thinking?

I asked myself the question so many times, each one getting me more attached. But right now, in the dark silence that settled over me, I didn't care.

14

"What the ..." Vadika's forehead wrinkled as she shook her head. "Just like that?"

"It isn't like we ever thought the Barnett community had much tact," I said.

The letter my roommate had promised I'd get, which Lauren had written, was cordial but certainly didn't mince words, like Natalie had suggested their apparent secretary did. The entire subject line of the email might as well have said, *You've been REJECTED*, complete with bold letters and an exclamation point, as if this were a pleasant thing to open in your inbox and see.

Like I'd told Vadika, I hadn't expected much, but a pleasant hello to start would've been nice.

"Let me read it again," Vadika said, turning my laptop toward her.

I'd reread the email at least a dozen times already for some reason. I was a glutton for punishment. I'd thought I was over the fight to have my campus Samhain event, and yet also, I wasn't. A new wave of frustration came over me when I read it again.

. . .

Fellow Barnett student,

After consideration, your request for on-campus funding for your upcoming event has been denied. Please see the attached list of well-developed and approved campus events funded by the student council below.

Best,
BUSC

I'D BEEN DENIED funding for my event on campus. No reason. No rebuttal. Seriously, if that was the best sort of email the council could come up with, I was sure to bet that Natalie had a better manner. She should run against her so-called courteous friend.

"Huh," Vadika commented.

"Huh," I repeated. Pulling my laptop back around, I read it once more.

Then one more time.

"You seem upset."

"I'm not," I said. My voice said as much. Strong and sturdy.

"You sure?"

"I'm just …"

I had just been denied funding. There it was. I'd tried.

Celeste and Gertie and the rest of the coven couldn't say that I hadn't put my mind to something and actually made a decision even if it didn't work out. And yet, for some reason, I thought of Ryan and how he had lit up at my plans. I thought of the nights I'd spent planning them from inspiration from my own Samhain celebrations, both alone and here, after I met my coven of eclectic folk-driven witches in their own right.

I'd been denied funding.

Funding.

I'd been denied the lifeblood of a fancy Samhain party on campus, but that didn't mean I couldn't still have it. For years before I came to Barnett, I'd been celebrating the witch new year on my own, with no budget at all—longer than that. Sure, I'd had high hopes for a slightly exaggerated and over-the-top extravaganza of sorts. I didn't want the Barnett University population to view the entire thing as a joke, but that didn't mean we couldn't still do *something*.

In high school, I would take a nature walk through a crowded park. I laid out on the cold grass for a moon bath one year.

I would light a match and blow it out to move forward into the new year.

I'd made wishes on stars like birthday candles once when I saw the moon at its highest and danced as an offering, however ridiculous that sounded now.

Denied funding didn't mean I couldn't fund the on-campus event somehow, right?

"Do you have any of that shea lotion bar thing in your bag yet? The soap in the lab is ruining my hands," complained Vadika. She leaned back against her own backpack, rubbing her palms together as she soaked in the sun.

"Yeah." I reached toward my front bag pocket and tossed her the mini canister. As well as being extremely intelligent, Vadika was also well coordinated. She caught the lotion with ease. "Here."

"Why, thank you." Popping the cap, she made the same motion as Ryan had last night, bringing her nose down to the salve. Her eyes closed as she breathed it in. "So good."

I chuckled as I shook my head. I couldn't help but feel delighted by the comment. I was always protective over my scents, afraid if they smelled too floral, too medicinal.

"You should really think about selling this stuff, you know," Ryan had said.

My eyes narrowed as I watched Vadika lather her hands in the melting oils. She capped the tiny metal container and extended it back without residue. I stared down at the square box in my hand. Orange and lily. Sweet and cloying.

"So, do you have a plan for what you're going to do next?" Vadika asked.

The brightness shining in my eyes must've been visible as she asked the words. Hers widened with interest, lips pursing.

"Well, go on. Share, mighty Luella. How do you plan on taking over the world today?"

Or maybe the look in my eyes might've been a little wilder than I'd thought.

Either way, she was right. I did have an idea. However, I was going to need her help. I was also going to need hands and mastery of the student handbook to see if I could pull this off.

I'd figured out the problem. I'd figured out exactly what I planned to do next.

I stared up at Ryan and his messy head of hair as he approached us across the grass. The answer for Vadika died on my lips. I might be looking at exactly the person who had solved my problem hours ago without realizing it, in all his light-eyed, wavy-haired glory.

"Hey, what's going on?" Ryan grinned, holding on to the straps of his backpack as he came up next to us.

Vadika gave a wave, eyes wide and just as delighted. "Hi there."

"Hi, I'm Ryan." He adjusted his bag's straps. "You must be the one and only Vadika."

"The one and only." Vadika grinned at her nickname. "I guess so."

"Great to meet you. Properly anyway. I think I was in a gen ed class with you second year."

"I think so," she agreed. "Lu has been talking about you."

"Has she?" Ryan's expression opened up as he turned toward me with pure humor. The longer I stared at him, however, the faster it dwindled. "See? I can say hi. Wait, why are you looking at me like that?"

"Remember what I said about a little sacrifice?" I asked, raising my eyebrows.

As he swallowed, Ryan's face blanched, but he didn't look away. "Plan on cashing in?"

I bit my bottom lip and looked between him and Vadika. Neither of them was running yet.

Good start.

15

"Okay, I'm not going to lie. You really scared me before with the crazy eyes," Ryan said from where he stood next to me.

"Crazy eyes?" Hands busy, I made a face.

"Yes. The way you were looking at me on the quad. Sacrifice talk, however, well-timed." Ryan's eyes widened in mock fear. "Crazy eyes."

Rolling my eyes, I turned my attention back down to stirring the boiling contents on Gertie's stove. It didn't take long for Ryan to understand that I was, for the first time, taking his suggestion.

"See, I have good ideas," he said. "Next, you'll be taking up my advice on doing what makes you happy."

For the first time, immediately, an answer sprang to mind that I stopped from saying outright.

I already am.

"Aren't you two just so adorable?" said Vadika. "What's going on in here?"

Both of us turned toward her teasing voice.

"I was just telling Lu that she's brilliant."

"Well, we all already knew that. Unfortunately that means that we are forced into hard labor on my one Friday evening off, but so be it. I'm officially done with my report, so I'm now officially free and all yours for the next few hours."

Ryan and I shook our heads at her.

"Are you setting me on canning or packing duty?" She tied one of the brightest aprons from the wall around her waist. "I'm ready to help get a nontraditional Samhain celebration off the ground!"

Ryan chuckled as he pulled away from the stove, heading toward the boxes. We set aside blank labels for Vadika's perfect, almost-robotic handwriting. I had the lists already written in my old book of shadows that fifteen-year-old me had promised to not let anyone see.

Yet here I was, with Vadika commenting on my poor, looping handwriting and Ryan reading out the words for each ingredient we added to glass vials, mason jars, and canisters. Lotions would harden overnight. Spells and scented sachets were labeled with intention-coded ribbons.

Gertie got in on the small factory of spells that was taking place, adding her own brand of knowledge. She showed Ryan how to properly crush herbs before sitting down next to Vadika. With swift, smooth motions, she curled each knotted ribbon with an old pair of sewing sheers.

"What are you doing?" I watched as she adjusted the now twisty, curvy bows I'd tied.

She looked softly at each one she traded off, as if wrapping a birthday gift.

"Uh, Lu, your one pan is bubbling again," Ryan called from behind me.

Vadika giggled, ignoring the panic in his voice as much as I did. She set another label on the finished side of the table.

"A little extra flare can't hurt, can it?" asked Gertie.

I smiled at the very pleased woman, turning over my shoulder to watch as Ryan aggressively stirred, trying to figure out which knob was off on Gertie's old and slightly senile stove.

"Guess not."

For the next few hours, the kitchen felt alive from all of us rushing around from one station to another. I only ever did one spell at a time. It was neater that way. To work slow magic, like patience, never was my strongest quality. But this sort of work felt somewhere in between. Careful yet chaotic. Peaceful and organic, yet loud and full of life.

Music floated in from the living room by the time the heat from the stove dissipated. The sound echoed off the turning record Gertie had put on, humming the melodious chorus of Billie Holiday and Janis Joplin.

* * *

I ADDED THE FINAL LABEL, numb fingers knotting the tiny tag of paper around one of Gertie's curly ribbons. There. *Perfect.* I leaned my forehead against the mounds of my hands. I shut my eyes.

Just for a moment.

"Done?" Gertie stood over me.

The kitchen was darker than it had been a moment ago when I shut my eyes for a second. It looked like it was maybe a few more than just one. I took a deep breath and rubbed the nagging reminder of sleep from the corners of my eyes.

"For now."

"Always for now." Gertie smiled knowingly.

I huffed a short chuckle.

"Did you have fun?"

"I did."

"You seemed ... alive."

I cocked my head. "I'm always alive."

More so with every minute, I felt like. Especially standing in the kitchen with them all. Again, I was reminded of the beauty of Barnett, of this house, from the moment I'd knocked on the door.

From the moment Vadika had said that she would have no one else as her orientation partner.

From hearing Ryan laugh for the first time to him reaching out to almost touching the crystal around my neck. Bright and curious and so unexpectedly kind.

That strange tugging feeling pulled gently in my chest. I glanced behind me toward the hall leading to the living room, where the music that had been turned down low had since disappeared.

"No, you're always *living*," explained Gertie. She placed her hands on the table to take the weight off her back. "People forget the difference."

"Do you think all this is actually going to do anything?"

Gertie glanced around her kitchen until her gaze landed back on me. "I think it already has."

After a moment, I nodded, looking back down to my hands. "Everyone else leave?"

"Vadika's parents came to pick her up," Gertie said.

The stove was off. Spells and the intention-filled apothecary I was set to take to the Barnett campus were ready for their owners and packed away. Only a few were still sitting on the sill, basking in the moonlight that caught through trees and passed the windowpanes.

"They did?"

"They came by a bit ago. She told me not to wake you." Gertie chuckled.

"What time is it?"

"Late." Gertie offered a hand. I gently took it as I stood up. "You should go up to your room and get some rest if you plan on doing anything tomorrow."

Gertie led me into the hall toward the stairs. We passed the living room.

"Of course, I also suggest that you find your friend somewhere more comfortable to spend the night. Neither of you is fit to leave at this hour."

Pausing, I stared at the tall form draped over the floral couch cushions. Ryan's one arm was flung overhead. He was breathing steadily, one leg falling over the side to the floor. His bad knee stretched up onto the coffee table.

He looked almost at peace for someone who obviously didn't fit. On the sofa. In this house.

Yet somehow, this image would remain ingrained in my head. I could see him and his soft lashes against his cheeks.

Even when I blinked.

Gertie nudged me in the right direction. "Go. This old woman is going to get some rest."

I watched my friend move away from me and toward the stairs, taking them up toward her room before I managed to reply. Slowly, I took my own steps forward. Crouching down, I leaned over Ryan, unsure of exactly what to do. How did you wake a sleeping man?

The one time I had woken my father when he fell asleep on the couch after Mom died, telling him that he should go to bed, he cried. Tears leaked down from his eyes worse than at the funeral we had all been so prepared for.

He hadn't, on the other hand, been prepared for the empty side of the bed. There had always been a reminder of how someone else should be there, so loud he couldn't fall asleep at night.

Before I could question it, think on it any further, I swept my hand down his arm gently. "Hey, Ryan."

He inhaled, slowly blinking his eyes back open. "Oh."

"Hi."

"Oh, man. Sorry. I was just going to sit down and rest a moment. Vadika was talking to me, I think …"

"It's fine. Come on, big guy. Get up."

"Are we going back to campus?"

I shook my head, extending my hand. "Just come on."

He took my hand without question. His skin was warm, and all of him was rumpled. He grunted as he stretched out his leg, knee hinging back and forth as he took a few steps with me toward the stairs. If anything, Ryan was still half-asleep until we made it to the top. I put a finger to my lips for him to be quiet, and he mimicked the same motion to let me know he understood.

Gertie's door was closed, but I was never rude when she put me up.

Even when that included me and someone else now.

I paused after another step, looking between the half dozen doors. At the end of the hall was Gertie. Ana lived here almost as much as I did. She stayed in the room near the front of the house, looking over the street where the roof bent around the doorway. The other rooms were almost always open. Ryan could very well choose any of them and call it his for the night. Forever, by how Gertie took to him.

"What are you doing?"

I put my finger back to my lips again. Before he could make any more noise, I pulled him directly into my room and shut the door behind us. He stood near the door while I maneuvered through the darkened room, reaching for the bedside lamp. The bulb flickered before it held steady. The light coated the space in a cool-yellow glow, and the sound was the hum of the river outside through the bay window.

I'd stepped into another world when I locked myself inside this room. Turning back around, I watched as Ryan scanned the space, much like he had my dorm room.

"Wow," Ryan whispered. "Is this your room?"

"Sort of. When I spend the night with Gertie it is."

"I think I like this room at the house better. You know, more than your other one." He tilted his head up in the direction of the window toward campus.

"Really?"

He started to wander around, making himself at home. "It's more you. This whole place is."

I thought about the difference between this space and the dorm room I'd tried to decorate. Most of it was under my bed in storage after a few too many threats from Natalie in the first few weeks. Even if she was warming up to me, I didn't believe that extended to my many objects that made the space the opposite of any minimalist's dream.

Ryan looked around, picking up the books I'd left, and smiled down at my new book of shadows I had left beside the window seat along with my book bag when we first arrived at the house with nothing but a mission. Still, he didn't touch it, knowing well enough now what it was.

This room was me, in a sense. What could be.

"Let me just get this straight. One more time."

I waited.

"She really wants to give you this whole place?" Ryan asked.

"Yeah. Sort of."

"Is it because she doesn't have kids of her own?"

I shrugged. "Probably. Gertie has never been a strict legacy person. It's not my story to tell, but she didn't have the best life, growing up. Then, she found a place like this for a while. She decided to make it her own. She wanted somewhere safe for us all, so …"

"She wants someone who appreciates it as much as she does to take over."

I nodded.

"You love this place."

"Yeah," I said again. I thought it a dozen times a day. "I do."

Get rid of the uncertainty that no longer serves me.

It was so much easier said than done, even when you metaphorically and literally tried to burn it.

Ryan nodded a few times. He was still looking around by the time I sat down on the bed and watched him look over my dried flowers and more of my tinctures, sniffing one and then the other, newfound understanding passing over his face for each one.

His gaze caught on me as he stood by the one window, looking at my assessment of him. He also took in the single bed set in the center of the room. Twisting back, he glanced at the foam-padded window seat.

"I can sleep over here."

I shook my head, hands moving away another layer of pillows and tossing them to the floor. "Don't be ridiculous."

I crossed my legs over one another. I reached back and pulled the blankets back, so I could tuck my feet under. I watched as Ryan explored more pieces of me from the past three years, biding time. This room, however, really had started to hold more than I'd realized.

Ryan made me realize.

Then, carefully, as if afraid to frighten me—which made me smile—he sat down on the bed with me. Maybe it wasn't only him who was unsure, as my heart pulsed in an uneven rhythm with each new movement.

"It is a nice bed." Sighing, he stretched his leg.

Letting myself lean back farther against the headboard, I stared down at where his knee and calf flexed. "Still bothering you?"

"Not as much as before. Just nervous."

"About what?" I asked.

"I don't know," he said. "Just worried that my leg and everything else will never be the same again."

"Is that a bad thing?"

"Says the girl who is nervous about taking a house and life she loves more than just about anything else," said Ryan.

"Touché."

Ryan smiled. This time, the grin was directed completely and wholly at me. It made me smile back. Soft and easy. His eyes widened along with his lips.

"I'm not sure I've seen that face enough."

"Has that been your goal all along?"

He shrugged, a little embarrassed all of a sudden. "Part of it."

Huh. I glanced down at my hands, taking a deep breath. "There are just a lot of unknowns. I want to do what I want, sure, but I know better than to think I can handle all this for that long."

"Why?"

"Because …" I didn't know. "Nothing is permanent."

"Not unless you want it to be."

I inhaled, leaning my head on my arm as I laid down to buy myself some time. Not that I needed it. Ryan slowly laid down next to me on top of the covers.

"No. Not always," I murmured. "We were so prepared. I was so prepared when she got sick again, and still … it wrecked me. It wrecked my dad."

"It was your mom, Lu."

"So, it was supposed to cause so much of a mess?"

"Yeah," he said, as if it were the simplest thing to understand in the entire world. "The things that matter and that you love the most have a tendency to do that. They take over. Isn't that kind of the point? Would you want it any other way?"

Pressing my lips together, I knew I didn't need to respond.

I stared at where his eyelashes tucked themselves against his freckled cheeks. I lifted my fingers, as if to touch each one. He was still slightly in whatever dream he had fallen into on Gertie's couch downstairs. Still, a smile hovered over his mouth.

"Are you staring at me, Lu?" Ryan's gravelly voice asked. His eyes fluttered halfway open. His lips curved to the right.

I inhaled but didn't move. My palm flattened on Ryan's chest, testing the waters. I watched it rise and fall.

"Yes."

He hummed with pleasure at the word before shutting his eyes intentionally. "We have found that we do fit well in bed together, huh?"

Silence settled.

Unable to help it, unable to close my eyes, I swallowed. "I just …"

"Yeah, Luella?" Ryan asked, amused.

"Thank you."

"For what?"

"Just … thank you. So much. You know, for all your help recently. I honestly can't believe that we got this far tonight, let alone the fact that you were willing to come back here and spend time with Gertie and Vadika. Before, I know that you found it strange and weird and everything."

"Maybe at the start, sure. But not weird."

"No?"

"More fascinating."

"Well, thank you."

His jaw clenched at my words. "You don't need to thank me."

"I do. It's been nice," I admitted. "You've been kind to me and gone so far above and beyond how I helped you with your class stuff once."

"Twice," Ryan corrected.

Twice then.

"Do you really think that is what this has all been about?" Ryan asked, amused. His eyes were once more fully open and alert as they studied my face, looking to see if I could possibly be telling him a joke. "Me paying you back for help on my classwork these past few weeks?"

The two sides of whatever argument I was starting must've been mirrored on my face.

"Luella"—he bit his bottom lip after saying my full name again

—"I had no idea how twisted and confused that head of yours is."

"It's not—"

"I think it is. Listen. I would stay up until the next day, every day, with you, making soaps and spells with bits inside I'm not even sure I will ever know the names of. I would do that not only because you are selfless in helping a poor sap like me, who made you feel awful once for such a stupid reason, but also because—"

"Because now you like hanging out with me?" I said, repeating a similar assortment of words that he had to remind me of all the time. Like yesterday, the first time we had lain in my bed together, a breath away from a kiss. Another kiss he had let fade away with calm refusal while all I'd felt since that night on Mabon was want. "I know."

"Because I like all of you."

My lips parted before I thought of coming up with something else teasing back. But this wasn't a tease. Ryan's smile turned into something more genuine, serious even, as he lifted a hand and settled his thumb in the center of my chin.

"I thought you just wanted to be friends."

"I did want to. I do. But I feel like, now, you need to know that I also really want to kiss you. I want to kiss you and tell you how extraordinary you are. That's the problem. I wanted to do that all night on the equinox. Couldn't you tell how my hands were shaking when I fed you those seven pomegranate seeds? Those stupid little pomegranates. I kept thinking I would drop them. But then I saw that maybe you wanted me back and the curse—"

"There's no curse."

"I know that now. Or I'm starting to see that even if it feels like the whole thing is a part of me now." He touched his chest.

"I get it."

"No, I don't think you do," said Ryan. "I more than just like you, Lu. As a friend. As anything."

My heart felt like it froze for a moment. "Like a good friend?"

Ryan chuckled. "Now you are making fun of me. More than a

really good friend. We both already knew that though, right?"

"I mean, you're sure about that?"

"I figured that you would've realized that by now," he said, bashfully.

I wasn't sure what I realized exactly. I mean, I understood that he wanted to be my friend. Maybe more than that. I didn't want to say the words and fully realize them aloud. I wanted it to be more. I wanted everything this year.

Ryan had certainly become everything for me, somewhere in the past few weeks.

I understood the pull I felt that startled my nervous system more and more when he was around before settling, soft and easy, all around me.

Everything was soft and easy and warm with Ryan.

"I only ask if you're sure because I'm not sure if I ..." I tried to figure out what I needed to say.

"You don't want me?"

"No," I quickly corrected. "I want you to be sure of all this because I know people are casual. I know you were talking with Ana and Celeste about relationships and how it might seem like, in our lifestyle, our feelings are casual when it comes to me being here. Kissing you. But I'm not. I'm not casual. Not when it comes to this."

"You mean us."

I loved those words when he said them.

"I don't want to be, nor can I be, casual with you," I said one last time.

"That's become abundantly clear," Ryan joked. "In case you haven't noticed, I'm not *casual* either. My life has been so much better with you. I haven't wanted to spend my time with anyone else. Ever since I got the courage to talk to you that day outside the dean's office, I realized how alone I'd been all this time at Barnett when all I wanted was to be a part of something. A group. A team. A home."

I was careful not to say anything as he spoke. My lips were dry. I couldn't form words if I wanted to. Was Ryan telling me that he liked me? Actually liked me more than just whatever sort of thing we were calling each other? It felt so silly to think that, like we were back in grade school. Hands shaky, voices nervous.

We just were together. And that was the most amazing thing.

"It makes me want to go back those three years to orientation, when I first saw you, and slap myself." Ryan licked his lips as he shook his head. "God, I was so stupid."

"Are you telling me that you can actually stand me?"

"I can do more than stand you, Luella. Did you not just hear me? I've been slightly infatuated with you for the past three years."

"Slightly," I tried to tease him, but it came out weak.

"I want to do a whole lot more than just stand you. You are everything I've ever wanted in a friend from the moment you looked down at me in the cemetery to make sure that I wasn't dead." He chuckled, holding on to the back of his neck while his other hand indented the quilt beneath us. "Then, we started hanging out more, and, Lu, I don't care what anyone else thinks of us. I couldn't care less about everyone else when I care so much about what you think. For years, I saw you and thought you were so amazing, but maybe the world was making us wait. For right now."

"Look at you, getting all spiritual. Already failing those traditional mentalities from home?"

"You bring it out in me," he agreed. His fingers slowly began to stroke the sides of my face. Our foreheads touched. "I'm ready to declare whatever you need me to, to the stars and moon if I have to, if it means that I don't have to spend another year of my life wondering, *What if …*"

"What if …" I repeated.

He glanced down at my mouth. "What if."

16

Eyes wide, I stared at Ryan. I stared at his lips that I'd wanted to slam mine against the other day without any fear of all the repercussions I knew could happen, wondering if this was still some sort of joke, a tease that Ryan would pull back away from. He would go back to his friends and his team and his sports house. I would be all alone again, save for Vadika—at least until she, too, ran away to whatever graduate school she was likely going to be fully funded to attend.

I would be that weird little witch girl who couldn't steal a soul for her own, so unlike what Ryan had said to begin with when we saw each other for the first time.

So unlike we were now.

"I know I'm hanging by a limb here—"

Before he could say anything else ridiculous, I stopped him. I stopped him as I reached forward and set my hands on his thighs that I'd always wanted to touch, feeling the muscles I had known were there flex beneath my palms as I leaned up and let my lips hover over his, waiting long enough to know he could pull away and set all things to right again. For now, I could get over it. I could pretend that I was still sleeping and this was all just some very wonderful, steamy dream.

No harm, no foul.

"Can I—"

He didn't let me finish before he met me halfway this time. No hesitation.

We kissed carefully, as if we were talking a soft banter that made him smirk and sigh when we pulled back an inch before tucking ourselves back into each other in a new form. More confident as his tongue traced the line of my lips and I could feel my body shiver.

"And here I thought, you said you didn't like me all that much before."

"We've both said a lot of things we didn't mean once," I whispered.

Lifting his hand up to my face, Ryan traced a path over my eyebrows, parting my hair away from my face.

We kissed until his breaths became a symphony in my ear. His and mine melted together. When we pulled apart, the world came back into focus—from the way the quilt twisted under our legs to the window shining moonlight over us. We gasped. Yet still, we didn't let go of each other. We were too far past that now. My hand still cupped the back of his neck before I came up for air.

"I really wanted to kiss you." His hand was flat against my stomach, curving around my waist. "You have no idea."

"I really wanted to kiss you too," I whispered.

The words caused a small groan to escape Ryan, making my wish come true twice when he kissed me again. And again, carefully pressing his tongue at the seam of my lips until I was the one melting with a soft whimper.

"What was that I said about waiting for this?" Ryan seemed to ask himself. "What an *idiot*."

Tilting our chins, we found new ways for our mouths to meet, feeling the crest and sighs of our breaths between each moment we broke away from one another. It was not like the last time. The almost-last time, where our lips had just met, as if a mistake were easily erased by exhaustion and misunderstanding. This was no mistake. This was meant to be. This was destiny.

This was me, and this was Ryan, and we were kissing as if we were talking like any other day, any other moment. We were both soft and easy.

Ryan held me to him as we continued to touch and feel over our clothes, trying to get closer.

I couldn't believe that this was happening. I almost wanted to laugh, smiling into his mouth.

How is this happening?

"Can I?" He looked over me, still very much clothed, where his hands were fisting the bottom of my shirt, right at my belly button. "I want to see you."

I hastily nodded, kissing him once more under his chin. His breath hitched. "Yes, please."

He broke away, pulling back away from me as his breathing remained uneven. "You need to tell me. You promise? You need to tell me if I'm doing something wrong."

I nodded, eager for him to kiss me again. "Promise. But I'm pretty sure that's impossible."

Ryan's nervous chuckle breathed through my lips, letting me part them open as his tongue gently slid along the inside. Hesitant, but oh so curious—exactly like him.

I lifted my hands up, and he pulled my shirt carefully over my head. Staring down at me, he seemed in awe for a moment before he realized where my hands were. They tugged at the hem of his shirt, trying to take it off and throw it down to the floor along with mine.

"Only fair."

"Only fair," he agreed.

He lifted his arms, his nose still resting against mine as we stared at each other. As the shirt passed over him, it gave us a second to fully realize how much of our skin touched. Nervous, exuberant energy vibrated between us.

"We don't have to do anything else," I say. "Not tonight."

After a moment, he nodded, a breath escaping his lungs. I watched his chest as it dropped beneath my hands. Running his tongue over his lips, he seemed to relax, eyes looking me over, as if he were caught in a dream.

"Okay."

"Okay," I agreed.

Because every little piece of this, right now, felt like a dream. Almost. But of course, it wasn't, and that was what made this second, these minutes, this moment in time all the more magical.

He ran his teeth along his bottom lip. "Staring again?"

"Well, I know how it gets you going."

Looking down toward his feet, Ryan chuckled and tipped his mouth back against mine.

Definitely not a dream.

17

Campus was oddly quiet as we set up, turning a few heads as students passed by to make their way toward the SUB. People's eyes stuck to the table before they carried on, so that was a good sign. Right?

"I wonder if anyone is going to care if we're standing there. They're probably going to think we're insane."

"Eh, there are worse things." Ryan shrugged, completely at ease.

Stacking another row of fresh lavender sachets, Ryan tilted them just so, as if he were a happy shopkeeper.

I watched each movement, completely at ease when, at any moment, there would be a stream of Barnett students crossing the usually busy walkway where we were now set up. "And here I thought you would've reached your quota of crazy at this point."

With his other hand, he reached around my shoulders and pulled me toward him, lifting my chin up. I stared at him straight on, looking at his tanned freckles. "And here I thought you'd be sunshine and optimism."

"Definitely one thing you got wrong about me."

He smiled against my mouth as he tilted his head down. "The rest makes up for it."

I whacked him gently in the chest.

Already, he looked mighty pleased with himself.

We'd mainly stuck around Gertie's for the entire weekend. The two of us finished the final touches on the dozens of things now set up along our folding table. I showed him the greenhouse outside and the other little magic places in Gertie's home. He had taken particular interest in the vines Ana had once fallen from after climbing back through the house late one night when she locked herself out. He admired the tiny stained glass windows that were hidden all over—from the crescent moon above the doorway to the bright stars and poppy flowers high up in the attic, which Ryan proclaimed was properly suited for any average ghost to casually haunt.

Faith would be thrilled at the assessment. She herself continually asserted she could feel a presence whenever we sent her up to get ornaments for the tree each holiday season.

I watched as people began to flood out of the academic buildings surrounding the main quad of grass in the middle of campus. I took a deep breath. "Here we go."

Ryan rubbed his hands together. "Let's do this."

Dozens of people started to walk by us. I tried to force a smile to draw them in. At the very least, they could pause and purchase any of the soaps, spells, or little bundles of herbs and help us be one step closer at last to making Samhain happen. All I needed was for even half of the things on this table to go to make a dent in decoration supplies, snacks, and the rest of the things I remembered from my notebook that I deemed absolutely necessary.

A few glances turned our direction as distracted students coming out from class veered around the table, where they, on any other day, aimlessly walked ahead.

"Don't worry," Ryan assured next to me. He reached out to

squeeze my hand, and warmth traveled up through my arm at the small gesture. "We just need one person to get it rolling."

With a nod at his own words, he took a step, rounding the table.

I raised my eyebrows. "You really think that's going to work?"

"I guess we will see, won't we?" Ryan smiled, picking up one of the sachets. He lifted the tiny cloth bag up into the air. "What a perfect little smelly thing. I could put this in my closet and make all my clothes smell like the wonderful Luella Pierce."

I bit the inside of my cheek, forcing myself not to smile. "Stop it."

"And this?" Ryan moved on to the other section, lowering his voice. "Spells. Like witchcraft? Woman seller, is this witchcraft?"

It took everything I had not to burst out into laughter.

"Oh, yes." I waved my hand toward the bottle of what was not one of the spells, but a canister of Sleep Better tea. "Only the finest in all of Barnett."

Oddly enough, my near combustion of laughter, as well as Ryan's intent looking, began to draw more glances, a few people looking over the table with a pause.

"What's this?" One girl stopped, glancing over the assortment. "Oh my goodness. Is this, like, a little artist market thing? What a cute idea."

"It can definitely be that," Ryan agreed without agreement.

"Hey, man!" Another group of people approached from the business building a little ways up the greenway, only this set obviously knew Ryan and hadn't expected to see him. All of them were fit and full of grins as they reached out toward him. Only after they exchanged greetings did the Barnett football team look over the table. "What's all this?"

"We're selling …" Ryan trailed off, looking at me, as if he was searching for the right word of what exactly we were selling on campus.

We had to be coy, according to Vadika, if we didn't want to be reprimanded for being an off-campus vendor or nonclub with no permission.

So, basically, we had one rule to exude. Confidence.

"Apothecary goods," I offered.

Ryan repeated the words, as if that were exactly what was stuck on the tip of his tongue.

"Is this some sort of joke?" One of them laughed.

If they thought it was, so be it.

Ryan maintained firmly. He raised his eyebrows, but the rest of his face remained calm and unaffected. "Nope."

There was a long pause, a few reconsidered nods.

"Okay then," said Ryan's teammate. "Cool."

"I think so." He grinned. "Want something?"

The one guy beside Ryan shrugged. "What do ya got?"

I dipped my head down, and this time, I didn't stop the small smile on my lips as I turned away from them as another someone stopped, picking up a few of the spells with tiny instructions on them. His fingers were gentle as he skimmed over each, forehead crinkling in concentration as he read over the instructions.

"What's this?" He lifted the small mason jar.

I glanced at it, seeing the flash of what was inside at once. "Motivation jar spell."

"How is it for motivation?" The guy rocked back and forth, looking this way and that as the table began to draw a few more people with wandering eyes.

Could this be working?

Hope surged.

I could answer that even better than the last. "Basil for luck, cinnamon for motivation, rosemary for clear thinking, coffee for a little energy during late-night study sessions. Plus, I added a bit of lavender for anxiety relief. Hard to be productive when you're dreading the future, right?"

At the words, his shoulders seemed to ease down from where they had been clenched to his neck. "Okay."

"Yes?" I asked, grabbing the jar he was extending to me.

He nodded, fishing out his wallet from his back pocket. "Are you going to help me do it?"

Softly, with care toward his hesitance, I tipped my chin, moving him over to the space of the two tables I'd left empty.

"Now, you are going to be the one who seals it," I directed as I moved him over with me. He followed with wide eyes as I continued to explain each movement. "We are going to be using orange wax for this."

"Why?"

He had all the good questions, and I beamed up at my first customer. Besides Ryan anyway. "The orange wax is for creativity, inspiration, attention, good luck, and a bit of positivity. Here you go. You take the candle. I'll light the wax. Be careful you don't get any on you, but this is the important moment. Think of what you hope to get out of this spell, what you want motivation for, or whatever it is you most need as the wax drips as the jar seals shut."

A small crowd surrounded the two of us as I flicked the flame over the candle, waiting for it to start to melt. It might not have been very ornate, but my tiny lighter got the job done.

"Whoa."

"I definitely need one of those," another joked, stepping up to the table next.

"This is so neat," a few more murmured as the wax locked in his intentions—from joy to creativity to a much more traditional protection—in thick globs

Lifting the candle, with a single breath, I blew out the flame.

More students began to line up for their turn, grabbing their own jars to purchase.

"This will work?" one girl asked, raising a thick blonde eyebrow at me after it was all said and done.

"Should," I agreed with a slight shrug of a shoulder.

Somehow, that seemed to set her at ease. "Thanks."

"Anytime," I said with a small smile, touched by the sudden sincerity as each new patron turned away.

Anytime, I supposed, if I ever got to make premade spells for sale again. It felt good.

Spell kits and sachets and interactive charms, soaps, and even baked goods—which Celeste had dropped off after Gertie let the rest of the coven know what I was doing—were picked through.

"Anything for acne?" one more asked.

"How about sleep?" another added.

I smiled, reaching over toward the soap and a tea combination, handing them to each of the interested customers. "I got you covered."

Girls I had never met before smiled at me with bright, interested eyes.

"I love your necklace," one complimented.

I glanced down at the crystal hanging at my chest.

"It's labradorite," Ryan chimed in next to me, sticking another few dollars into the collection pouch.

I scrunched my nose at him, and he snorted at my tease before I turned back to the girl. I hadn't ever seen her before. Still, I pointed up to her fluffy brown hair. "I really like your pins."

"Thanks." She beamed. Her light eyes remained soft, cautious. "It's vintage."

Vadika waved as she jogged past toward the science building. She lifted her hand in a thumbs-up.

I smiled. I'd kind of hoped that she would stop. I knew she was busy with the big project she'd been working on. Half of everything we had made over the weekend was gone anyway.

Over half.

This was going to happen. This had actually somehow worked. Before I could turn to Ryan and tug on his arm, close as I ever might be to jumping up and down from glee, the girl cleared her throat again.

"So, um, you make all this stuff?"

I nodded. "With some help."

"What if I need something a little more … specific?"

Pausing, I turned away from the table, wiping down my slightly sweaty hands. "Like what?"

"I need a spell or something that isn't here. At least, I don't think it is." She looked over the quickly depleting table again. "I need to get over my ex."

"I don't really do love spells."

"I don't want a love spell. Not really," she tried to explain. "He graduated last year, and we ended things. *He* ended things, and I'm just—I need to let him go. I'm ready to let him go."

"You need a new beginning."

"Yes." Her shoulders sagged. "That sounds … magical."

Immediately, I thought of the candles I needed. Slowly, I nodded. Ripping the label off one of the remaining jars, I turned it over and wrote my name and number. "Come see me later, all right? I'll set you up with something."

"Really? It's not like selling my soul or anything, right?" she joked.

"No," I assured her, chuckling. "It's harmless. Mostly. It will give you some peace of mind."

She nodded slowly. "I could use a little of that."

"Good." We all could, I was certain.

She took the note, rolling her shoulders back as she walked away through the trees.

Taking a few steps after her, I wanted to say something else, though I didn't know what. Something was guiding me toward her. I didn't know her name, nor did I thank her even if the interaction had been nothing more than the other few I'd already had. Glancing back at Ryan, I put up a hand, so he knew where I was.

He didn't see me, as he was talking to someone else, telling a story with his hands rather animatedly.

I smiled again, shaking my head.

She was already gone, maybe late to a class. I hoped that she would message me, but either way, it was what it was.

Sighing, I shrugged to myself as I turned back around toward the table setup. That was, until another body stepped out in front of me. I nearly came up short on my toes. The sound of my heels clacked back down on the sidewalk.

Natalie's friend with a sharp bob cut stood in front of me.

"Um, excuse me." I attempted to step around her.

She moved with me.

Blinking, I extended a hand. *What the ...*

"What do you think you're doing?" she asked, terse.

"Standing here or ..."

"You know what I'm talking about."

"Well, I've created a small apothecary business today after my recent rejection of funding for my campus event," I said, proud of myself. "If that's what you are talking about. I think we'll be open for a little while longer. What have you been doing on this fine fall day?"

Her jaw unhinged as she narrowed her eyes at me, as if I were the most idiotic individual she'd ever seen before in her life. She must not get out much. "You know that I had a thing with Ryan, right?"

"You mean, back in first-year?" I asked. Oh, I knew, and I wasn't going to back down. Not from Lauren, the awful emailer of all people. "Are you still holding on to that? It's been a few years now, you know. I actually have a new spell I'm going to be making for moving on, if you need it."

"Natalie said you were weird."

"We love to exchange those sorts of love notes. Thank you."

"Cut the shit. I'm telling you to back off," Lauren said, finality in her tone. She crossed her arms.

At least she knew how to get to the point.

"Ryan might not know that we are getting back together, but

he hasn't been with anyone else. That's because everyone knows he's going to end up mine. Get it?"

Hers? Was this like she was peeing on her property or something? Because, for one, gross.

"No."

"No?"

"No, I don't understand. My tiny brain just can't understand why someone as stunning and powerful as you think you are is coming up to me to let me know that I can't have something. As well as the fact that Ryan isn't something. He's a person. So, maybe next time, before you look at me like I'm the desperate one, you look at yourself first. Also, for future reference"—I took a step forward—"don't threaten people who have rumors going around that they worship the devil. It really won't end well. At least, not for you."

She took a step back.

Thought so.

"Honestly, I'm just trying to warn you," Lauren said, her voice taking a softer tone.

I stared at her.

"You may think you know Ryan, but he's just like all the rest of the guys. A boy's boy. He might be having a little crisis right now since he lost football—*if* he decides not to come back and play with the team again."

"He won't."

What was it with everyone acting like that simple fact was the end of the world? It wasn't like Barnett had a renowned team. They sucked. The entirety of Barnett sports sucked as a whole, and it had become nearly a fun joke at this point.

At least to most, apparently.

"Even so," Lauren continued, "you're a passing fancy. I just want you to be prepared for after he has whatever college experience you are to him as he heals mentally"—her eyes trailed over my frame pointedly—"and physically."

I gritted my teeth, tearing my face away from her.

"The rest of the guys thought it was a little funny, making jokes, not thinking it would last this long. They didn't even think you'd give him the time of day. But we were all wrong there."

But I wasn't. I knew Ryan—or I had been getting to. *I do know him.*

"Eventually, Ryan's going to miss his friends and his life, and then you'll be wherever it is you normally are. I just don't want you to be unprepared."

"How considerate of you."

Noting whatever expression was on my face, Lauren took another step back, as if she was done here. Her mission was complete.

Well, that just wouldn't do.

"Like I said," I called out, stopping Lauren in her tracks, "if you need help with the whole self-confidence and desperation thing going on that makes you unable to get over a boy you made a joke out of, because you couldn't help but act like a child, let me know."

I knew my words were harsh. I didn't care as they flowed. I knew I would probably think of something better to say later—I always did—so I let my words fly as they formed. They were meant to be off the tip of my tongue for her to hear.

"Oh, sure," she muttered. "But then again, didn't he make a joke out of you once?"

Something stabbed me below my ribs, but I didn't dare look down to show how hard her words had hit me.

Didn't he make a joke out of you once?

I huffed, rolling my eyes as Lauren retreated, walking as if she were stepping on clouds. "You make a joke out of women supporting women!"

Lauren didn't turn back. Of course she hadn't. She was making it really hard for me to be supportive of other women right now. I'd thought all the cliché mean girls had been left in high school. There was always one that stuck around, it seemed, and it turned out, she was on the student council.

Ryan's eyes narrowed, but he looked oddly amused by the time I stomped back into view of our table. "What was that all about?"

"Oh, y'know, just scaring the student population."

He nodded thoughtfully, as if this were an everyday occurrence.

"How are you doing?" Ryan tried again.

I let my teeth drag over my bottom lip. "Good. Really good actually."

"You look good."

I nudged him. "Dork."

"I'll take it." He laughed. "The guys from the team bought, like, five things of tea."

"You're kidding."

"I doubt they'll ever drink it, but no one can say I'm not a salesman."

You're amazing, I wanted to say.

But Lauren's words came back to mind again.

I might be just a passing fancy to him. He'd get over me and miss what he left behind.

Then I'd be left behind.

I shook my head, shaking off all the nasty words with it. Since when did I ever listen to anyone, including the likes of Lauren?

"Thank you. I guess that means you are also going to help me get silly supplies with all our earnings? There's going to be plenty of fairy lights to untangle." I batted my eyelashes.

And streamers and lanterns to set candles firmly inside of. And marshmallows to stack in piles out of the sun and out of sight, so Ana wouldn't find them and they wouldn't melt or be eaten if I kept them at Gertie's house.

"A new challenge with you? Always," he said, seeming even

more excited before he tilted his head down. All merriment disappeared. "But I do have a really serious question for you."

My smile dipped down with dread, all the way to my stomach. A question ...

Have you realized I actually think this entire thing is a joke?

I don't actually like you.

I don't want to kiss you anymore.

Okay, those final two weren't questions, but they ran through my mind all the same.

"Yes?" I finally prompted, swallowing.

"Will you go to homecoming with me next weekend?"

I whacked my hand across his chest as I looked him in the eye. What a ridiculous boy I'd gotten caught up with. "Absolutely not."

18

I was going to homecoming.
Even Vadika was shocked. Her exact words had been something along the lines of, "You're kidding."
Unfortunately, I was not. Ryan was the most delighted at my caving in to his peer pressure—and the kisses he'd trailed down my neck and between my chest, whispering his pleases and other encouraging words of how much I would love it.

Like him.

I blinked at myself. The thought had come unbidden.

Um, *no.* I was good for right now, thanks. Still, I couldn't help the smile that was brought to my lips as he rambled on about his plans.

"You'll see," he said. "So will I. This is going to be my first homecoming not on the field, you know?"

I gave him a hesitant smile each time after he mentioned it. But I played along.

He talked about homecoming like it was his Samhain celebration. After a week of his constant chatter, I was almost starting to find his excitement infectious. That, or I was still immensely grateful after he did spend a good three hours untangling lights with me on my dorm room floor, covered with the other dozen candles and other decorations, while I leaned back in his lap, earning a rather strange glance from Natalie.

Nothing was going to ruin my parade I had been marching onward in ever since that day of selling spells on the greenway. I imagined the strings of sparkling white fluorescent lights hanging across the center of the campus's low-hanging tree branches like a fairy tale.

Getting ready for Samhain was my thing. Now, it was Ryan's day.

Homecoming.

I nearly snorted at myself as I stared in the mirror, getting ready while Ryan got a shower down the hall. Over the past week, he'd also begun to make himself at home in the house, and it felt as if he had always been meant to be there.

A loose purple dress fell below my knees, complementing my scuffed boots. I'd found the dress in one of our attic raids at Gertie's. Homecoming wasn't a dress occasion and yet—

"You look …" Ryan stood in the doorway, eyes wide and hair still slightly wet as he patted it dry with a towel patterned with irises and begonias. He looked me up and down. "Wow."

"Wow?"

He bit his bottom lip. "I think I need to brush up on my adjectives."

I shook my head, glancing at myself again. The dress was loose and easy, but I would need to find a sweater or something to cover my arms when the sun went down. "I'll take wow."

It felt right.

Everything right now felt right.

Slipping the jersey over the top of my dress, however, I paused.

All right. I barked a laugh. This felt a little wrong.

Pressing my lips together, I tried to hide my distaste behind my sudden elation. The question of when the boxy jersey had last been washed was also up for a debate I didn't want to think about. I cinched the hem up and under around my waist, trying to find something to tie it with. A hair tie, a ribbon left over from the decorations we had found, anything.

As I turned around, in the mirror, I stared at the name on the back.

Gardner.

I let the extra foot of fabric fall from my hands once more for a second. Instead of grabbing the tie, I reached for my phone. Lifting my phone, I took a photo of my reflection. Ryan stood in the corner of the mirror with his hands on his hips, like a proud spectator. I sent it directly to Vadika. I waited with bated breath for her assurance that I didn't look completely ridiculous.

Or that I absolutely did.

Either or.

After a few minutes however, she didn't respond.

Well, at least I'd see Gertie's reaction once I made my way downstairs. My cheeks started to hurt, flushed from all the withheld smiles.

"I thought you'd look good in my old jersey," Ryan proclaimed with a swift nod. "And I was right. You do look good in my jersey."

"You mean, branded like a cow?" I teased, turning around to face him fully.

He shrugged, reaching out for me before he was close. He wrapped his arms around my waist. I could almost imagine us swaying, dancing. "If you'd like. Now, you really look like those other girls you used to glare at all season on campus."

I put my forehead down to his chest, and I muttered, "I did not glare at them."

"You did. For a while, I thought you were glaring at me."

"I *was* glaring at you."

He snorted.

"Seriously"—I looked back at the green and purple color

combination—"I look like a strange, unripened grape. Or an eggplant." I was sort of hoping it was the former now that I thought about it, however.

Peering at my face again, nervously, as if he were afraid I'd jump through the window in an attempt to escape, Ryan placed a small kiss on my forehead. The kiss sent sensations all the way down to my toes. I stared at him quietly as he pulled back, hands sliding down my elbows to my wrists to my hands.

Little hesitance hindered Ryan's physical touches anymore.

How far we'd come in such a short time. The understanding of how quickly things moved forward, like most things since arriving at college, dug deep into my stomach.

How long could this last?

"You look tired."

"I am tired."

The past few days felt like something out of a dream, a life I hadn't realized I could be a part of. Other thoughts kept bothering me, nagging at the corner of my mind.

Leaning forward, Ryan placed another short kiss against my lips. I leaned back in. The soft, warm feeling dragged on as our lips parted over one another's before finally sliding away once more.

We stared at each other for a long moment. His bright eyes and crooked smile were really hard to look away from.

Blinking a few times out of his own trance, Ryan tugged at the hem of my jersey, making it look like even more of a dress I'd need to fix. Reaching for a tie, I carefully looped it around the bottom and tucked it under. The jersey looked slightly better. Less T-shirt dress and more oversized sweater.

"There." He smiled, noting I was careful not to hide the number nine emblazoned on the front. "Perfect. Now, you are Barnett homecoming ready."

Those were a few words I'd never thought would apply to me. Those were three of them.

Barnett. Homecoming. Ready.

* * *

Gertie put three fingers to her mouth, but they did nothing to hide her smile when she caught us sneaking out the front door. "You two have fun!" she called out.

Ryan waved and assured her that we would. He kept assuring me all the way up to campus, where it was more difficult than usual to find a parking spot. Cars with BU bumper stickers lined the narrow streets and admissions parking lot.

"I've never seen Barnett as such a popular destination," I mused.

"Only on homecoming," Ryan agreed, still looking just as thrilled as he tried to back into a space for the second time.

I was still looking at all the green and gold streamers that were tangled and taped anywhere they could be by the time Ryan ran around the car and opened my door for me, as I was too frozen to do so. Perhaps for good reason when I stepped out and could already hear the noise emanating around us.

Music pulsed through the air, getting louder as we walked toward Barnett University's stadium.

"What is that?"

"Spirit," said Ryan. He laughed at the lack of amusement on my face at his reverent tone. "Trust me."

"I'm here, aren't I?"

"You're going to love it."

Now, I wouldn't say that, but I'd give it a chance. Cars were parked in the back, along with tables set up for games and food being passed out. Everyone had a drink in their hands—from the students to the others who had returned to campus to relive their youth, who, I could only believe, owned the cars with BU alum plastered on the rear. All of them were dressed in different shades of green, as if they were preparing to make a run for it into the woods nearby and see who would blend in the best.

"Hey, Ryan!" someone yelled, running directly up to us. "You finally got here. For a while, I thought you weren't going to make it."

Ryan grinned, looking down at the can of beer that was pressed into his hand. He tipped it to the side in thanks but made no move to drink from it. "How long have you guys been here?"

"We have to get moving soon. Coach wants us ready for the game early so that we won't be a mess like last year."

Ryan snorted, as if recalling the distant memory.

"So we had to start the tailgate early."

Laughing, Ryan nodded. He noticed the rest of his old team, appearing just as enthused as the guy I had seen before, sitting in the sports house.

"Trevor, right?"

He gave a small smile, flashing his teeth. "That's me. You're Lu."

"That's me."

"Well, come on." Trevor wrapped an arm around Ryan, pulling him farther into the condensed group of people. "For a little while, we weren't sure if you were going to show. The team misses you, whether you think so or not."

Ryan cast a glance over his shoulder before his hand snuck out, grasping onto mine so that he knew that I was following behind. Immediately, as we approached the group of people, some sitting on the tailgate of a truck, they got up to greet Ryan. It truly was almost a homecoming as they asked him where he'd been and if he needed a drink. A few of them glanced toward me as Ryan held on to my hand still, making sure that I didn't get lost in the collision of people.

With a hand squeeze, I let go of his hand as he was pulled farther along into the group.

You okay? I saw his mouth move.

I nodded. *Go.*

Along with the mass of broad football players with streaks of paint over their cheeks, other girls stood, also looking at me up and down as I stood on the edge. Practice jerseys were knotted high under their boobs, much like mine. Their stomachs, however, were painted in different letters to spell out their cheer when they stood—hopefully—in the right order.

"I like your dress idea." One girl with braids over her shoulders approached me after about a minute of me looking around.

It was a scene of organized chaos. Even the school administrators looked to be taking part in a few parking spots over.

The girl was short, yet she didn't let that stop her eyes from scanning down at the way the skirt draped over my legs. "It's really cute."

"Thanks." I looked for anything on her expression that wasn't sincere. I found nothing. "I like your face paint."

She lifted a hand, careful not to touch the gold lines that looked more like petals coming from the outer corners of her eyes. "Thanks! You've never been to the homecoming game before, huh?"

"I think I've been to as many games as I can count on my one hand alone."

She laughed. "Don't worry. As long as it doesn't get too hot out and you don't end up sweating for most of the day, it's fun. Just relax. Most of the girls are nice if you want to sit with us while the game is happening."

"Oh," I said with a small shake of my head. I looked over to where Ryan was talking with his teammates. "I'll be with Ryan, but we can sit near you guys if he'd like."

"He wasn't cleared to play yet?"

"He's doing his physical therapy." I paused. "But I don't think he's coming back."

The more people who kept asking, insinuating otherwise,

made me question it. I cocked my head toward Ryan again. He fit in well with the other guys, loud and charming.

I could see why everyone looked at us so strangely.

I was also starting to see why I was so obviously falling for him hard, so sudden and easy after so long of building up a wall, brick by brick, from the first time he'd noticed me. All that hard work. It had ended up being so flimsy.

"I heard that might be the case." She sighed with emotion as she, too, turned to look at Ryan. "A shame since it's senior year."

I took a deep breath. "Yeah."

It must've been a bigger disappointment than I'd imagined.

"It was really a hit," she admitted.

I had been there that day when Ryan got hit. Vadika had wanted to go to the first game of the year. Ryan had been slammed to the ground, his leg flexed as he tried to stand back up. Coaches had rushed out to stop him before he could do any more damage.

"I don't blame him. He looks like he's doing decent now."

"He's been doing well, I think."

"I didn't even know that he had a girlfriend. I'm not sure if I've seen you around before."

Another girl, tall and with a high blonde ponytail, came up beside the petite one. "She's the one Lauren was talking about," she murmured.

"Oh." The first one's nose crinkled. "Really?"

"All good things, I hope?" I asked, as if I were overhearing a different conversation.

The blonde tilted her head to the side, as if she didn't put much stock in whatever it was that she heard. "Eh, I wouldn't worry about it much."

"Let me guess." I tried to sound casual. "I'm a devil-worshiping slut who stole her boyfriend."

The one who had first approached me nodded, as if she was

shocked at how closely I had been to Lauren's exact words. She wasn't very creative. "Just about."

"We all knew they weren't dating or anything really. Not like you two are, obviously."

"Oh, we aren't …" I paused, trying to figure out what I was about to say.

In the past week and a half, Ryan and I might not have gone out on dates, but we had been spending nearly all of our free time around classes and in the evenings together to get ready for Samhain. He'd been crashing at Gertie's with me, often in my bed or on the sunporch with me, where we kissed and touched and breathed so easy that it felt like I never had been able to take a full breath before.

But we weren't dating. We were just … Ryan and Lu, I guessed.

My meaning must've gotten across.

"Really?"

"We're …" I let the conversation trickle off again, still unsure of exactly what I was trying to convey.

The blonde again raised her eyebrows. "Right."

Right. My lips pulled to one side in something like a confused cringe.

In the moment of silence, Ryan made his way over. The two girls in front of me smiled before I noticed him at my side. "How are we doing?"

"How are you doing?" one asked.

Ryan looked down at me. "Good so far."

The girl—I hadn't caught her name—smiled as she swayed back into the rest of the thick crowd, toward the people she had left.

The other taller blonde also looked between us with a shake of her head, as if I were clearly blind from the last part of our conversation. "See ya."

"See you," I agreed.

Ryan looked between me and the retreating girls, who had turned out to be more pleasant than expected. "Look at you, making friends."

"You bring it out in me."

He looked more than pleased by the compliment. "Come on. You're hungry, right?"

19

"You all right?" Ryan asked.

"Mmhmm."

"You seem quiet."

"You know you can still go and hang out with them, right?" I said. "It's your homecoming day. I don't want to hold you back."

Ryan scrunched his nose. "Stop. I want to hang out with you. Honestly, it's nice to see everything from the outside, and they'll be going in to get ready for the game soon. And that's not something I want to think about."

"Sad?"

He shrugged. "Is it bad if I say a little?"

"No, it's honest."

"And I'm allowed to feel how I feel." He repeated the words I'd once told him about not needing to downgrade his grief over leaving the game and his team so suddenly. Just because it was the right thing for him to do didn't mean it always felt that way.

"Now you're getting it," I said.

The parade of the small yet enthusiastic band traveled down the greenway as we sat on a bench. We watched as the plumed hats headed through town, where people were lined up along the sidewalk.

How had I missed all these festivities in the past three years? No matter if I didn't attend, but to not have heard any of this from either being tucked away in my room or down a few blocks in town, hunkered over a flower bed in the back of Gertie's house, seemed like an impossibility.

Or perhaps, at the time, I just hadn't cared.

"How are you liking it all so far?"

"I'm liking that they have a food truck specifically dedicated to french fries." I took another off the top of the paper basket, dipping it in one of the four sauces we had gotten since neither of us could decide which would be best.

They were all delicious.

"I'm still a little peeved the dean thought this counted as just as good as my Samhain celebration."

"You're right. That's going to be much different."

My eyes widened at his tease. "It is!"

He took stock of our surroundings. "Yep. There won't be snacks or music or people having a good time at all."

I shook my head. Now, he was just goading me.

Ryan dipped in one cup and then the other, mixing the two.

"Now, that's just disgusting." I pointed a fry at him.

"Deliciously disgusting," he proclaimed. "Go on. Give it a try."

"No."

"Come on."

Sighing, I dipped my glorious length of potato into two sauces before taking a bite. I let my head loll side to side. "It's not awful."

"See? Look what life has to offer. We are opening each other up to a world unknown."

I really didn't think it was the same thing. Though I would admit, it was true that Ryan had a whole other talent for blending in with new, strange things. In the house by the river, he thrived. Looking around at all the other students and parents, however, I still didn't feel like I quite belonged here. I spent so long actively trying not to after my freshman year, at peace with the fact I was destined to be a social pariah until Ryan came along.

"I still hate football."

"That's a lie," Ryan said, shocked.

"You're right. I like football for one reason."

"Me?" He put a hand to his chest.

"You got it, Ry-Ry."

"Aw, stop it." He waved me off. "You're making a man blush."

"Aren't you two such a cute couple?" a woman fishing through her bag beside us commented. Tucking her fluffy, light curls into the clip she'd finally found, she placed a hand over her heart. "How long ago did you two meet? Was it here on campus?"

"Oh, we're ..." Something? I waved my hand between the two of us, as if it would come to me.

Friends? No. Associates? Gods, no.

"Together," Ryan insisted easily before I could manage anything else. He casually looped an arm around my shoulders. "We met at first-year orientation. Love at first sight."

I glanced up at him, knowing that the surprise was clearly on my face. Like the rest of the girls attached to the team, I knew that we were something. Of course we were something—more than just something. Yet it still sent off sparklers in my chest at his certainty.

Together. Ryan Gardner and I were together. We must've looked like an odd couple.

Yet the overly enthusiastic woman clasped her hands with a tiny squeal.

Ryan chuckled at the sound.

"Adorable," she said, delighted as she continued to look around for someone else. "My husband and I met on campus too. Honey! Matt, get over here."

As we watched the woman steadily march over to where some of the older men were all gathered around, much like Ryan and the team had been, I wondered what they had been like back so many years ago. I always questioned what the town of Barnett had been like through the years, but for some reason, my curiosity never fully extended to the university. It always felt like a piece of the town—and not my piece.

Not until right now.

"Now, what was that look for a minute ago?" asked Ryan.

I knew what he was talking about.

"*Together*," I repeated quietly, just between us, as he weighed my expression. "Sounds so very ... tangled. Permanent."

"You seem shocked."

"I just don't want you to regret it."

"Why would I ever regret you?" He stared at me like I had breached a whole new level of crazy. "This might sound a little weirdly macho possessive and all, but you're mine."

His. Any other time, I might've rolled my eyes, but the phrase was ultimately right. It might have been one of the best things I had ever heard. I almost had to look away, but I didn't.

"You might not think people look at you like I do, but they do, and I'm the one who gets to call you my girlfriend because I want to."

"You do."

He tilted his head down until our faces were almost touching, noses brushing. "You've become my favorite person, Lu. So, yeah, I have a magical, stunning girlfriend, and I get to kiss her and tell the world about it since I never got to do that before in my entire life. Okay?"

"Okay."

"Good. Because I have pretty big feelings for you."

"So you've said." And I wanted to say it too even though the casual idea of letting those sorts of words loose made my legs feel like jelly.

"And I get to keep saying it."

I wanted him to.

"Here he is." The woman came back. This time, her husband, broad and a little burly in comparison to her, was in tow. "Matthew, I was just talking to these two. Aren't they adorable? Reminded me of us."

"I'm Matthew now?"

She rolled her eyes. "Matt."

"Nice to meet you two," said Matt.

Ryan extended his hand immediately, shaking Matt's. "Ryan."

Before I needed to offer my own palm, I answered as well. There was something about shaking hands that always sent off a string of nerves—a feeling I'd been having a lot more recently, especially when I needed to be tall and confident when standing next to Ryan. "I'm Lu."

"Ryan and Lu," Matt repeated, as if committing our names to memory. "How did you happen to win over Hannah?"

Ryan thought it over. "Turns out, we are adorable."

Matt glanced at his wife out of the corner of his eye. "Of course you are."

"Forgive me if I'm a little hormonal," Hannah said with a roll of her eyes. It was then I noticed her hand gently reaching up to settle on the tiny curve of her stomach.

"Weren't you on the team? I feel like I've seen you before." The man eyed my green jersey.

Ryan opened his mouth before seeming to rethink whatever it was he was going to say. "I was on for the past few years, yeah."

"Position?"

"Running back."

"Fantastic. I was on the team for a bit."

"For one year, Matt," Hannah said. "For one game."

"Yeah, I wasn't very good," Matt conceded. "But it was fun, being part of the team anyway. You aren't playing today?"

"How could you tell? By how calm and at ease I am?" Ryan asked, attempting to joke.

After another moment, the woman offered a small laugh, leaning into his humor.

"I've been getting over an injury from the first game actually."

"Ah." Matt nodded in understanding. "But you're going to make it out there before the senior game soon enough, right?"

"Well…" Ryan lifted a hand to the side of his neck.

"Leave the boy alone, Matt. You don't know what is going on," his wife intervened.

"I could go back and play again," admitted Ryan. However, he went on. "But after a few hits to my knee—"

I cut him off with a smile. He didn't need to make any excuses. He didn't owe these people. "He's going to need his leg to travel before settling down to teach our youngsters."

"Is that right?" Matt's eyes widened with a nod. "Good for you."

"Thanks." Ryan nodded along with the man, seeing this reason was now perfectly acceptable for all.

"We were class of … a little more than a decade ago. These days, I'm working in business."

"And you?" I asked Hannah.

"I was in marketing. Copywriting really," Hannah said, looking up at Matt. "We met in class, though I find the actual work terribly boring now. Figured I would try being a mom for a bit."

"So, you two are graduating. You're going to be a teacher," Matt pointed at Ryan before looking at me. "What are you studying?"

Ryan laughed before I had to piece together an answer, as if he knew I needed time. "She's taken basically the whole course catalog at this point. All she needs to do is declare."

"I didn't know they let you do that so late."

"I guess since the credits are already taken, it's just a matter of paperwork," I offered.

Hannah nodded sympathetically.

"If you ever lean toward the business end of things, you let me know. I have a card here somewhere." Matt patted his pockets before handing over the small card. "There you are."

"We're also in the school directory, I think," reminded Hannah.

Matt dipped his chin in agreement. "That too."

"Thank you."

"Well, we'll leave you two alone for now. I have one more person I want to see before we take our seats for the main event."

"Have fun," said Ryan.

"Well, one of us is going to have more fun than the other," she said, running a hand over her *Future BU Alum* bump once more. "Have a good rest of your homecoming, you two!"

They walked back toward the people they had wandered away from.

Waving goodbye, I twisted back to Ryan in disbelief.

"Were you really about to say you would go back out there and play the game today for those people you don't even know just like that?"

Ryan, the people pleaser.

With a roll of my eyes, I lifted myself up on my toes so that I could ruffle his hair. He let it happen.

"You really are a mess."

"They didn't have to know whether or not I was being honest."

"You're a terrible liar."

"You think?"

To be honest, I wasn't sure. "I figure."

He huffed a laugh as we started to walk back closer to the small stadium. "You think that'll be us?"

"What?"

"Matt and Hannah. Do you think that will be us one day?" he asked, clarifying.

"Attending the BU homecoming game?"

Ryan stared at me with a small shrug. He didn't correct me because, immediately, I knew what he was thinking. Ryan and me at the BU homecoming football game, teasing and holding each other without notice. In love. Me, I could see it as well, standing next to him, pregnant and pleased with ourselves.

I never thought about babies much before. The idea always felt so far away. Ryan, on the other hand, from the look in his eyes, he thought about them, and it was easy to see why. Ryan would be a good dad, patient and smiling.

I snorted. "Head in the clouds?"

"Only a little." Looking up, Ryan grinned with his arm around my shoulders.

"Well, you'd definitely be Hannah."

"Seriously?"

I scrunched my face. "The sweet ramblings."

"My ramblings are sweet?" he asked. "You know, that makes you Matt."

"I'll take it." I chuckled.

"Having fun yet?"

"Oddly enough."

My answer appeared to have been the right thing to say as he tugged me along farther into the crowd, heading inside the stadium, but not toward the stands. "I want to do one more thing before the game starts. You showed me some of your world. Now, it's my turn."

"Your turn?"

He meant that the whole terrible cookout in the parking lot wasn't already a part of that? I asked him as such.

He nodded, pulling me down toward the field instead of the bleachers. On the grass, parents and young children were learning how to throw and catch the ball with other players.

Understanding bloomed the moment he let go of my hand, rushing in his strange jog toward a lone football no one else was using.

"You can't be serious."

"It'll be fun," he promised. "Isn't that what you said you were going to be today? Fun Lu-Lu."

"Please stop calling me that."

"Why?" he asked. "It's so fun to see your face blush when I do."

"I do not blush."

"All right," he said, obviously saying so just to appease me.

"I don't."

"I said you didn't," he conceded, though he was a little liar.

I could feel how hot my face had gotten, and it wasn't just because of what was likely the final day of the warm sun beating down on us.

"Anyway, I have to practice if I'm going to be teaching the youngsters how to throw a ball next year, as you said."

I was eating my words. "And I'm your practice run?"

"No one better."

"No one less coordinated."

* * *

"To be honest, I really thought you'd be slightly better than this," said Ryan.

"I don't have superpowers."

He laughed as I picked the ball back up and practically rolled it to him. "You never know."

"Just throw it again," I grumbled.

"You got it this time," Ryan encouraged, one hand gripping the football. "I'll be gentle."

I narrowed my eyes at him but lifted my hands. "Well, let's go."

"Ready?"

"Ready."

"Are you sure?"

"I said I was ready," I insisted.

I was going to catch this stupid thing at least once. I had no luck thus far, and I was pretty sure time was running out before the actual game started and the people filing into seats didn't have to watch my incompetence at the American game.

Watching the ball, I reached up, barely able to catch the lobbed ball as Ryan hurled the object toward my chest. It flopped between my hands, bouncing between my palms before I grabbed it. I was holding the football.

"I got it!" I might've screamed.

"Now, run! Run, Luella!" he called as the others with much smaller and less enthusiastic children stared.

Still, I didn't pause. I had the ball. I had done it!

I turned toward the other goal behind me, sprinting as quickly as I could in my boots that sank into the patches of dirt before I finally crossed the line for a touchdown. Turning back, I extended my hands to either side as Ryan carefully jogged toward me, favoring that one side, though he didn't seem to be in any pain.

He didn't stop as he got closer, lifting me off the ground and throwing me around in a circle as he continued to cheer, as if I had done more than run a few yards against no one.

"Woo-hoo! Look at you. Maybe Barnett will make you the new running back for the team."

"Doubtful."

I couldn't stop the laughter that rolled off my tongue as I let the football fall behind his back and onto the ground. It bounced once before rolling away. Carefully, after another moment, he set me down. My arms still looped around his neck. A light bead of sweat spilled on his forehead from where his hair stuck up.

I wiped it away as I glanced down at his lips again. What would he do if I kissed him again right now, right in front of everyone? His lips were right there, perfectly parted.

"Attention, students, faculty, and visitors. Please find your way off the field and into your seats as we reset for the game in fifteen minutes," the announcer called overhead.

"Well …" Ryan pecked my lips quickly, sweetly, for a long, lingering second before he let one hand go from around my middle. He smiled at my gobsmacked expression, mighty pleased with himself. "Better find our seats for the main event. Shall we?"

* * *

"Finally! I found you guys," Vadika called out as she moved through the crowded row of other students in the stands. Glancing down at her wrist, she checked her watch, as if she'd truly been on the search for hours.

I scooted over, giving her some room on the seat next to me. "Where have you been?"

"A little bit of everywhere. I was running late," she admitted without any more details.

Vadika running behind schedule rarely ever happened. With how she'd talked about it before, I'd thought that she would be here earlier, taking part in all the tailgating and schmoozing alumni connections.

"I have approximately three hours before I need to be changed and ready for my graduate presentation in the SUB," said Vadika.

"That's tonight?"

"That's tonight," she confirmed. "Don't worry about it. I nearly forgot too."

She'd nearly forgotten about her capstone thesis project that she'd been working on nonstop for the past two years?

I raised an eyebrow. "Who are you, and what have you done with Vadika?"

She only laughed.

"You're seriously risking that?"

"It's all done. It's been done. I finished the final touches on my poster board a few nights ago and have my clothes in my car. Do you mind if I change in your room later?"

"Of course not." I narrowed my eyes at her, still a little confused. "Seriously, where have you been?"

Not hearing me or maybe not wanting to, Vadika looked out across the field, where the band was starting to play, echoing.

"So, how are you liking your homecoming adventure?" Vadika nudged me.

Ryan leaned around my shoulder. "Lu caught a football."

Vadika's eyes widened, incredulous. "She did not."

"She totally did."

"Look at you, getting all collegiate. I'm so proud. Oh! Here they come out on the field!" Vadika screamed as the rest of the stadium clapped and listened to the music pounding over the speakers.

Ryan cheered as his teammates took the ball, raising his hands into the air. I pressed my lips together as I smiled and shook my head at the sight. He screamed out bad calls and clapped his hands together until it created a rumble and then a wave through the stands.

Perhaps Ryan had missed his calling as a professional cheerleader. A few others turned their heads—from the players waving at him to other spectators. All of it only made me laugh until my cheeks hurt. We both stood out in a crowd. Perhaps for different reasons, but all in all, the two of us were weirdos in our own right. I liked it.

I might be his after all.

But, stars, if that was the case, it turned out, he was going to be mine too.

20

The only parties I had ever been to were university-approved events in one of the campus buildings or the few in cramped college houses Vadika and I showed up to for approximately ten minutes before we got claustrophobic and sweaty, prompting a hasty retreat.

The post-homecoming party was not either of those kinds of parties.

For one thing, it looked like everyone was having a good time. Whether it be from the fact that some had pregamed all day or the fact that some alumni from the sports house had shown up, gifting better booze and a more confident air to the likelihood that the party wouldn't be shut down. No one, after all, wanted to upset the people whose donations kept a close-knit university like Barnett running.

I couldn't believe this was me. This was my life.

The feeling was one that I'd only ever had once before—right after I finally felt at peace in Barnett. I found my place in school and, most of all, in my coven. I had a strange sort of family after so long of feeling like that, too, was being slowly stripped away from me. Now, I felt it more than ever. The shock, the awe.

The joy.

Ryan was right there with me because he was kissing me in a hot, crowded room, and I didn't care who saw. I felt alive. My insides were sparking like they were on fire, and I was ready to explode with delight and something even deeper dripping down my insides to the bottom of my center. Pulling away, I licked my lips to taste him.

Over the deep bass of the music, I could hear Ryan groan.

I kissed him once more, letting myself delve into the heady moment with the thick, gyrating motion of everyone around us.

Was this what life was supposed to be like? Was this what was waiting for me all along with a bright and glorious feeling that spread through me, just like Ryan's smiles? My better next?

If so, it was stunning and brilliant.

Maybe Vadika was right in her determination for so long to take in the entire college experience, though I never would tell her that. There were nice moments, whether or not they lasted long. For now, I wanted this one to linger for a very long time as I held on to the hem of Ryan's soft T-shirt, keeping him only a breath away.

"Even your kisses taste like magic."

I peered at him as he slowly swiped his thumbs back and forth over my cheeks. "And what does magic taste like?"

"Sugary sweet."

I giggled. "Are you sure that's not just your imagination?" Or one too many drinks?

"No," he whispered, leaning back in. "Definitely you."

I hummed into him.

"I love you."

I pulled back a few inches to make sure it was him who had said those words. "What?"

He shrugged, as if it was the simplest thing. A weight off his shoulders. "I think I love you, Luella Pierce."

"You think?"

"I know." He laughed.

"You love me," I whispered, staring at him.

Ryan ... loved me. Emotion surged through me as I looked at him, pushing me to want to slam my body back into his and kiss him or ... run away.

I licked my lips, trying not to laugh. "Really?"

"I love you," the boys had said as they dipped their hands below my shirt. *"You're so free."*

"You're not like the other girls. I love that."

"I love you so much, Luella. So much," I heard my mother say in the very back of my mind, covering the rest of the taunts and teases, a voice tangled in my memory that sounded so close to Ryan's confession.

True and honest.

"Do you want me to say it again?" Ryan asked a little louder over the rest of the voices and music as I came back to myself, obviously not averse to the idea. "I'll scream it if I have to."

I swallowed. "Maybe."

"I love you. A piece of love, all of my love." Ryan said, smiling at the strange phrase. "Whatever kind of love or magic you call this sort of feeling I have for you, it's yours."

He loved me.

Maybe he didn't know yet, however little or however much, but he was right; it felt like magic all the same. Powerful and extraordinary.

I finally gave in and kissed him again. "Ryan, I—"

Over his shoulder, I noticed Vadika waving at me frantically. She tapped her wrist.

Her presentation. The reminder flooded back through me as I turned my shocked expression to Ryan.

Until I pulled back. "Wait."

"Wait?"

"I have to go let Vadika into my dorm to get changed."

"You do?"

"Yeah, remember?" I asked, laughing. "I'll be right back."

"Right now?" he yelled over the music.

Luckily, there was no anger in his expression at me running out on him like this. If anything, it was pure humor.

Especially as Vadika looped around, tugging on my one arm. "Sorry to steal your girl, Gardner. I have to go!"

"Bring her back."

"I'll be right back," I assured him with a grin, pulling on his hand to let me go as I leaned back toward the path toward my dormitory.

"Promise?" He grinned at my renewed excitement as I looked at him.

"Right back," I said again. "Promise."

* * *

RYAN LET ME GO, the force giving me another bit of speed as I headed back toward my room with Vadika close at my side. We passed the library. Its fluorescent lights were still dimly lit, someone inside staying later than the librarians. People were scattered all over the place. They chatted as they perched on the edge of the curb outside as well as in the stairwell as we raced up the flight of stairs.

Vadika ran through her presentation she'd be giving in a room with a half dozen others—possibly scholarship granters and graduate school department heads. Her voice remained cool and confident, even while out of breath.

"This is definitely one college experience you can check off your list," I said, giving her a smile.

She smiled, reaching out to squeeze my hand. Her eyes were a little sad, but knowing at my pleasure. "Might be one of our best yet."

"You know you can tell me anything, right?"

"Of course."

"I'm saying that because I know you have been busy and I know that I have been busy."

"Have you?" she teased.

If I could tell any better, I'd say she knew exactly what I was talking about and was deflecting.

"Don't joke. I'm trying to be honest here. Ever since you came back from the wedding a few weeks ago, I know that something happened. I'm trying to ask you."

I stopped talking as we turned the corner.

I paused as I stared down the hallway toward my room. The door was already unlocked. The passage open. Voices teemed with volume inside. More than ever before.

"Should I …" Vadika paused for a second before taking a step away in the other direction from whatever was happening.

I waved her on toward the other bathroom.

"It's fine. Go get changed and get ready." I forced an easygoing smile I wasn't feeling. "Make sure you don't forget to take off the face paint."

"Maybe they like a little school spirit."

"Big risk."

"Could be an even bigger payoff," she joked, turning down the hall with hasty steps, catching her one heel as it almost fell off the top of her professional clothing pile. "We can talk later. After my presentation, if you're around."

Making sure she saw that I would be, I took a deep breath. My heart hammered in my chest. I knew, somehow, what waited for me beyond the threshold of my dorm room, yet I walked inside anyway.

Still, I was unprepared. All of my Samhain plans, detailing where things would be set up on the greenway, and Ryan's perfectly comprehensive checklists of our decorations were yanked from where they had been organized on my desk. Decorations were torn apart. Pieces scattered all over the carpet. Candles were toppled. The glass windows of the lanterns I'd planned on lining the path with were cracked and shattered. Everything I'd kept safe here in my closet or under my bed, where it wouldn't be in the way, it was all there. Ruined.

My mouth hung as I took in the view, turning my head to meet Natalie's eyes that went back and forth between the mess and me.

She stood in the doorway, her arms crossed over one another. Next to her was the friend who had stopped me the other day, as well as our RA and an administrator. I remembered her from student housing the first time Natalie and I had gone to see if there were any other single rooms available at the start of the year. Her eyes scanned the room before they finally landed right back on me.

Lauren raised her eyebrows, cocking her head to the side.

The world paused. Gone was the thrill and delight I'd had, rushing around campus from the party with Ryan. It turned into thick guilt that coated the inside of my throat and dripped toward my stomach, sinking.

"What is going on?" I asked. I stepped into the room, shrugging beside Lauren to the RA, who was glancing around.

Lauren nudged Natalie, sending her into stuttered-out syllables.

Finally, Lauren, Natalie's good friend, took over for her. "Natalie told you to stop bringing all your weird stuff into your room. Did you know that things like your candles and some of your decorations are forbidden? Not to mention the essential oils or your salt lamp, which could easily cause an allergic reaction to other residents. These aren't allowed, are they?"

The RA looked as much at a loss for words as Natalie.

It wasn't the two of them—I knew that. But the fact that they even entertained this, that this was going on at all when everyone else was out, living life and participating in homecoming, like I had been for the first time felt like a knife, slowly sliding into my gut.

I clenched my teeth tight.

There was nothing I could say, and a dark laugh was starting to bubble up in my chest, if only so that the wave of emotion going through me wouldn't pulse behind my eyes. That would be even worse.

With a deep breath, the woman from housing gave a short nod. "I understand that this might not be expected, especially not today, Ms. Pierce, yes?"

I gave a sharp nod.

"Unfortunately, you have violated the housing code that you signed at the start of the year. It did state that items like the candles are prohibited, as they could, as Lauren mentioned, pose a hazard in such an old building such as this one," she explained.

"I did not leave my things like this. These items were for an organized event on campus."

Blinking, the housing woman paused, as if she hadn't known this, looking at the others in the room. "Oh, I—"

"Either way, she isn't allowed to have these things. My friend's living situation has become inhabitable, both emotionally and physically," Lauren cut in.

"There have been complaints in the past between the two of you," the housing office woman said. "This is true. I'm here to let you know that you will have the next forty-eight hours to clean out your things. I will find you another placement, but there will be consequences put in effect due to the three strikes you already have from previous incidents with your roommate. If you have questions, please stop by my office on Monday."

Without further ado, the housing woman made her way out, her night obviously interrupted for no reason.

Lauren didn't wait long after the woman made it out the door along with our RA. "Too bad. Looks like your weird Halloween party that you and Ryan were trying to put on in the quad isn't going to happen. It can't, after all, with those consequences the woman from housing mentioned. They include participating in on-campus clubs and events—in case you didn't know. Sad, after everything that you did to try to make it happen."

She had no idea.

"How does it feel, Lu, to have everything fall down around you and no one care?"

Anger flared deep in my stomach, all the way up through my neck and into my face. "What is wrong with you?"

"I like to follow the rules." Lauren glanced away, looking at the walls. "I'm just doing exactly what everyone else expects me to do as a good BU student."

"Be a complete bitch?"

"At least I'm not a bitch witch who goes around pretending that they are someone they aren't. You've been sticking your nose into business and people who don't belong to you."

"People don't belong to anyone," I insisted.

"Maybe not. But rooms certainly do. And this one is owned by BU."

I closed my eyes, clenching my fists on either side. I couldn't stand to look at all the things I'd been storing for Samhain. They were ruined. My housing in the old yet strangely homey building, tucked into the trees, no longer felt like a sanctuary. I could, on the other hand, look at Natalie, who had been oddly quiet this entire time. "And what about you?"

"Natalie doesn't have to say a word to you."

"I'm not talking to you." I put up a hand as if that could block Lauren out. "Natalie."

She lifted her head, her own eyes glassy from whatever had gone down here now that I was in front of her.

"I thought we were starting to be friends," I whispered.

"Us?" she asked, genuinely confused and a little unsure.

"Yes." When she didn't answer, I shook my head. Why did I ever assume anything anymore? Suddenly, nothing was right at all. "But I guess that was just another disappointment for a little bitch witch who doesn't deserve much in this life, huh?"

"Lu …" She trailed off.

"Let the RA or whoever it is, know they'll have one less person to worry about soon. I'll be living off campus."

"Where else will you go?"

"To my real home. Where people actually give a shit about me and where I give a shit about me. What? Surprised that not everyone is a sad, narcissistic backstabber like you? Or just that I'm a person who has enough feelings to finally tell you how I and everyone else see you?"

"Lu, I—"

"No." I stopped her. "You don't have to say anything. Like your friend here said."

Her mouth opened, eyes changing as if she was about to apologize. I didn't want it though. I didn't want anything else but what had been taken away from me. It didn't matter—the party, the possibility of Natalie being a somewhat decent human being, kind enough to me, unlike so many others. I'd had just enough …

I had.

"You should probably leave if you are going to look at me like that," I suggested. "I'm really not in the mood to witness another one of your pity parties. You get your bed all alone now. Lie in it."

Smoothly, face unchanging from the sad shock, Natalie turned herself around from where she stood and strode back down the hallway. A few people behind us opened their doors, glancing toward the commotion we had caused.

But this was it, wasn't it?

Lauren stood there in a state of shock, it seemed, by my cold yet truthful words. Then, I followed Natalie out the door and back down the stairs onto campus.

21

My stomach was in my throat, and it was choking me. My eyes watered. The muscles in my back pinched as I tried to hold myself up straight and make my way toward the Row, where I'd last seen Ryan, who was still likely oblivious to what had happened. The roads felt quieter than they had a short time ago, and the only beacon other than the parties I began to stumble on was behind me at the center of campus, where Vadika must've sprinted to make her presentation on time without coming back to check on me.

I took a deep breath. Then, I took another until they came back out less shaky, exhaled on shards of glass.

Entering the house, I scanned the living room. Everyone looked like blobs, sounds carrying and blending together as I searched for one thing. One person.

"You okay?" someone asked me.

"Do you know where Ryan is?"

"Gardner? He's upstairs, I think."

I nodded, unable to thank him as I made my way up the steps. I didn't even care if there were potato-shaped mice in the walls or whatever was going on in the other rooms, where the doors were closed. I was crumbling.

It pained me to admit how much I needed Ryan. I needed his optimism. His ceaseless smile that made me think it was all going to be okay, if not completely all right. I needed his arms wrapped around me so that I wouldn't completely fall apart as I made it to the open doorway at the end of the hall.

A girl kicked her legs up on the worn chair in the corner. She sat directly on a guy's legs. For a moment, I wouldn't have maybe recognized him. I would've thought he was just another one of those guys on the football team who had huge enough egos to think that no one else was better than them.

But I saw him. I saw a girl sitting on Ryan's lap, smiling up at him. His own grin was bursting with slightly tipsy sunshine. He laughed like he did when someone made a good joke.

And I froze.

"Honestly, man, I didn't know you had it in you." The guy, still up among the five or so people and not otherwise sprawled around on the bed or floor, patted Ryan on the back with a forceful hand.

"What do you mean?" Ryan reached around to rub the back of his head. He squirmed underneath the girl in his lap, but he didn't ask her to move.

They looked good together.

They looked like they fit.

"I mean, getting with Lu Pierce. The weird girl you were always making fun of?"

"I didn't make fun of her."

"Whatever. I'm just saying, that's seriously a new level of commitment. I've always thought the weird ones were oddly good in bed though. Right? Or did she just give good enough head?"

Ryan shrugged, blinking rapidly as his jaw worked left and right. "I—"

"You might not be with the team every day anymore, but you're still a part of us here. You know, so you don't have to keep running around with those other people who have no fun. We're still your friends. At this rate, you'll be competing with the rest of us to hit a Barnett home run now that you got her out of your system. Lauren's been talking about you, too, you know. She's probably around here somewhere."

"Maybe."

Something stabbed me through the chest as well as the stomach.

"That's our Ryan. Took you long enough."

Took me long enough to see it. To see all of it as I glanced one more time toward him and the girl still in his lap. Everything screamed at how I didn't belong here, just like Lauren had. I was hollow as I took a step back, catching Ryan's eye as I headed back out the door.

As I turned, I heard his voice call out, but I was already halfway down the stairs. I couldn't be here right now.

I couldn't stand to be anywhere.

"Luella!"

I kept walking. No one seemed to notice me as I pushed through the crowd to the front door to get outside where the party was. I went right through them until I was in the front yard.

"Lu. Wait!" Ryan called again.

"Why?" I flung back around to face him. "Why should I wait, Ryan? So I can listen to you and everyone else talk about me like I'm some sort of joke again? So you can tell me that maybe we were wrong this whole time? I hope you came up with better punch lines this time around."

"What are you talking about?"

As if he didn't know or didn't understand. He was much smarter than he let on, and anyway, I'd heard him. They were talking about me like I was dirt, just like Natalie had. Just like those stupid people back home. I kept waiting to hear Ryan say something, anything at all. I was hoping he'd defend me. Instead, he just let it go. He'd shrugged like he hadn't held me like I meant something.

My face scrunched with emotion as I pressed my lips together.

"Lu …" He reached out a hand, staring at my distress. "What happened?"

"Samhain on campus is canceled."

"What do you mean?"

"I mean, I just went back to my dorm." I tried to calm down as I spoke, but I still wanted to scream. This didn't matter anymore. None of this mattered when Ryan shouldn't even be standing in front of me, so composed. "All the decorations and the plans—they're gone. Ruined. That bitch and my roommate made sure of that before they called housing on me."

"You're kidding."

"It's done."

It was all over. I should've known better than to put my energy into something that was never meant to happen. I kept doing it, even after I was told by Gertie and Celeste and the rest of them that I was only setting myself up for disappointment by avoiding the real things in life that I needed to figure out. But for one moment, I'd thought maybe this was all meant to happen.

The party.

Me and Ryan.

"But otherwise, nothing. Nothing happened. Nothing ever happened or should've happened or anything. How stupid was I to even try or think that something in my life so good was meant to be?"

"You don't mean that."

"I do. What was I thinking to consider the fact that I could be someone or try to make life a little more magical for myself?

Stupid Luella. Always the odd one who stands out too much," I told him.

"That's not true. Please tell me what else is going on," Ryan pleaded, reaching out to me.

I took a step back.

"You're not making sense. So what if some decorations are ruined? They can be fixed. We can still figure something out."

There was that optimism I had been looking for ten minutes ago. I felt the tears start to pool in my eyes, and I knew he saw them too. But I wouldn't cry. I was not going to cry in front of him.

So, instead, I sneered. I looked over each shoulder toward the nearly empty sidewalks. Still, I doubted that I was quiet enough that no one on the thick-columned porches of the nearby houses couldn't hear me. But so what? So be it.

It didn't change anything.

"That girl was sitting on your lap."

He had the decency to look ashamed. "I know. She just sat down, and then I felt weird, asking her to move. I should have. I know I should have."

"I'm not even mad about that."

"You're not?"

"A little. I'm just … I don't understand how you don't see it," I said.

"See what?"

"Luella, the witch. Luella, the stealer of souls. Luella, whose mother died. Luella, who should know she's always just been Luella, the nobody!" My voice rose. "I never cared about how anyone saw me before. But I know you do. And I saw how perfect you and that girl looked together."

"It doesn't matter how we looked together."

"But I care now, okay? I cared about how you saw me. And in the end, it looks like you didn't see much."

Not enough.

"Obviously you didn't care enough to think about how I would feel to come back here and see a pretty girl sitting on your lap. Obviously not to try and stop someone when they boast of how you're probably just using me," I pushed.

He needed to understand what I was trying to say.

Yet, right now, Ryan's face looked perhaps as distraught as mine.

I couldn't focus on it, not when I needed to stop the water that was flooding my vision. I couldn't cry. I didn't cry. Someone really needed to tell that to my body right now, which was prepared to revolt from the rest of the world spinning around me.

"And you should go with them and be happy with them, like you were before your injury. You should go back, and you should be with someone like her."

"I don't know why you are saying this," Ryan said, his voice still careful as we stood in the middle of the sidewalk. "I told you I love you. Does that mean nothing? Did you just expect that after that, I'd just get bored or feel like I'd met some goal and walk away?"

"I don't know."

"You do," he said seriously. "Those guys were stupid. I care about you, Luella. I care about you so much more than I ever thought I did after following you around for years. You know this. I know you know this."

I held my breath until it felt like a tightly wound spool of thread, fraying and coming loose. Twisting and turning for some sort of relief as I squinted tears back. I had too much hurt. I didn't want to hurt anymore.

"I don't know what you saw. I'm sorry if I'm not as strong and loud as everyone wishes and thinks I am. I'm working on it," said Ryan, a bit more edge entering his tone. "I'll always be working on making myself better, and I thought I was getting there with you. I'm sorry that I didn't stand up for you in there like I should've and made you question things like this. So, I'm going to ask you, why are you pushing me away?"

"You belong with them," I repeated.

I'd tried to belong here on campus. I'd tried to make something that I could be proud of—from Samhain and then Ryan—but it was becoming very clear that I was forcing myself into a place that obviously didn't want me.

"You belong here with your friends. With the girls who think it is okay to sit on your lap while people joke about me and others behind their backs. But I don't. That's not me. No matter how much each of us tries, I just don't think we'll ever quite fit. We'll never be exactly what we want each other to be."

"I want you, Lu." His voice cracked. "I'm sorry."

"It's all right," I said even though it wasn't. I wasn't. "I'm sorry too."

"Lu!"

I needed to go. I needed to leave before I broke down in the sobs lurching forward inside of my entire body.

"Maybe you just need some time. For so long, to keep the peace, you've always wanted whatever it was other people wanted. Maybe you need some time to figure that out too. I'm glad that I could make you see that, but Lauren was right. Maybe you don't know what exactly you want right now. But you will and …" There was no other way to put it.

I couldn't handle another person, another thing important to me being stripped away when there was nothing I could do to stop it. I just couldn't do it. If this was how I felt now after a silly party getting torn from me, how could I survive someone who would thrive without me leaving?

Because nothing was permanent. No one was.

"Since when would you ever listen to something she said?" Ryan was dumbstruck. "You need to stop this. I'm not going to let you do this just because you're upset. You're not being honest with me."

"I am."

"Then you're hurting me," he cried. Unlike me, maybe Ryan was the bravest out of the two of us after all because he let a tear drip down the side of his face and he didn't push it away.

Well, right now, I hurt me too.

So, I turned away.

22

What did I do? What did I just do?

I was possessed. I felt like I'd just decided to jump off a bridge without testing how cold the water was first, and now, my body shook with the terrible aftermath. Only now, in the aftermath, I had no broken bones and was unable to scream for help because I knew no one would come running.

I made my way back onto campus. I turned this way and that, unsure of what to do by the time I nearly collapsed onto my knees on the sidewalk outside of the SUB.

My head felt so full and confused and ruined.

I could still see how Ryan had looked at me, so full of hurt …

What have I done?

My throat shut, choking me. I closed a hand over it, as if that would help when I was sure the same palm had reached in and ripped my own heart out of my chest.

I forced myself not to cry. Not yet. I wasn't that far gone into whatever was going on yet. Whether or not everything was crashing down on top of me.

When I peeked inside the SUB meeting room, everyone was

dressed in shades of black, white, or navy blue. Scanning over faces drinking tiny bottles of water, I found Vadika gently smiling, sleek and fascinating, until her eyes caught on me.

"Can you hold on for just a moment?" she seemed to say to the older man, waving her hand as if she'd be just a second.

The clicks of her shoes echoed louder with each step, but there was nothing else. Not the voices inside the room. The clanging plates serving tiny hors d'oeuvres were cast aside from the flurry happening inside my head.

"What are you doing here?"

"Vadika, just for a minute, I need to talk," I said, trying to keep my voice calm.

"What are you doing here?" she repeated the question almost so sternly that I wasn't sure if I'd answered her audibly the first time.

Her eyes scanned down me, looking at me like I was insane as she pushed me into the empty hall. The door shut behind us.

I mean, I must've looked a little wild from my flushed face to the Barnett football jersey sliding off my shoulder. I stared down at the number nine for a long moment before turning my attention back to Vadika in her sleek black dress and cream blazer.

"How did your presentation go?" I found myself asking.

"It went fine. Lu, why are you here?"

"I, uh—"

"You need to go."

I paused, looking around. There weren't that many people left inside, and she had said the presentation went well.

"But you said you were done. And please, you know you've already been let into the school of your choice. You already knew that last year when they basically offered you more than I'll ever make my entire lifetime, just to go and continue the work you started here anyway. You don't need to worry."

"I'm not worried about that." Again, she looked me over, her eyes scanning so quickly that I almost didn't catch it.

I had been getting a lot of those looks lately. Brow furrowed, I just hadn't expected the same appraisal from Vadika.

No matter, because I had bigger things to worry about, so I ignored it. "I just need you for a minute or a few."

"I can't just—"

"Please. I know it's a lot, and I know we've been distracted, but I just need you for fifteen minutes, max. It's important. I need someone to tell me—" Tell me that I was being crazy and needed to screw my head back on because I was pretty sure I'd just ruined everything and I didn't know how to properly put anything back together.

Not when, for all my life, I was always surrounded by things falling apart.

"I still have to stay, Lu."

"But I need you. For once, I need you," I nearly begged.

Still, Vadika hesitated, looking back and forth from me to the door, leading back inside to her fancy alumni friends and people she didn't want me around.

"You need to go," she said once more, as if I wasn't already starting to understand her meaning.

Had I been blind to her as well all this time?

"Why?"

"Lu."

"I don't even understand you anymore."

"This means a lot to me, Lu," Vadika said, a crease forming on her forehead.

"No, it doesn't."

Not like this. She was already locked in. She had the graduate and PhD program in her pocket from the Ivy Leagues of the world. This wasn't about that.

"It does."

"You mean, those people in there?"

She didn't answer.

"Why?" I finally asked. "Because your parents want it to?"

Vadika jolted back a step, as if I'd physically pushed her. "No. Why would you say that?"

"You've always conceded to them."

"I have not."

"You've always done exactly what they asked of you, whether or not you wanted to. You chose your major because of what they wanted for you. You won't date like you want to because it isn't the certain type of person they want you with. You went to a school and are still close to home because they didn't want to let you go," I told her, one after another. "You've wanted to live this grand college life, and yet you keep just doing what everyone else wants, so they can step all over you. You don't even realize it. Your parents or aunts probably even arranged whatever it is between you and the guy you've been messaging and trying to keep all hush-hush."

Vadika's lips parted with hesitance. "I didn't tell you about him."

"You don't tell me a lot of things anymore because you're so scared of not fitting what everyone else wants for you," I said. "Your parents, your aunts, me, college boards. I hope you don't give it up to be some guy's housewife next."

Pressing her lips back together, Vadika nodded as she looked around the space. She gave small, distinct nods to each thing said. "Wow. I really didn't think you saw me that way."

Shutting my eyes, I replayed my words. I flinched, putting a hand up to the side of my face. That wasn't how I'd meant to say those things. "I don't."

"Obviously, you do. Good to know right before I leave and take on the biggest moments of my college career."

"What do you mean, leave?"

"I'm graduating early."

"In the winter?" I asked.

"My program wants me by the end of January," Vadika confirmed, barely looking at me.

"Why didn't you tell me this?" That was fantastic. I'd expected no less, and yet her words were cold. "So, what is going on here? Did you think I wouldn't find out? That you would just disappear on me and that would be okay? I'm asking you for five minutes here, Vadika. I've been by your side this whole time, and you've never once stood by mine."

She ignored that. Just like she ignored me most of the time and my problems and my little coven that meant the world to me, compared to her grand and sparkly life, all taken care of for her. I always let all the little things go.

But how long ago had she already let me go?

"Who would've thought that my best friend was also one of those people just walking all over me like a doormat, as you put it?"

"I didn't say that last part."

A fresh wave of hurt crossed Vadika's face anyway. "I want you to leave."

"Vadika."

"No. I might give in to what a lot of people want for me, but I don't want you here, Lu. I thought you were my friend and supported me."

"I do support you."

Or had she forgotten the hours of time I spent with her quietly so that she could work in the lab? Did she forget everything I did for her so that she could focus on what was important to her?

"If you did, you'd know that I love what I do. Here, in there"—she pointed back toward the room she'd left—"people think I'm astonishing. They think my work is groundbreaking and better than everyone else's, especially half these other students here in Barnett that can't even figure out what they want to do with their lives."

A Barnett student like me.

"So, now, you're saying, all this time, you've believed you are better than me?" I stammered.

"I'm telling you that I love the choices I've made even if I feel a bit trapped by them sometimes. At least I let myself make them."

"That's not fair."

"Neither are you," she snapped, looking around so that I wouldn't notice the glaze coating her dark eyes. "You're picking a fight when I'm clearly done with them. Where's Ryan, by the way? Did you finally scare him off, or can you still not make up your mind about if you're actually willing to like him?"

"If you had been around more this year—if you cared how much I've been your friend, no matter how busy you always are for me—you'd know that I did actually love him. I do. And I wanted to tell him."

But she was right. I'd pushed him away. He was gone.

Everything was my fault again because who better to blame in the end than me?

I shook my head at Vadika, realizing everything I'd said—everything she'd said. Tears began their descent down my cheeks, and there was no stopping them anymore.

"I'm sorry. I just … I need to go. Good luck in there." I heard my voice hiccup.

"Lu. Wait," I heard Vadika call out after me, but I was already halfway down the hall leading back outside, and she didn't speak up more than a whisper in case someone else might hear.

I needed to get out of this place. I needed to get away altogether.

* * *

I WONDERED what would happen if I just started to run without a plan.

What would happen if I closed my eyes and kept walking away from BU and the tiny town of Barnett? And went farther and farther and farther away until no one recognized me and I recognized no one and nothing.

Would I end up at the magical house of wayward women, like Gertie had told stories about? Could I look up to the stars and end up at that unknown location they took me to?

I wanted to be swept up by the night sky. I wanted to be taken away, never to return. I wanted to have a reason to keep going as tears caked down my cheeks, but my eyes remained turned down, watching as my feet took me to the single place I ever wanted to be.

Home. Home. I needed to go home.

I stood in front of the Victorian home alongside the river, trying to turn the stupid, slippery brass knob of the door that wouldn't open.

Nothing was working.

The door whipped open at my struggle, and I nearly sobbed in relief as my hands fell to my sides.

"Luella," Gertie exclaimed, shock and worry coating her voice. "What happened?"

"I just wanted to get away. I closed my eyes and wished that I would end up somewhere else, be anyone else, like that home you were taken away to when you had nothing left."

"You have so much left, Luella."

"I asked the universe to take me home."

Gertie inhaled with understanding as she wrapped her arms around me, leading me inside, where it was warm. "You're home now, Lu. You're home."

And yet I still couldn't help but feel empty.

23

I shut off my phone after I couldn't stand watching the fact that there was never an incoming call from Ryan. Maybe he'd fallen asleep from exhaustion. I had too.

I slept until eleven the first day.

Then, I did it again.

Usually, anytime past eight in the morning, and I felt as if I'd wasted the entire day. I'd had so much to do. I had things to plan and Vadika to see and deliver coffee to, if I didn't have any classes until noon.

Now, in the past week, I'd had none of that. My professors didn't seem at all concerned either if I showed up to classes or not after I sent them brief emails that I wasn't feeling well. Most of my work for the upcoming quarter had already been submitted, they said.

So, they didn't need me either.

I knew, eventually, I would have to make the walk back up to campus. I would have to go back into the room I hated more than ever, knowing that all the hard work, time, and energy I had exerted likely still laid in pieces over the ugly throw rug Natalie had bought. There was only so long I could wait before I cleaned the assigned space out, packing away the postcards Vadika had sent to me from her family trips to Europe and Asia, which lined the back edge of my desk, and folding the twin-size bedsheets that scratched my legs, unlike the ones at Gertie's, which I laid in and tried not to move, no matter how hard the sun streaming through the sheer curtains pushed me.

I knew I could only roll over so many times before I ended up on the floor. My legs tangled in sheets and the large shirt I'd finally changed into the last time I woke up to Gertie knocking on my door, promising that it wasn't all as bad as it seemed.

But it didn't matter if it was or it wasn't. It didn't matter if I felt guilty enough from ignoring Gertie then or when I'd sat silently next to her outside with my knees in the dirt in the vegetable garden as she prattled on about how fresh air was good for me.

Either way, everything that had happened so swiftly and so strong with the current of emotion the other night was all my fault. Or at least, partly.

It was my fault.

Leaving the decorations in my dorm room.

Trusting Natalie.

Trusting Vadika to see me as more than someone she needed to take pity on for so long apparently.

Even trusting Ryan, though I still wasn't sure how I felt about that. I knew that it wasn't just him at fault here. That was for sure.

I was a plain awful friend to the one person on campus who had ever cared about me and laughed with me and made me feel alive. Though there was still truth to my words. Still fairness to letting Ryan go, so he could flourish and be who he was meant to be without me getting in his way and messing things up any further for him.

My phone remained silent from when I had turned it off.

I squeezed my eyes shut.

If I wasn't ready to deal with returning for my salt lamp and clothes, I certainly wasn't ready to face that.

Another small knock clattered against my shut door. "Darling, you should be up by now."

"I know," I whispered, the words muffled as I huddled in my blankets.

"Are you getting up?" Gertie asked, her voice a little louder between the thin barrier.

With a huff, I pushed to a sitting position. Everything in the room was still the same as I'd left it. It was as it always had been since Ryan had begun to share the space with me over the past few weeks. Dirty clothes had been strewn over the colorful rug beneath my feet. My legs hung over the side of the bed as I tried not to look at it all.

"Yeah, I'm up."

"Good." I could nearly hear her gratification at the fact. "Someone's here for you."

Ryan?

Clutching the sheets to my chest, I tried to see if I could feel my heart still beating through the layers. It was. However faint and stilted, I breathed. In and out. For some reason, I hoped that, somehow, he'd show up eventually, yet I also didn't.

But a week had passed now, and there still was nothing.

Maybe once and for all, I wasn't worthy of forgiveness. It wasn't like without me, he or Vadika had nothing left on campus, like in my abysmal case. They had friends. They had lives and joy and love neither of them wanted to include me in.

And things had ended.

The self-pity was strong in the morning, sometimes stronger than late at night if I lie around long enough.

"Who?" I finally built the courage to ask.

"Get dressed. Or don't. That's up to you." Gertie didn't answer the question. "I'll be downstairs."

I pushed myself the rest of the way up. My legs, even with all their rest, still felt unsteady. Leaving the bed unmade, I stripped out of my oversize shirt, sliding on comfortable drawstring pants and a loose sweater.

When I had been outside with Gertie the other day, already, I had been shocked by how cold it was getting now that October was in full swing. Still, I didn't complain. At the time, I let the brisk chill seep into my bones until I was forced to retreat back inside. It had been nice in the moment to feel something other than the strange quality I hadn't felt for years now.

Grief.

Sniffing, I barely looked in the mirror before I headed down the stairs, listening for any voices. I noticed that no one stood by the front door. Sounds of dishes clattered down the hall with quiet murmurs.

Standing in the doorway of the kitchen, I looked at the four other people scattered inside, sitting at the tiny round table, cluttered with delicate teacups and spoons they stirred with.

Faith stood. Her chair screeched as she pushed it back. "Good, you're actually up. I wasn't sure."

"What are you all doing here?" I looked between Gertie, who said nothing, and the rest of the women.

Ana looked half-asleep herself, and Celeste pulled a batch of scones out of the oven, nudging the door closed with her hip.

A cup of tea was immediately pressed into my hands.

"We came to help," said Faith. "Or at least provide company. What else are sisters for?"

"We also have very boring lives and nothing else to do this weekend," added Ana.

I sat down, slouching in my chair.

"The house hasn't seen this much relationship action in just about forever," said Faith.

Ana agreed, thinking about her last relationship. "Truly forever."

Such a lie. I knew it as they prattled on, adding a teaspoon of sugar to my cup, swirling it around. Still, I didn't reply.

"So, what happened?" Ana finally asked.

Pursing her lips, Gertie shook her head. *Too soon*, she mouthed.

"No, it's fine," I said, my voice scratchy. Taking a sip of smooth tea, I felt the heat of it begin to warm my insides. "I was stupid to think that anyone would ever like me, and I ruined everything."

"Well, that just can't be true," Faith said immediately. "You don't ruin everything. You are like glue. And isn't your Samhain celebration coming up? I wanted to ask about flyers, if I could…" Her voice drifted off as she again noticed my eyes and the small shake of Gertie's head.

"I feel like I missed a lot," said Faith.

With a sigh, I swallowed another gulp of tea and tried to fill them in. It was harder than expected. I told them about how I was kicked out from housing and how I had seen Ryan with some other girl—which had Ana bristling—to me running off from him to Vadika, which I really didn't want to get into now as a fresh wave of misery overpowered me.

"This can be fixed," Faith said, sure. "It was just a time where you were caught up in the moment. Ryan knows you. He's called, right?"

"What do you mean?"

"Well, he showed up at the library the other day when I was there."

"He did?" *Was he looking for me?*

"I thought that maybe he was looking for you since he went upstairs and came back down quickly afterward into my office. He didn't look much better than you, and he told me what happened," she explained.

"Then, why did you ask?" I asked, looking around in case

anyone else in the room had already heard my stupid homecoming tragedy already.

But they, too, were focused on listening to what Faith had to say.

Faith shrugged. "I wanted to hear both sides. He told me that you seemed really upset and that you had been under a lot of stress lately—not to mention the whole roommate thing. I told him to give you a little space, but to give you a call. He did, right?"

I shook my head. "I turned it off."

Faith's well-meaning expression fell a bit.

Celeste hummed at the situation from where she stood against the kitchen counter, listening in. "It's probably best that he doesn't come around, honestly. He was quite a challenge for Lu."

I bit the inside of my cheek. *A challenge?* "Excuse me?"

"He seemed very down to earth, that boy."

"Ryan," I corrected, knowing very well everyone knew what his name was.

"He obviously values family and perhaps small-town life. You said that he was going to be a teacher, correct?" said Celeste, though everyone knew that. It wasn't a question.

"Elementary teacher."

"Right." She pointed as she scooped the set scones onto a plate and placed it at the center of the table for us all.

Quietly, Ana and Gertie took one. Ana picked up a few before settling on the one with the most blueberries inside. Then Ana leaned back in her chair, looking between the two of us like she was getting ready for a show and didn't want her breakfast treat to be involved.

"I'm not quite sure that I understand what you are saying, Celeste," I said, narrowing my eyes. "It almost sounds like you are saying that I wasn't good enough for Ryan."

Though, of course, I wasn't.

She shrugged with a hesitant smile. "Wrong fit, is all."

Wrong fit.

I imagined reaching up and holding her cup to her mouth until her dark, soulless black tea spilled down the front of her blouse. But wasn't that what I'd basically told Ryan? We were the wrong fit. We didn't match up.

He deserved someone who matched him.

My forehead creased as I studied the chipped edge of my teacup.

"I know that you offered Lu to take over the one task of the Samhain ritual coming up in a few weeks as well, Gertrude, but I figured that, with all of this going on, Estrella could surely pick up the slack. We understand, of course."

Oh, of course. How kind. How thoughtful.

I wanted to roll my eyes more than they already did, taking half my head with them.

Ana must've caught them because she snickered.

Gertie gave a small shake of her head, not looking up from her plate. "I don't think that will be necessary."

"Still," said Celeste, "Estrella will soon need to be a more active part of our little coven and begin to understand the ins and outs of things."

I couldn't stand it as she continued to go on.

All this time, all I'd done was mess things up. There was only one thing left, and I could have it, and I wanted it, and I should have accepted it from the start. It shouldn't have taken Celeste and her whiny disposition for me to come to my conclusion of what I planned to do next, but now, it didn't matter. I gritted my teeth as I turned my gaze back up from my tea, a retort no one had asked for sitting on my tongue.

"Truly, Celeste, let's not get ahead of ourselves when we are here for a calm morning. We are showing support to a sister, as we have all shared support with each other in the past," Gertie assured.

"Right. I understand. I just figured, why not bring it up early?"

"Because I'm taking over the house," I said finally, cutting off her "benevolent" tirade. My tone was a Venus flytrap of conversation. Sound halted in an instant.

Celeste's eyes met mine. "What was that?"

Gertie cleared her throat, her own eyes stuck on me. They widened, as if in warning, as if she could feel my mood turning from ennui to complete frustration. "I believe what Lu is trying to announce is that she has taken time to consider and has decided to take me up on my request. I asked for her to be next in line as high priestess here in the house and in Barnett."

Blinking, Ana was the first to recover. "Well, I'm not surprised."

That seemed to make one of them.

"Congratulations, Lu," Faith whispered, a small smile bridging the gap as she lifted her cup for another sip of her own herbal concoction.

Celeste appeared catatonic. "This is up for discussion."

"It isn't," I corrected her.

I would correct her a hundred more times if she would look at me for once like I was more than a grain of salt sent to make her recipes go awry. I was more than that, and all this proved it. I was meant to be here, whether she ever accepted me as a part of this mismatched coven or not.

"Of course it is. This is a coven, not a dictatorship."

"I've made my choice."

"The choice was made long ago," Celeste argued, turning her chin in the other direction, unable to simply look at me.

I wanted to bark a laugh. At the very least, I still had enough sense of mind to hold back.

"Celeste." Gertie took a deep breath, "I know this might come as a shock from your previous understandings, but Luella became very clearly seen in my eyes and in my prayers as the successor of this house. It was my choice to make as well, though I will not stop you from sharing any concerns you have with me."

"And she is simply going to be staying in Barnett as if it were her home?"

"It is my home," I said. Warmth spread through me at the words. I had asked the other night, when I was feeling lost and unseeing, for the universe, the stars even, to take me home. "This is my home."

Celeste stared at me, pressing her lips together. "I see then that the decision has been made. Thank you for inviting me over, Gertie, but I need to go and ... reflect on some things." The final words twisted sourly in her mouth.

"I understand," Gertie said calmly.

No one said a word as Celeste gathered her purse and turned back toward the front of the house, leaving us behind her. She was supposed to be here for me and for the coven this morning even if it didn't end up as she'd so perfectly planned for herself. But then again, she had obviously never been my biggest fan. So why would she pretend to be pleased?

What is wrong with her?

"Well, for one," said Ana, "I'm excited."

I stood up. No. I was not going to just let this go. Not anymore. Whatever was on my expression must've conveyed that as Gertie attempted to reach out to grasp my hand but missed.

"Lu, don't," Gertie called out softly in a warning. "This isn't the time."

Then when was? I was already up. My blood boiled over, and I couldn't help myself anymore. I might have been making all the wrong moves, all the wrong choices recently, but for once, all at once, I was making them.

"What is your problem with me?" I spat the words out at Celeste when she was out the front door.

The door snapped shut behind me, so no one inside would have to hear as I stood, looking out on her from the small porch.

The put-together woman blinked at me as she turned around.

At least she now had the decency to look me in the eye. "Excuse me?"

"I asked you a question."

"And you assume that you are owed an answer because you barked it at me?"

"Just as much as you feel you are owed to somehow take over this entire coven for yourself or your daughter. So, yes, I do feel, after the past three years of my life, that I'm owed an answer as to why you constantly feel the need to pick and pick and *pick* at me. Why do you try to make me feel so small and insignificant compared to your perfect life that you didn't even have to work for to get here?" I let it all out. There was nothing holding me back any longer.

I had so little to lose.

Pursing her lips together, Celeste paused at the final part of my exclamation. "That was never my intention."

"What?"

"To make you feel insignificant. That was never my intention," she clarified.

"Then, what—"

"What my problem with you and all of this is that you have so much to learn yet, dear," said Celeste, working her jaw as she stared at me. "Obviously."

"What the hell does that mean?"

"You should want to go to school and be whatever it is that brought you there to be. You should desire more. To flourish."

"You, of all people, acting like you care about what I possibly want or don't in this world is funny, Celeste. For once, I am finally doing something for me. You told me to figure out what I'm doing in this world when I really have no idea. You might've meant a major so that I could get out of your hair and run off into a corporate job, where I'd be in a cubicle all day, but no. I've decided. I'm choosing me. I was brought here for whatever reason for me."

All I could think of then was the story that Gertie had told me so many times. Over and over, I'd thought of that story since it'd reappeared in my head last week, of the house that brought in wayward women when they had nowhere else or didn't know where else to go. Drawn by the stars.

I had been drawn here. I had been, godsdammit.

And I wanted to be here for the rest of the messy, unsure people who might eventually come here too.

My hand flexed in front of me with the ferocity of the words, my breathing heavy. I expected the same hatred back threefold. Instead, I received worse, and I was willing to take it all.

"I tried to be nothing but a mother to you since it was clear you didn't have one."

"I do!" I screamed at her. I screamed at the woman I'd wanted to scream and scream at from nearly the day I'd met her with her appraising looks and words of advice I hadn't asked for. "I have a mother. She was the most beautiful and wild woman I'd ever met —that anyone had ever met. She died, not that you ever cared to ask because you never got to know me beyond what I was worth to you. But I have a mother."

Celeste stared at me, stunned to silence.

"She sure isn't you," I said. "So, stop lying and trying to act like you want what is best for me under some sort of guise to get ahead with your own real children. I'm sorry that I, the girl who came from nowhere, found something worthwhile here. Love and family and this feeling that I finally belong when all you've ever wanted from me was to leave and be unworthy."

Of Barnett. Of Ryan.

Gods, what had I done to Ryan? To myself?

"That isn't—"

"It doesn't matter. Love …" I nearly laughed now at the word. "Didn't you once say that was the purest form of magic we could make? Is that what this all looks like to you?"

It looked like I wasn't the only one who still had a whole lot to learn in this life.

But I was the one who decided to never stop.

Standing still on the front steps of the house, for a moment, I thought it was my chance to turn and head back inside even if she followed me. I didn't have to resort to it though, like a child running away.

Celeste nodded once, twice, three times in understanding before she met my eyes—both pairs lined with tears—and then she turned away down the path and toward the beat-up hatchback.

When she got inside and drove away, I finally saw the other person in on our conversation, standing across the street. With fluffy hair at the top of his head, he stood there. He looked just like how I'd left him the other night. His eyes looked so bright and clear, even from this distance.

Pressure built in my throat, pulsing with the tears behind my eyes. I wouldn't let him see me cry. I had promised the other night that I wouldn't let Ryan see me cry.

Especially not when his lips parted in despair at what he must've seen transpire.

I wanted to rush across the street. I really did. I wanted to feel his arms back around me again. But they hung limply at his sides.

Who am I?

Because maybe I was evolving and this was my next great *next*. But maybe I wasn't the pretty, extraordinary person I'd imagined. Maybe I was still just me, a little bright and shiny, sure, but also a little ugly inside.

"Hi," I gasped, though I wasn't sure if it was loud enough to reach him.

His hand rose, however, just a little. "Hey."

"I'm not able to talk to you. Not right now."

"Okay. I'll be here."

I nodded over and over again as I turned around, heading

back inside the house before the tracks of tears fell. So, alone, I gasped for air around all the terrible words I'd said today, constricting my throat and lungs. I wanted him so much, and yet this was not how I wanted me. It was not how I wanted him to want me when he deserved so much better. So, maybe Celeste was right; I couldn't have him.

I pressed the mounds of my hands into my eyes, trying to make myself stop. I should've been all out of tears, but not yet.

Not today, not today, not today.

Slowly, a presence knelt in front of me and carefully peeled away my palms from my eyes. I had done this for her before, more than once before. I thought we both realized that as she tipped her head in understanding.

Ana's mouth screwed to the side as she looked me over. "I think we need a little me time, huh?"

24

"You finally gave Celeste what was coming to her," Ana said after a long time, carefully parting my hair.

After picking me up off the floor of Gertie's, Ana had been very clear with what she planned to do next as she took me down the road. At first, I thought she was taking me to her apartment for a change of scenery. Instead, she sat me down at one of the two hair-washing stations of the only hair salon in Barnett. No one else was inside other than her manager, who hadn't looked at us twice, from my puffy eyes to Ana's swift determination.

She took her time, lathering my scalp with solutions that smelled like a thick meadow. Her fingers were like magic as they slowly massaged around the nape of my neck and temples. I shut my eyes and let her continue, drying me off and taking me to her station in silence, save for the hum of pop music running over the radio.

Without a word, Ana walked to the back room and returned with a fresh bowl of color. I didn't ask what she was doing. I'd never had highlights before, no matter how many times before the two of us always talked about doing something with my hair since the moment I'd let her cut it off years ago.

I trusted Ana in her zone. Long black lashes touched down over her cheeks as she concentrated. One sweep of her brush at a time, she added streaks of color, covering before moving on to the next section. Once she was on the third section, she spoke, pulling me out of whatever trance I'd been put under.

"Even Gertie said, when we sat in the kitchen awkwardly, that the whole blowup was bound to happen eventually."

"Was I that loud?"

Ana snorted. "Yes."

I didn't know if that made me feel better or worse about everything. At this point, besides the understanding that I was officially a high priestess in training—which sent a sharp bolt of fear and excitement through me—all I felt was numb.

"You'd been planning to confront her for, what, three years?" Ana asked.

I met Ana's gaze in the mirror. "Two ... two and a half."

I openly aired my ire toward Celeste and her *well-intentioned* comments every time she wasn't close enough to hear, though I had a feeling Gertie passed along the abridged versions of my dislike and distrust to Celeste. That woman somehow managed to get under my skin, unlike anyone else.

"She had to know that at some point, you were going to burst," Ana commented calmly. As if this entire situation was an everyday occurrence. "Tell me about the house. Has Gertie been showing you the ropes of the place and your future duties now that you are our soon-to-be fearless leader?"

"She's been giving me space, but, yes, she has been. And now that I've been there all week, I know where the breaker box and all the supplies she has stored for special occasions are. The rest will come in time, she told me."

"It will. And just to let you know, I think we all figured that you would be the person to take over the group."

"Really?"

Ana nodded, as if it wasn't surprising in the least. "You were called there. Faith said that about a year ago."

"That's what Gertie said too." And Ryan.

"Well, she's right. You fit there. In the house, with us messed-up women trying not to fuck up lives anymore. You've always been good with us. Besides Celeste, of course. Otherwise, it's like you're our new, younger mommy."

I chuckled.

"You'll do good," assured Ana.

I appreciated the vote of confidence. "Even if Celeste wants to burn me alive?"

"She already knew too," said Ana. "She just didn't want to believe it. Essie might be a great girl and a great leader in her own soft and stern sort of way, but her soul just isn't the one we need. She's never been called to the coven. Not like you. We all saw that. We were just waiting for you to realize it."

I stared at her.

"And look, you have now."

"I guess so," I whispered as she folded another sheet of tinfoil into my hair.

"That's good. How is Ryan?"

"How long have you been holding that in?" I asked. I didn't bother to ask if she had seen him outside or heard my struggling words as I called out to him across the street.

She shrugged, flipping another piece of hair up and over my head. "Long enough."

I huffed, unsure of what to say.

"I know I'm not the one to be approaching you with this. But you decided to finally step up and do what you want. So, why aren't you trying to be happy and go after that? All of it?"

"You're right; you're definitely not the person who should be bringing that up." With her messy past relationships and terrible taste in men that left her aching in her own pity parties worse than my own, Ana was the last person that anyone should've been receiving decent personal advice from. Especially not after her last boyfriend, who was surprisingly kind of sweet, until something happened and she pushed everyone away, even the coven, for a short while.

"Don't be rude. I'm doing your hair."

"Sorry," I muttered, but I noticed her small smile. "I really hope you aren't dyeing my hair orange or something for some sort of revenge."

"Revenge? For what?"

"Like I said, I've been doing pretty well, making everyone mad these days."

"No," she insisted. "You've just been terrible at listening. A trait that should be rectified in our great and future high priestess, don't you agree?" Ana raised her eyebrows.

Probably.

"Ryan isn't the sort of person I think any of us pictured when we told you to get out there. And obviously, he isn't the person you pictured. But he makes you happy, Lu. Anyone would have to be blind not to see it even if it sounds like you both have made some pretty poor decisions in the moment. You love him."

I did.

"He loves you."

So he'd said.

"What's that face for? He doesn't?" Her face shut down, as if she was personally affronted.

"I just …" I took a deep breath, poring through my thoughts that all did indeed sound ridiculous.

Ana finished the final section of my head. Letting the foils sit, she sat in the chair next to me, spinning around once before making the chair stay still.

"What if he deserves better?"

"Why would you say that?"

"Like Celeste said—"

"I thought we stopped caring about what Celeste thought today."

"We don't fit," I stressed.

"So?"

"We look, well, we don't look right or at all like we're meant to be together. I'm all …" I looked down at myself. My dark-green nails were chipped, and I was pretty sure Ana had clucked at how greasy my roots had gotten before she washed my head.

"Screw meant to be."

"He's so nice. He smiles all the time and makes cheesy jokes. He has friends, and everyone has said that we don't make sense."

"You're going to believe them?" Ana seemed shocked by this. "What happened to my strong, independent Luella, who pried me out of bed after the last asshole I was with? What happened to the girl who made Gertie literally scream from joy that we had another witch joining us for the long haul?"

She was still in here, I was sure, somewhere.

"I wanted to give him a choice. I wanted to make sure that he was sure of what he wanted and that he wouldn't regret it," I said.

I couldn't handle being a passing fancy. I could barely handle whatever this was.

"You're hurting me," Ana said with an exhausted sigh.

"Like I said, I've been doing that a lot these days."

"You need to stop hiding from all the heartache, Lu. How else are you ever going to fully take life by the balls and live? You've had enough, and if the world throws you more, you already know that you can handle it. Just like you can handle Ryan. He's amazing and sweet, and he actually somehow didn't run screaming from us when you brought him to the house."

I huffed a short laugh, trying to stop the sadness welling back up.

"You are starting to live your life and make decisions. I can see it. Things are going how they should be," Ana assured me. "But I think that you are a fool if you don't get your ass up, find Ryan, and fix whatever it is you both broke. You'll be the one regretting things if you don't."

I knew she was right. I did. I glanced at my head again as she stood back up to check on how things were going.

Meeting Ana's eyes in the mirror again, I raised my eyebrows, faux serious. "Did you just call your future high priestess a fool?"

"Yes. Do I need to do it again?"

I pressed my lips together and shook my head.

"Good."

"Thank you, Ana."

"Don't thank me yet," she said.

For the next few hours, I sat with her, listening to the stories she had about other clients she did hair for, both from and not from BU, who seemed to always have strange requests that Ana took on without question. She talked about not dating for a while, which was different for her. I couldn't remember the last time she wasn't seeing someone, coming to coven meetings with a fresh first-date story that never ended well.

"I just don't want to keep forcing things," Ana said, reminding me of the words I'd told her the last time she was going through that last breakup. "My hopeless romantic days, as you called them, are over."

"You'll find your person," I said.

"Yeah, well, I'm in no hurry now." With a twist of the chair, she swung me back around to face the mirror. "It's your turn."

I stared at the reflection.

"Time to stop hiding," said Ana before she took off the cloak and presented me back into the world.

25

I put on a loose dress and wrapped one of Gertie's thick shawls around my shoulders. I looked so unlike I ever had. I also looked so much like myself. My feet grounded themselves in my worn boots. After a few days, my hair wasn't so shocking to see. The vibrant color struck me with how fantastic it looked every time I turned my head in each direction to get a better look.

Ana had outdone herself.

Today, it was time to stop hiding.

Pulling out my phone, I listened through the messages Ryan had left, each one more pitiful than the last, until I couldn't any longer. They made my heart ache. Then, I opened a new message.

I know it's not enough, I wrote underneath Vadika's name. *I'm sorry.*

I didn't wait to see if she'd respond. I didn't truly expect it, nor was I sure if I was ready for her to. I heard, according to Faith, that she had received more offers for her spot in postgraduate programs, but they all were vying for her to go on last-minute visits before the end of the semester, when she graduated. I'd be surprised if she and her parents hadn't packed up and rushed from Barnett right away now that nothing was holding her back.

I was happy for her even if I made sure not to pass the science building on the way to the sports team housing.

Taking a deep breath, I knocked.

No one answered. I knocked again, waiting. There was always someone home. At least, I always figured as much with how many athletes they crammed inside.

A guy next door yelled over to me. He stood up from where he had been lounging against the railing of the frat house. His hair was askew, and the coffee in his hand looked like it had long gone cold along with the rest of him, wearing little more than shorts. "Who are you looking for?"

I cleared my throat before I called out, "Ryan. You know, Ryan Gardner?"

"Yeah, I know him." The guy blinked. "Oh, uh, honestly, I thought I just saw him. Maybe he went to training?"

"The sports complex?" I repeated.

He nodded, looking me up and down, as if he recognized me as the crazy girl who had screamed at Ryan outside the house a week ago.

So be it. I was past the point of caring what other people thought of me once again. It took being shoved to rock bottom to get back in that mindset, it seemed.

"Thank you," I said.

"Anytime. Cool hair, by the way."

I glanced up at it again from the corner of my eye. "Thanks."

Turning away, I walked on the sidewalk up to campus, the same way I'd walked the other night after I ran away from Ryan. I walked past the swath of trees that created a dome overhead on the Row and kept going around the bend until I passed the library and stood in front of the sports complex.

I took another deep breath.

Take two.

Going inside, I looked around, wondering exactly where he could be. If he had decided to go back on the team after one week of lessening his amount of physical therapy, Ryan was going to get a piece of my mind. He wanted to walk. He wanted to travel and see the world and climb mountains or whatever in the future, and now, he was throwing that out of the window?

I pushed into the football locker room to find it quiet and empty. Bags laid on the floor alone. Practice jerseys were stacked to the right, still holding on to the faint scent of body odor. Unsure of where else to go, I moved toward the other door that led toward either the gym or out toward the field. After a step, someone pushed through.

The guy I recognized from the other day—and forever ingrained in my mind as the guy eating cheese puffs on the sports house's couch—stared at me for a second before he continued his direction back toward his own cubby, searching through his bag. "Hey."

"Hi, Trevor," I said, hesitant. Then again, he didn't look like it was completely out of the ordinary to see a random person standing in the middle of the football locker room. "I was looking for—"

"He's not here."

"What do you mean?" I asked, my voice turning more high pitched and ill-humored with each complaint. I was never going to find him. With each place and step I might come across him, my chest felt as if it were caving in a little further as I lost my nerve. "I was told that he was coming here."

"He cleaned out his locker early this morning, but then he headed out for the rest of the day," said Trevor.

Cleaned out his locker. I looked over to the corner, seeing the number nine above the empty space. Here I'd thought he was here because he was going to ruin his leg again. But he wasn't. He was seriously done playing, and I hadn't been here for the day when he cleaned out his space on the team once and for all.

I put a hand to my head, letting go of the fear and anger that had festered in the past ten minutes. "Oh."

"Yeah, I don't know where he went, but he had one of his lists with him."

One of his to-do lists. My body softened at the mention, though that meant he could be anywhere, on or off campus.

I turned back around to give Trevor his privacy that I'd invaded, heading toward the door. "Thanks anyway."

"No problem. I hope you find him."

"Me too."

"Hey." He stopped me as I opened the door. "I heard what Lauren and her friend did to you. That was pretty shitty."

I stared at Trevor. I wondered how he'd found out. Was it from Ryan? Someone else? Or did Lauren think that it was cool to hurt others and show her achievement off like some odd sociopath?

"Yeah, it was."

"Like I said, I hope you find him." Lifting his arm up in a wave, he turned back out toward the gym he had arrived from.

When I pushed my way outside back onto campus once more, the breeze that ruffled the branches of the trees around me felt like an odd relief as I looked this way and that, debating which direction I should go next or if it would be better just to head home and regroup. I let myself wander unthinkingly along the path, along the edge of campus.

As if out of a dream, however, I stopped.

I just wanted to find him. And like magic, I did.

There he was in front of me on the sidewalk, carrying a box of things in his arms, looking like he was heading somewhere.

There he was.

And next to him, carrying another box as he tilted his head closer to her as he talked, was Natalie.

26

I must have stood there long enough for, after a few more steps, Ryan immediately found me. His eyes stuck to me like we were magnets, constantly pulling one another toward each other, hearing the buzz when we were close. But I took a step back from the image of him and Natalie side by side, smiling and laughing.

I turned around.

Regroup. I needed to regroup.

"Luella!"

Shit. I paused.

People sat on benches. Others went about their day while mine slowly, silently imploded. My back was still toward Ryan, and whatever that scene was that I'd just witnessed with him being all buddy-buddy with Natalie sent a new shock wave of uncertainty straight to my brain.

"Hey," he whispered when he found himself in front of me. His eyes were soft, tired.

"Hey," I repeated back, my voice a single breath.

"You ran off again. Is that a new habit I'm going to have to start learning to like?"

I had never been a runner before, yet somehow, I was changing all over the place, it looked like. For better and for worse. I shrugged. My mouth opened and closed on the words I wanted to say. I'd had it all planned out when I first arrived at the sports house and then again when I opened the door to the locker room. The script had been in my head this whole time.

Now, it was caught in my throat.

"Maybe."

Ryan only nodded. He reached up a hand to scratch the side of his neck. "All right."

"You look nice," I said, looking at his crisp business attire. He looked like a teacher.

"I had a presentation today. They are placing us for student teaching next semester." He stared at me as if I were a ghost.

I nodded a few times, watching as others began to stream steadily out of the humanities building. "Right."

"Luella—"

"Please. Just wait." I shut my eyes. This had been going on long enough. I needed to get this back on track. His eyes flared, uncertain, as I cut him off. "I'm sorry. Just let me talk."

I had a lot of talking to do.

"Okay."

I swallowed. "I came here, hoping that there was still a reason for me to. You can try to stop me if there isn't one. Then again, that might not stop me either. Once I start talking, I don't know if I'll be able to stop because I haven't been able to stop falling in love with you from the moment you first gave me that reassuring, crooked smile, like you saw right through me, that day outside the dean's office when we both were waiting to get our ruined new beginnings."

Ryan's lips closed, but he didn't stop me.

"I wanted to call sooner. I did, and I didn't, but I really did," I rambled. I was getting lost again in what was supposed to be coming out of my mouth. "I didn't know how I'd sound on the phone because I'm terrible at phone conversations, and I wanted to see you. I really wanted to see you. But like I said, I get it if I'm too late. I really made a mess of things. I know that I did. I was just—I was so scared."

"Why were you scared?" he asked, voice quiet and sad.

"Because you deserve better than me and I feel like you haven't had the chance to see that. Plus, everything seems to just fall apart around me."

"That's not true."

"Which part?"

"Any of it. Lu, you might think I'm better off in some other alternate reality, but I get to make those decisions," said Ryan. "I decide what I want my life to be and who I want to be in it in the end. Screw everyone else."

"Really?"

"I told you that I was working on trying to be less of a people pleaser." He shrugged.

I nodded. "I'm so sorry I ruined things, that I sent you away the other day. I see I'm probably too late. Maybe you did take my advice. I can't blame you for that, but I just needed to see you even if it took me going to your house and then the sports complex and then here to say this. All of this."

I really wanted to stop talking now and plow back into his arms. I hadn't realized how much I would miss them.

"Why would you be too late?"

I peered back over his shoulder toward where I had seen him first. Natalie gave a hesitant wave toward me, but headed off in whatever direction it was she was heading. She didn't try to wait for Ryan. "You and Natalie, after everything and—"

His shoulders slumped as he sighed. "Let's get out of here. Can we go back to the house to talk? Gertie's?"

And mine, I wanted to tell him.

In the past few days, Gertie had already prepared the documents to sign the property and everything else over to me. She'd been preparing, it seemed, a lot sooner than when she brought the proposal up to me.

I swallowed. He wanted to go back to the house. With me. "Okay."

He didn't offer his hand, but he waited until I was behind him as we headed back together.

* * *

"I like your hair," Ryan said.

I resisted the urge to thank him and tell him that I really liked it and how I'd always wanted to color my hair something a little more extravagant, but never had the courage to. Until recently, anyway. But if I said that, then I would also have to tell him again that I missed him. I'd have to tell him that I wished he had been the first person who saw my bright-purple hair when Ana was done after hours. I could imagine the smile he would've given me, and it made my heart hurt all over again.

So instead, I swallowed the thick saliva coating the inside of my mouth.

He settled himself further on the window seat of my bedroom. Right back at home. I sat down next to him on the edge.

"I didn't get to say that before." He reached up and touched a strand of his own.

"Thanks. Ana just did it."

"So, you really ran around campus for me?" Ryan asked.

"I needed to find you," I said. It had been so simple before.

"And you did."

"You know, you don't have to forgive me." I should've said that before. "I mean, I understand, like I said, if I'm too late or if I hurt you. I know I hurt you. You don't have to just forgive me because you feel bad or are always too nice."

"Stop, Lu."

"I'm just saying—"

"Luella," Ryan said sternly.

I stopped talking.

"I'll forgive you because I love you, Lu," he said. "But now, it is my turn to talk. You had your chance, right?"

Finally, I said nothing. I didn't interrupt. I let him take over and say what it was that he needed to say. It was fair even if I didn't want to hear it. I'd wanted him to come here all too much. Desperately, if I was being honest. And now, he was here.

I was done hiding.

"You have to know, I wasn't thinking the other night. I don't think either of us was thinking clearly," Ryan started. "The only reason I didn't show up here, banging down the door sooner, is because I was terrified you'd throw me right back out. I wanted to give you some time, but then I realized that you weren't coming back to campus. You weren't at your library spot or anything. My witch wasn't managing to piece herself back together, and I knew I had to come find you, whether you wanted me to or not," explained Ryan. "And I thought about that too—if we should have each other. Because you are right; we aren't perfect pieces of a puzzle."

I looked down, but not before I caught the shake of his head.

"But somehow," he said, "we fit. You are the best thing to happen in my life in a long time, Lu. So, no, you aren't too late. You had a reason to come back on campus to look for me, and I'm so glad you did."

I stared at him, pretty positive my heart had stopped.

"You could never be too late," he whispered.

"How do you mean that?" I didn't try to hide the way my voice shook. "I'm terrible to you."

"Now, who's lying?"

We both chuckled.

"The last week has been hell. I'm sorry I didn't stop you from walking away. I love you. That hasn't changed. Loving you might be the only courageous thing I can make my mind up about and not question in the slightest. The rest of the decisions in my life were made for me. They were fine decisions, but in the end, they were never mine. So, I'm going to be courageous again, Lu. I'm going to make my own decision. I'm choosing you, whether you like it or not. I hope that's all right."

I stared at him. The miserable look on my face must've been enough of an invitation for Ryan. He extended his arm, and I couldn't help myself any longer. I fell over to the side, resting my body on his chest, letting my head mold up and into his broad shoulder that took the load.

A shiver racked my body against his warmth.

Ryan held on tighter, pulling me into his embrace with his other arm so I couldn't escape.

"It's definitely all right," I murmured.

"You're not so scary that you're going to make me run away from you that easy."

I inhaled, smelling him and a scent I knew well. I pulled away, narrowing my eyes at him. "Why do you smell like me?"

"Oh, right." He pulled back a fraction. "When you saw me and Natalie, we were cleaning out your room with most of your stuff. All of your things are back at my place. Housing isn't going to let Natalie go too long without another roommate, it looks like. While I was clearing off your desk, I might have dropped a bottle or two of your perfume."

I dipped my nose back into his chest and smelled him again, taking in the aroma of spring flowers and citrus.

"Please tell me you dropped them all over her floor on purpose?"

"Now, that would be devious." He smirked. "She's sorry. She told me about what had happened. She hasn't spoken to Lauren since. Not since I lost my shit after I heard what actually went down that night."

"You?"

His eyes widened, as if remembering. "Oh, yeah. Don't worry; I'm sure you'll hear about it when you get back on campus since you can stop avoiding me now. Big thing here is, Natalie wants to apologize."

"I'll believe it when I hear it." I knew deep down that Natalie hadn't done what she did on her own. I saw it in her face that night, however angry I was. It was all Lauren. "I'm still much more interested in Ryan Gardner causing chaos on campus."

"Another time."

I chuckled, and he held me closer. My chest shook somewhere between relief and wanting to cry all over again.

"I missed you, Lu-Lu."

"I missed you too, Ry-Ry," I tried to joke as I ran my fingers down his cheek and along his jaw. I cupped him there, so he couldn't move as I stared at him, trying to commit every freckle and speck of blue in his eyes to memory. "So much."

Not pulling away, Ryan instead carefully slid forward until our noses brushed against each other and then our mouths. It was a whisper of a kiss, smooth and sweeping. Gods, I missed him so much.

We spoke sadness and joy as we kissed, grasping onto one another as if it would keep us afloat in this weird, messy life that never stopped confounding.

And yet here we were.

We were here, together.

It was all *pretty magic.*

27

Each kiss. Each touch.

Each word of love I'd never thought I would be so afraid of.

With Ryan, it was magic, and I couldn't bear to send it on its way.

I leaned closer for another kiss, another lick, another touch, as if I wanted to slowly devour him once and for all and make us one person. Perfectly evening out the other in cosmic unity.

Every other time we kissed and touched, it felt like we were exploring. We listened to quiet sounds and breaths the other made just as we learned more about each other through words. This time, we already knew. We still waited for something new, found a breath of fresh air in one another as we came up for oxygen we didn't want unless it was found between open mouths and the gentle scrape of teeth.

But now, when Ryan reached for the straps of my dress, he didn't hesitate as he pushed them down. His hands reverently skimmed over my skin. He wanted to see me as much as I wanted to feel every piece and part of him.

I pushed at the waistband of his pants that he stepped out of.

He didn't want his fancy presentation pants getting wrinkled before meeting my lips again in one last sweeping kiss as he pressed me back onto the bed.

"Are we really?"

I paused, staring up at him. My legs hooked around his waist. I nodded, looking around. Quickly, I grabbed my shirt, pulling it on over my arms and wiggling out of his reach and off to the other side of the bed. "Just a second."

"Where are you going?"

"I'll be right back."

I wasn't sure I'd ever run faster. I held Ryan's shirt to my chest as I raced down the hallway to the bathroom. When I swung open the cabinets under the sink, hair and personal care items burst out at me. I slid one of the bottom drawers open, knowing that when Ana had lived here for a few months, she wouldn't go without stocking some other necessities.

"Aha."

By the time I made it back to my room, Ryan didn't look like he'd had time to move.

Shutting the door behind me, I jumped back up onto the bed next to him. The square package dropped between us. "In case."

His teeth began to show as he smiled.

"There's no one I would rather be with," Ryan said.

The words made it hard to breathe, with the emotion catching behind my eyes. He couldn't mean that, and yet he did.

"From the moment I saw you, I knew it somewhere inside me."

And I didn't doubt it for a moment. Not anymore.

Ryan stared down at the gray packaging. "Can you help me put it on?"

I stared down at the condom between his fingers, reaching out to smooth my hand over his. "I would love to put it on you."

"But for now …" His lips carefully followed the path of where he pulled away his shirt I was still clutching to my midsection.

He followed with his hands this time, as if he didn't want to miss a single spot, as I remained on my knees, watching as he pressed his damp mouth over my skin, as if worshiping each line and freckle he came across. The pad of his finger swiped back and forth along the top of my thin bra, sending a shiver through me.

"I think we should take this off."

"I think so too." Meeting his hands around my back, I gently reached to help him undo the single clasp, but he already had. I slowly let the material fall forward, slipping down my arms. "You sure you've never done this before?"

"I said I was a virgin, not that I never managed to get anywhere before with a girl," he said, gesturing back to himself. "Who could help themselves with all this?"

"So humble."

"Did you think I ever was?"

"For a minute there." I giggled.

"Once I get over the fear of making a fool of myself, I'll make sure to fit expectations again."

"You can't make a fool out of yourself right now," I said.

He let his thumbs brush over the tips of my nipples. I sat up straighter, feeling it strum a chord low in my stomach.

"Especially not while you are doing that."

"How about this?" He lowered and immediately took one of my breasts into his mouth. All bravado.

Oh, how I loved his self-confidence. I shivered.

Each of us used our fingers and palms, dragging feeling over each other as we got undressed, shaking with anticipation as I settled underneath him. Heat radiated between us.

"Are you nervous?"

"Right now?" Taking a deep inhale, Ryan met my eyes. He nodded, then shook his head as I traced the pattern of his freckles along his cheeks.

I smiled. "Good. Because I literally think I might die if you stop touching me."

"Is that so?"

"Very so."

As if to prove it, I shifted my hips, leaning down to take a tiny bite alongside his neck. He moaned, grunting to keep himself together.

I wanted to watch him fall apart.

"Is there something you need to tell me?"

"Like what?" I asked.

"Like you're a vampire as well as a witch?"

I laughed, the sound warm and gooey, like honey. I'd never thought I could laugh like this. We were bare and vulnerable, the pair of us. It was perfect, soothing. The muscles in Ryan's back tensed as he settled over me. He hissed with pleasure as he shifted, rubbing between my legs. I inhaled with him in a small whimper, all sensation.

Catching each other's eyes, we laughed again, low and breathy.

"Ready?" I asked.

Dipping his head low to give me another kiss, Ryan positioned himself as he kept his eyes on mine, never straying. I couldn't help the low groan as he sank deeper inside me. It was unlike anything else I'd felt before. He was perfect.

"You all right?" He sounded as if he'd already run a marathon.

"I'm perfect," I breathed. "So are you. You feel so good. You are so good."

Slowly, he began to shift, his thrusts gentle and soft for a moment as our mouths held over one another. Each breath and tiny gasp were shared. We built and thrummed with tender sway until we couldn't seem to stand it anymore, crashing down in a pile of quiet murmurs and tangled limbs.

I clutched on to Ryan's chest as he slowly draped over me, breathing in the smell of love and him. "Stars."

"You're seeing them too?"

I chuckled. "I really love you, Ryan."

"I'm bewitched by you, Luella Pierce," he said, still catching his breath as he ran a finger from the top of my forehead to down my nose. "You've bewitched me, body and soul."

It took only a second for me to succumb to laughter. "You really like *Pride and Prejudice* too much."

"We really need to watch the movie."

"We can if you want."

"Not now." Ryan grinned with his eyes closed, pulling me back into his chest and holding me there. "Right now, this. This is right where I want you."

A good thing, I thought as I let myself relax into his hold, *because there is no other place I'd rather be.*

28

I knew where to step so that my feet didn't creak on the stairs as I made my way down. Conversation drifted along the hallway, and I couldn't help myself but listen as I turned the corner.

"Slow craft was always the one thing Luella struggled with at first," Gertie said softly to Ryan. "It was all or nothing. She'd get so frustrated while creating magic before she realized that some things took more time than others to sort and evolve into what they were meant to be. She still forgets at times when the walls are crashing around her. But she doesn't give up."

Ryan nodded. "She certainly doesn't."

"You're welcome here always; I hope you know that as well."

"That's good." Ryan chuckled. "I think I'm going to be here a lot more now."

Rolling my eyes, as if Gertie couldn't guess what Ryan was insinuating, I hopped down the final few stairs and made my way to the doorway of the kitchen. Gertie filled up her watering can under the sink faucet to take it out back to the garden.

Ryan smiled wide when he saw me. He wore clothing he'd left

here from the last time he'd spent the night. This morning, his eyes were bright, and his face was full of a healthy flush.

I shook my head, trying not to laugh at everything going on here. "Morning."

"Good morning, Lu," said Gertie. "Sleep well?"

Glancing at Ryan and back to her, I held my smile. "Exceptionally."

"I'm glad."

"You ready?" Ryan asked after a minute, walking over to meet me with his car keys in hand.

As ready as I was going to be. "See you in a bit, Gertie."

"Good luck."

"See?" I shot a pointed look up at Ryan. "Even she knows I'm going to need it."

"You're going to be fine."

"So *you* say. Haven't you learned that when a witch is saying good luck, you should really look into why?"

"You're going to be fine," he repeated.

Once we made it outside, he held open the car door for me and nearly pushed me inside, like I was on my way to jail. This didn't feel much different. I was pretty sure anyway.

"It's not like she is going to yell at you and throw you out."

Now, that I wasn't so sure of. I was about eighty percent sure that was exactly how visiting Celeste was going to go. I knew that I had to be the one to confront her and smooth whatever it was between us over, but I also really didn't want to.

Her home wasn't far down the road, and we stopped in front of the brick house on the corner. I'd really thought I had more time to prepare.

"Go on." Ryan nudged me until I opened the car door.

"If I'm not out in twenty minutes, rush in."

"I will."

"You'd better," I said, getting out and shutting the door behind me.

Then, it was just the walk up to the very clean, organized front porch. Rocking chairs were perfectly angled. Throw pillows on top were chopped down the center.

Lifting my hand, I shut my eyes. My fist floated midair for a long few seconds. What was it that I was doing here? I didn't want to be here—that was for certain—and yet here I stood, staring at the obnoxious olive-green door I'd been through once before and quickly made an exit out of after.

I let my hand fall three times.

A few calls were heard about inside the house until the door at once swung open. Celeste paused halfway before extending it farther. She wiped her hand on a tea towel clutched between her palms.

"Hi," I said, my voice softer than I'd thought it would be.

Staring at my feet, Celeste looked me over with a short sigh. "Would you like to come in?"

Without waiting for an answer, she held open the door, and I stepped through the passageway and inside the home. It opened straight toward the living room and kitchen, much more updated than most of the other homes in Barnett. A crisp wooden beam ran across the ceiling, and the kitchen of the open concept clearly took precedence. It looked like I'd wandered into a farmhouse in the middle of a field somewhere instead of a tall house on the corner of downtown Barnett and the isle.

Dishes and baking sheets were spread along the counter.

"You've been cooking a lot."

"It's what I do," Celeste said simply. "Some see it as me, the happy housewife. But it's my own place to send out the best of my energy into the world. My craft. Estrella also has a bake sale for the National Honor Society. She was recently inducted, so I got a little carried away."

"Ah," I said quietly, still looking around.

The sliding back door opened. A man stepped in. Adjusting

his thick tortoiseshell glasses, he looked to be about to say something to Celeste before he paused.

"Oh." Her husband smiled as he turned back toward me. "Is this ..."

"This is Luella, dear."

"Of course. I think we met once before on a picnic."

"Last year," I agreed. "Nice to see you again."

"You as well. I'll be upstairs if you need anything," he said to Celeste, never taking his eyes off his wife.

He gave her arm a little loving squeeze before he headed toward the other end of the house. The movement almost reminded me a bit of Ryan.

Then we were alone again.

"That was your husband."

"It was," confirmed Celeste. "He works with computers. Forgive him if he was a bit brief."

I shook my head as I stepped closer to the counter she was on the other side of. He'd seemed nice.

"I really don't like talking to you," I admitted.

"I'm aware."

"I also don't feel like I should apologize."

"Nor should you."

"Right," I said.

We were at a standstill.

The silence went on for a long moment. Maybe I should carefully back away until I was in sprinting distance of the front door. If I came out running, I was sure that Ryan would start the engine before I even buckled up.

"I wasn't aware of your mother," Celeste said carefully.

Blinking, I took a deep breath. "I don't talk about it much."

"As I realized shortly after our last conversation."

If that was what my bellowing at her could be called.

"It isn't because she wasn't important to me. It's just ..." I sighed. "When she died, she sent this wreckage into my life. My father's a wonderful man, but after that, he's never been the same. I wasn't the same, so I couldn't blame him."

I settled my forearms on her stone countertop, cold against my skin. Celeste stared off toward my cupped hands.

"For so long, it was as if I was trying to piece together who I was and who she was. I wanted to be this perfect person I always imagined she would've kept being. In the end, I only set myself up for disappointment. I could no longer count on her or my dad. I could only count on myself and who I was. Keeping that in mind, it brought me here, to Barnett. For better or for worse."

"It was wrong of me. To say the things I said to you," Celeste admitted.

"Trust me, you aren't the only one with words that have come back to haunt you threefold."

She hummed respectfully. "I suppose not. My mother died when I was young as well. It brought out this sort of nurturing in me. It's part of why I wanted Essie to be so strong within our little coven all these years. I saw strength in her I never had. I also saw a bit of legacy I wasn't sure for so long I was going to get."

"I never thought this was where I would end up," I said in a similar vein. "Once I got here, I had no idea where I was going. I barely make much of a decision when I don't have to, but I'm done being uncertain about things and what I want out of life. I hope you can respect that."

Slowly, Celeste nodded. "I can."

"Thank you. Sorry to interrupt, though it smells delicious in here," I said. "I'll leave you to it."

"Thank you for being honest with me, Luella. Next time, however, I would prefer when we disagree on something that we don't have it out on the front lawn, where your poor boy—Ryan—is frozen, watching in horror, from across the street."

I huffed a small laugh. That seemed fair. "See you on Saturday."

"See you at the meeting," she agreed.

Without anything left to say—at least, not as much—I turned back down the hallway of the house toward the front door I had come in from.

"Hey, Lu."

Pausing in the hall before the hooks of discarded coats and rain boots, I glanced behind me toward Essie, standing on the steps.

"Eavesdropping?"

"Just happened to overhear," Essie said, though she grinned with mischief.

I gave her a knowing smirk right back.

"I wanted to catch you before you left. I wanted to tell you that it's all right about the whole priestess thing and all." She leaned over the railing. Seafoam eyes softened. "To be honest, I'm sort of relieved."

"Well then, I'm sure your mother will get over it soon," I said, though we both knew that wasn't likely.

"Maybe in the next decade or so."

"I was thinking at least until she shared her strudel recipe."

"Her deathbed then?" Essie raised an eyebrow.

"Maybe."

Essie pursed her lips in another small smile to herself. "How have you been, by the way? I heard that things weren't exactly good the last time everyone else was over."

"You mean when I was upstairs, hiding in my room for a week?"

After a long moment, she nodded.

"I'm okay. Or I will be. I am now." I thought about Ryan outside in his car, waiting on me. I wasn't sure how much longer I had before he came barging in. "Things are good."

"I'm happy for you."

"Thank you, Essie. Will I be seeing you at the coven meeting on Saturday as well?"

She shrugged. "Probably."

"Then, see you then. Blessed be, Essie."

"Blessed be, Lu," she said playfully, turning back to head upstairs as I opened the door and slipped outside.

* * *

Ryan was halfway up the walk, pausing when he saw me shut the door behind me.

"Oh, good. I was really thinking I was about to break down the door to come and get you." He let out a relieved breath.

What a dork.

"What's wrong? How did it go in there?"

Before he could ask anything else, I walked right into him, my arms open and clasping him to me. He swayed side to side before he realized that he was meant to hug me back.

"I'm just glad you're you." I hugged him tighter.

He settled his chin on top of my head. "Right now, I am too. I guess you didn't bring back any baked goods from in there?"

Slowly, I pulled away from him, checking to make sure that he was joking.

His crooked smile told me he was. "Ready?"

I nodded. Still, I didn't let go of him, instead holding on to his hand. Since when had I become the sappy one in this relationship?

Relationship. The word ran through my head again with the foreignness of it. The perfectness.

I was in a relationship with Ryan Gardner. I was in love with Ryan Gardner. How many days would it take for it not to feel so wild and beautiful?

Dropping into the passenger seat, I peeked at him as he got into the other side of the car.

He had his seat belt halfway on by the time he noticed, giving me an odd look right back. "What?"

I shook my head. "Nothing."

"Do I have something on my face?"
I shook my head again. "Just drive."

"Hey, Lu." Ryan nudged me with a hand. In one smooth stroke, he let his palm travel down my arm before tugging me up from where I laid.

I'd collapsed on his lumpy bed back at the sports house at some point between classes, working on a new project I needed to turn in next week and waiting for him to return from his adviser, where he found out what grade he'd be doing his student teaching in.

Slowly, I'd forced myself to get used to the idea of invisible potato mouse pets. As I never had to see them, I could handle hanging out in his room for the short amount of time we did. In the past two weeks since we had made up, Ryan and I still spent most of our time back at the house.

I groaned, rolling over toward him. "What?"

Laughing at my exhaustion, he leaned in close, falling next to me on the lumpy as well as now squeaky bed. It sounded like it was going to fall apart. I remained unmoving, not letting my evening nap be interrupted.

"Come on. We have somewhere to be."

"What are you talking about?"

"I have something to show you."

"You can't show me here?" I blinked an eye open, feeling like I was moments away from shutting it again.

The past few days had been utter chaos. Not only had midterms felt like they had burned me out to my core, but I was also planning my first Samhain ritual for the coven this week. I'd also finally declared my major today, much to the academic office's relief. I deserved an irresponsible late nap.

"Nooo." Ryan laughed. He poked me again. "Come on."

"I'm tired," I moaned.

"Trust me, you're going to love it."

When he put it like that, I raised my eyebrows, sitting up.

"That's my girl."

I let Ryan pull me the rest of the way up off the bed. The next thing I knew, he was wrapping me in my jacket before tossing on his own. I looked him up and down—from his forest-green shirt to his dark jeans and worn sneakers.

"Where are we going?"

"You'll see," he said with a grin.

So far, I did see why I needed my coat. At the end of October, it was turning from brisk chill to cold. Fall days might have been granting us a reprieve from the humidity of summer, but now, the nights were settling in heavy and on the verge of frost. I let Ryan lead me through campus, where the lamp lights were turning on to light our path one at a time, all the way until we headed up the hill toward a spot I hadn't been visiting as much as of late with everything going on. I was pretty sure we'd already missed the sunset, if a relaxing walk was what he had planned.

Ryan, ever the romantic.

Only he started to pull me toward the right, and it didn't take long before I saw it. I gasped.

As I turned into the off-campus cemetery looming above Barnett, no one laid between headstones, contemplating the state of the world. No, there was so much more.

Candles lit up the rows. Headstones were draped in fairy lights and pumpkins. There were so many pumpkins and jack-o'-lanterns everywhere with a variety of faces and carving talent. Large comforters, likely torn from their dorm room beds, and picnic blankets from springs past lay over the dewy grass. People were squeezed side by side on them, together in gathering.

"Happy Samhain, Luella," Ryan murmured into my ear.

It wasn't everything I had planned. But with the lights, the people, it might as well have been everything and more.

I put a hand to my mouth, unsure of what would come out of it. My jaw dropped, and strange laughter huffed from my chest.

Faith was wandering in the distance. Ana sat down to look up at the bright and sparkling stars with Gertie, Celeste, and Essie. Even Celeste's husband and son were enjoying the night.

"How did you—what did you do to make all this happen?"

"You'd be surprised how excited football players get over pumpkin carving," explained Ryan.

That didn't cover the half of it.

"You're kidding."

"I'm really not," he said with another chuckle. "You like it? I know it isn't your dream Samhain celebration, but I salvaged what I could and figured that we could still at least try to do something near campus even if we weren't allowed to host it in the quad. The view would make up for it—"

"Stop talking," I said, reaching up to kiss him. "It's amazing."

"Yeah?"

"Yeah." I swallowed. He was making me become a softy. "Thank you."

He smiled, hugging me tight into his arms as we found our own seats a short space away from where, of course, Ryan always found himself in the cemetery. I laughed as I sat down, and he pulled out a black witch hat from behind him.

He promptly flopped it on his head. "Now, we have everything."

I adjusted the hat on my head, twisting around the floppy brim so it wasn't in my face. "Is that right?"

"I don't know about you, but I think we did pretty good."

The two of us looked over the quintessential setup for our early Halloween. Lanterns burned, and people rushed back and forth in dumbfounded delight at what they found lighting up the hill above campus.

It was the exact event I had planned—and hadn't—but it didn't need to be perfect anymore.

"We?" I scoffed jokingly. "I'm pretty sure this was my idea to start with."

"I'm the one who decided to share my secret spot."

"You're the one who infiltrated mine," I argued, thinking of my seat in the library.

Ryan chuckled as he leaned down toward my ear. An arm looped around my shoulders. "Is that what we are calling it now?"

"You're such a weirdo." I rolled my eyes as I held on to his hand. "How did no one find that out before now?"

"No one cared to notice much about me. Not even me until you. Do I need to remind you that you bewitched me? I'm yours for every weird and crazy way you have planned out for me in this life, Luella Pierce."

There he went again with the *Pride and Prejudice*. I never did ask him how he had done on that first paper to end his literary courting saga.

"What a monster I've created." I reached up, brushing a loose wave of his hair back over his head. It didn't stay still in the wind, which whistled before there were bursts of conversation around us. "A witch and a sappy ex-jock."

"I'm not sappy. At least, not full time."

I let that hang in the air, fueling another string of laughter. I loved to hear him laugh.

"Fine. We created that wonderful combination," he conceded. "Along with our forever."

I glanced back up at him again, undeserving of him and all the amazing things that came with him I never gave thought to ever having. It still didn't quite make sense how all this had happened to us so simply, so quickly.

"Is this some sort of record or something?"

"Us?"

I nodded.

"College time is different," he explained with a shrug. "Though we did have a good three years before we managed to finally be each other's, so…probably not."

I giggled into his side.

"But that's all right," Ryan made sure to add.

The moment I had first seen him at first-year orientation felt like decades ago. When I'd found him sitting in my chair, it felt like a year ago. Now that we were side by side, it didn't matter what two months later was. I looked forward to all the rest of the many days, months, and years we could sit right there together.

There might not have been a charm for forever, but I was pretty sure, right now, being together, looking up at the stars, was close enough.

"Happy Samhain, Lu."

"Happy Halloween, Ryan."

EPILOGUE

"Congratulations!" Faith burst through the door again with a fresh box of empty jars.

I took them from her hands gratefully, finding a safe place for them in the immediate chaos around me. I shook my head. "You need to stop."

"Why? If you stop doing wildly amazing things, then I'll stop congratulating you for them."

I'd believe that when I saw it.

Two weeks since graduation, and Faith was still in an oddly celebratory mood, even after I informed her this meant that neither I nor Ryan would be in the Barnett library anymore to help her with her last-minute research and or archival projects. That had dimmed her spirit for about five minutes.

Ryan had convinced me to go to graduation, and I had worn my oversize poncho of a bright-green gown along with a few hundred other graduates. After walking across the stage to the most obnoxious of cheers from a certain blonde ex-football player and future teacher who somehow managed to pull off any shade of green, I looked down at the degree in my hand and took a deep breath at the words on it.

Luella Pierce had been granted a bachelor's degree in business with a minor in graphic design and botany.

Even the career counselors we all had to meet with at the end of the year appeared shocked that I managed to get the final credits in before the end of the year.

I might have even surprised myself as Ryan reached back into my row to run my tassel from one side to the other, and I, his. He scrunched his nose, beaming his bright smile at me as they announced us as the newest graduating class of Barnett University and sent us off into the world.

Though our world was a lot closer than most.

During my final semester, it had helped that for my business capstone, I'd already had a business plan in mind. I wanted to open my own. Ever since I had stumbled upon the old building just off Main Street that had been empty for years, I couldn't get it out of my mind. The sage-green paint on the facade was chipping off in hunks, and the windows were covered with strips of old newspaper, but they were huge. When I'd peeked inside, past the layer of dust, I could see the shelves appearing in my head immediately, perfect for setting jars of tea leaves and tables for rows of soaps, oils, and small spells I planned on selling with user guides from my redesigned book of shadows, meant for anyone who wanted to find magic, like I had.

Now, it was all coming together with a little help from Gertie, the coven, as well as my mom, who had left me a bit of extra money I'd never cared to look at previously. The note, along with the account, had said that it should go toward doing something worth dreaming about. It was like a bright, shining sign. Because this shop certainly was all of that even if there was still a lot of work to be done.

The only thing that we had managed to do was scrape the windows and replace the one above the door with a stained glass mosaic of a crescent moon, like the one back at the house. The moon kept me company now day and night while I sweated profusely from the lack of air conditioning.

Earth tones splattered all over me and the floor from where I'd been painting.

"Do you need any other help or …" Faith looked around the place in her clean, colorful dress and kitten heels.

"Not with you dressed so nice, no," I said. "Could you go and get me another paint roller out from the back office though?" I wanted to start on the cream shelves for the wall behind the counter later.

"That, I can do," Faith sang as she headed into the back room. Her heels clacked in the empty space to the melody of the radio playing the Top 100 hits.

I'd just gotten to painting again when I saw another shadow pass through the door I'd left wide open, hoping a semblance of a breeze would float in.

Instead of a brisk wind to cool me off, Ryan stepped inside. He was still dressed in his crisp button-down and dress pants I had seen him off in from the house this morning.

His face dropped as he looked between his feet and me. He took a deep breath. My own stopped in my lungs.

I set down the paintbrush I had been using on the edge of the can as I moved toward him, trying to curve my head to see his face. "What happened? Didn't the meeting go well? I thought since they asked you back again, that was a good sign."

"I just … I don't know how to tell you this, but … guess who is teaching at Barnett Elementary this fall," Ryan said. His sad face transformed into one of elation.

"You little—" Relief spread through me.

He'd really had me worried there. We'd talked about what we'd do if he didn't manage to get a job right in town. We'd make it work, especially since our housing situation was taken care of for the rest of our lives, but it still wouldn't have been ideal.

Especially as the rest of our world slowly began to come into focus.

"They liked my enthusiasm," he said.

"Don't we all?"

"I was, and I quote, 'the only candidate we actively considered for the position.'"

"Now, you're just getting a big head."

Ryan wrapped me in his arms and took me straight into the air as he twirled around. When he set me back down on my toes, he looked around at the place, less full of dust and mold and coming together. "I told you, Lu, we got this."

"We got this," I repeated, not caring that I was sweating all over him as I looked around my tiny, forming shop.

It was all happening. This time, I wasn't going to stop it. This was a life I'd hardly imagined for myself, yet here I was. Every day, I slowly felt as if I was filling it up with more love. From Ryan. From the coven. From the house and all the hope it held, now and in its future, and from myself.

We all had a little magic in us, and ready or not, we were going to use it.

A small gasp caught our attention from the doorway leading to the back room. Faith held up a paint roller in one hand, her eyes wide with excitement.

"He got the job?" Faith squealed.

Pulling back from one another, all smiles, we both nodded. We knew what was coming the moment Faith started sprinting on her teeny tiny heels toward us, already starting to laugh.

"Congratulations!"

ACKNOWLEDGMENTS

Bewitched By You struck like magic. I had hardly finished my last novel, *The Way We're Meant To Be,* before I suddenly had a craving for fall a few seasons too early. Lu and Ryan simply would not stop the constant conversations. Strings of dialogue formed in my head—Particularly, the first cemetery scene when a happy go lucky golden boy takes time to reflect between the headstones. I knew that I was going to have to write their story, and quickly. I wrote during lunch and whenever I had a break, afraid that the modern witch who fell in love with a sweet football player would disappear if I didn't.

This book has been completely different than my others to write. At times it felt light and fun as it took on a much more mellow pace compared to my other contemporary romances. In other moments, it felt like a race to the finish. I needed to make sure my characters managed to say everything they set out to. Even though some side characters may still be nudging me eventually for a story of their own …

Now, as I finish *Bewitched By You*, I need to mention some wonderful people and give some big thank you's.

First, to Taylor Whelan, who taught me what the word "himbo" was after I first attempted to explain the sweet, adorable and funny character of Ryan. You may not have gotten to read this one first, but your support whenever I needed to you to read over the summary more than anyone should ever have to. You are so appreciated, as are our late movie nights where we end up just rambling about books and our latest theories. Those moments keep me whole.

To the work family I developed while writing and substitute teaching, who encouraged and supported me as if I was as amazing as any NYT Bestselling author, thank you. Vonnie Lessard and Katelyn Jackson, I appreciate being able to feel accepted and surrounded by kindness as I find myself in this big world as an author and person.

To my wonderful fellow indie authors online who are some of my biggest supporters, and never mind the casual question being sent to their inbox. Julie Olivia, Amanda Chaperon, and Taylor Epperson— thank you for starting to make me feel like I am a part of the book and writing community I always dreamed of.

To my family, thank you for supporting and encouraging me to continue to hope and look forward to the future as I continue this writing journey both on the page and in life.

A big thank you as well to Sam Palencia for crafting the stunning art for *Bewitched By You*. The moment I realized that this book was going to happen, I could picture no better person to design the cover. I am in awe of your talent.

To Jovana Shirley, you have my immense gratitude for helping me make sure my story is perfectly told for readers. Thank you so much.

To all the books, people, readers, and moments that made me feel like magic could be at my fingertips— most days, *you* are why I write.

And finally, thank you to my small-town college alma mater

that certainly inspired a few locations and scenes. For some reason, a cemetery on a hill outside campus now just feels right—even if there has never been a Halloween party or Samhain celebration held there (that I know of).

ABOUT THE AUTHOR

Kendra Mase is the author of emotional, steamy, and at times magical romance novels including the Ashton series and *Bewitched By You*. She holds a BA in English Publishing and Editing and is a graduate of The Columbia Publishing Course in New York City.

ALSO BY KENDRA MASE

Ashton
The Strings That Hold Us Together
Everything You Never Had
Words That Burn Like Ash
The Way We're Meant To Be

Barnett Witches
Bewitched By You

Printed in Great Britain
by Amazon